Destiny's

SECOND CHANCE

by Kate Vale

PROMONTORY
P R E S S

Promontory Press
www.promontorypress.com

ISBN: 978-1-987857-00-9

Cover design by Marla Thompson of Edge of Water
Designs
Typeset by One Owl Creative in 12pt Bembo

Printed in Canada
0987654321

Destiny's Second Chance

Dear Reader,

This story is dedicated to my mother, herself a foundling, back when that term was frequently ascribed to children first cared for in an orphanage and later adopted into a family. Her story and those of other women and men who claimed two sets of parents—one left behind, the other joined some time after birth—refused to let me go. I wondered what it might be like to *want* to know one's birth parents, to feel pulled in different directions by the knowledge that one's birth parents were not the same family that raised her or him.

Additionally, I was convinced as a young child that I must have been adopted. Why? Because I didn't look like my parents, nor did they seem to "understand" me. How could they be expected to, if they hadn't given me life? Of course, they had, but the conflicts between parents and children can sometimes spur such thoughts. And when I raised these thoughts, my mother was hurt. But I wasn't privy to the knowledge that she had been adopted until many years later, when she showed me the grave of the woman who had adopted her.

Special acknowledgement goes to Nurse Jeanne Brotherton, Doctor John Raduege, Maryann Angus, and to the mothers, fathers, and children of those families who shared so much with me: the good and bad, the positive and negative, and their own dawning understanding and acceptance of the complexities of how families are created.

I love hearing from readers. Email me at: katevale@sent.com or go to my website: http://katevale.com and click "Contact Me."

Enjoy!

Chapter 1

ISABELLA CAMPBELL RELAXED IN HER SEAT ON THE plane, glad to be going home. Her best friend, Zoe, had texted that she had big news.

Bella could guess the news had to do with Tör, Zoe's boyfriend. She smiled. Zoe deserved happiness after all the grief she had suffered; breast cancer and then the death of her brother overseas. Tör, with his pronounced Swedish accent, adored Zoe, called her his forever sweetheart. Bella smiled and sighed. *Good for Zoe.*

Ever since her disastrous falling out with Ethan, a geology professor at City College, she'd sworn off men. She recalled sliding her fingers through his thick black hair that last time they'd made love. Something she should never have agreed to. Something she regretted at the time, in spite of how he'd wheedled her into going back to his house for a nightcap. Oh, their lovemaking had been hot at first, but later, not so much. And make-up sex with him had been less than fun. More like he was trying to teach her he was in charge. Something she now wanted to forget.

Before they broke up, Bella would have expected Ethan to meet her at the airport, perhaps even embellishing it with a surprise marriage proposal. But she'd told him they were done, and now he was at the Grand Canyon. What she'd thought was a minor disagreement had escalated into yet another shouting match—he yelling, she trying not to listen. She'd been surprised at how relieved she felt, days after their last big fight. Now, all she felt was a quiet dullness that the future she'd dared to dream about wasn't in the cards. *My last, most recent, love affair bites the dust.*

Bella looked out the window as the Seattle skyline came into view, the early evening rays competing with the lights going on around the city and on the surrounding hills. She sighed and closed her eyes. *Home.* Maybe next year, she'd ask Zoe to attend the library convention, perhaps consider it a special time to get away with Tör, married or not. San Francisco was a nice city for a mini-honeymoon.

The announcement of the arrival of Bella's flight echoed in the terminal as she walked past a Starbucks kiosk and into the baggage claim area. Zoe trotted in her direction, waving both arms and smiling.

"Well?" Bella asked. "Did he propose? Show me."

"He did. He wanted to come with me, but there was an emergency at the hospital. He said he'd call after he finds out how long he'll be tied up." Zoe wiggled the fingers of her left hand, one of which sported a large diamond solitaire.

"It's gorgeous, Zoe. And you're glowing. When's the wedding?"

Zoe shook her head. "We haven't pinned that down yet. He wants his whole family here, and that's going to take some extra planning, since they're all in Sweden, except for his older sister. I want you to be my maid of honor, Bella. Will you stand up for me?"

"Of course, but promise me I don't have to wear a hideous dress in a color that doesn't work with my hair. Especially not something pink. It'll make me look like a giant Pepto-Bismol bottle."

Zoe giggled. "Not to worry. We'll pick out something that you love, something pretty you can wear to the annual library dinner. How was the conference?"

"Really good. My suitcase—there it is." She pointed to the carousel and grabbed her bag before it could angle away from her. "It's loaded with all kinds of new books. The session I liked best was all about story times for children of different ages. Gave me lots of ideas."

Zoe snorted. "As if Mitchell will let you implement them. Especially if it means spending any money."

"We'll have to convince him. You and me. Together."

Bella and Zoe headed for Zoe's car. She stopped walking when the theme of the Swedish national anthem sounded from Zoe's left pocket. "Tör's checking in. He must be on a break."

"Let me talk to him." Bella reached for the phone. "Congratulations, Doctor Lundberg. How does it feel to be engaged to my best friend?"

A prolonged laugh erupted from the phone. "Just fine, Bella. You two are coming home, right? And you had a good conference?"

"That's the plan. Are you stuck at the hospital tonight, or can you join us for dinner? My treat."

"I'm not sure. Let me talk to Zoe, if you please."

Bella handed the phone to Zoe and concentrated on tossing her suitcase in Zoe's trunk while Zoe chattered with Tör, her cheeks blooming with color at something he must have said. "He says he'll give me a call in an hour. Or as soon as he knows when he can meet us."

"His hours at the ER have to be long, Zoe. Are you ready for him getting home late or having to rush off for some emergency when you've planned a nice dinner, or a special dessert?" She waggled her eyebrows at Zoe, who blushed again.

"Am I ever." She glanced back at Bella. "And now that I'm engaged, we need to find you someone really nice." When Bella shook her head, Zoe reached over and grasped Bella's hand. "I mean it, especially after that awful Ethan. Someone who *really* loves you. Who sees how wonderful you are, caring and everything. To say nothing of beautiful, with that gorgeous red hair and those green eyes that remind me of Ireland."

Bella looked away, her heart thudding at the thought of that last fight with Ethan.

"I mean it, Bella. You *are* beautiful. You *are* caring. And smart. I can't imagine him accusing you of being selfish when he's so, so—" She made a face. "Anyway, he's off on one of his hiking adventures, so you don't have to worry about running into him at the library or any other place around town. It's the perfect time to forget about him and find someone else to love. You deserve it."

"I'm not interested," Bella insisted. "Maybe I'm not marriage material." Another one of Ethan's accusations, right before she'd broken up with him.

"Ethan's the one who's not marriage material." Zoe pulled out of the parking garage and headed for the highway. "Let's talk about something more pleasant than Ethan Butler. Like what we're going to have for dinner. And where. Since it's your treat." Zoe's laughter joined with Bella's as they turned right onto the road leading to Evergreen.

That evening, after dropping her suitcase at home and getting her car, Bella toasted Zoe and Tör at their favorite restaurant in Evergreen. The lights that winked at the water's edge reminded Bella of a similar scene when she'd gone with other librarians to a bistro on the San Francisco waterfront. But tonight was sweeter. Zoe was her best friend and Tör loved her. Bella liked him for that, and for himself, too, how modest he was, never calling attention to his position as second-in-command at the Evergreen Hospital emergency room. She'd been surprised when Zoe had shown her around his unassuming little house, thinking that the good doctor lived on the hill, near so many other doctors, in those mini-mansions with views of Lake Geneva, or in one of those luxury high-rises on the lakeshore.

Tör's cozy bungalow sat in a neighborhood known for attracting newly married couples and those starting families. Bella smiled to herself. *That will be them in a year or so.* She glanced at Zoe and Tör. They were silently gazing at each other, seemingly unaware that she sat across from them. *Time for me to get home and give the lovebirds a chance to do their own celebrating.*

Bella cleared her throat. "Hey, you two. I'm worn out. I'm going to say good-night and head on home."

Tör nodded his head and reached for his wallet.

"Don't you dare. This dinner was my treat. You two stay as long as you want." Bella reached forward and planted a quick kiss on Tör's cheek before hugging Zoe. "I'll see you tomorrow at the library and we'll go over all the great stuff I brought home. So we can attack Mitchell together. United front and all."

Zoe laughed. "It's a deal."

Bella returned home, tossed her dirty clothes in the laundry, and spotted the large stack of mail that had accumulated in her absence. She opened the windows to allow the cool spring-time night breezes into the house, and microwaved a cup of tea. While it cooled, she reached for the mail. *Might as well go through it now.* She began sorting. One pile for the recycling bin, one pile for magazines and brochures she might want to review more carefully before tossing, and one pile for "real" mail.

The pile to recycle, as usual, grew quickly. She set the cluster of magazines and brochures aside for later review. Three letters remained. She opened the bank statement and tossed the envelope into the recycling pile. The second letter, from her mother, was replete with news of her activities with the garden club, where she was approaching the final month of her presidency.

Bella's pulse jumped when she read the name in the return address on the last envelope, staring back at her in stark black letters. *Harris?* But the address, at least the part not smudged, looked like Austin, Texas. Had they moved? And why were her baby's adoptive parents contacting her after all this time? The letter had been sent to her parents' home in Portland, said address scratched out by her mother's firm hand. To one side, Bella's address was written, along with a command to please forward. The two different postmarks were dated months apart.

Had her mother steamed open the envelope before sending it on? She'd heard nothing from the Harrises for years, concluding that their silence must mean something she didn't want to contemplate, something she couldn't bring herself to ask. Was this the proof she feared? Bella stared again at the envelope.

With trembling fingers, she opened the envelope and

pulled out a piece of paper, its message neatly typed. Her eyes scanned the words until tears blurred what she was seeing and she could no longer read. She scraped her sleeve across her face, not bothering with a tissue, and tried again.

```
I, Nolan Harris, father of Destiny
Harris, give you permission to con-
tact my daughter directly. Her ad-
dress is …
```

More tears. Bella couldn't read further. Whatever information the letter also provided was less important than the words now burned into her brain. Destiny was alive. His daughter. *My* daughter. But that wasn't right. Bella hadn't raised her. She glanced again at the letter. It was dated on Destiny's twenty-first birthday. *Last August.* What had caused Mr. Harris to write? Why hadn't her mother sent the letter months ago?

Should Bella make contact? How could she not? By letter? No phone number was provided. Maybe she would do a Google search for a phone number. Or perhaps she should meet her face-to-face, on the doorstep of the Denver address she'd been given. But would her daughter want that? The letter was from her father. Was Mrs. Harris deceased? And Destiny's address was not the same as that on the envelope. What did that mean?

Bella stood up from the table, inadvertently knocking over her mug, the remaining tea soaking into the envelope on which her mother had printed the rapidly blurring forwarding address. She snatched up the letter to protect those precious words from smearing.

I have to contact her. But did she dare? Maybe she should just go to Denver and knock on the door where she was living. Bella's pulse ratcheted upward at the thought. Who would answer the door—Destiny or her mother? Maybe they wouldn't want to see her.

She couldn't just take off again after being gone for three days, without angering Mitchell Hargrove. She could use her sick time, but then Zoe would be left trying to convince Mitchell to give serious consideration to Bella's plans for offering story times to different ages of children, something she and Zoe had chatted about on the way home.

Bella patted the envelope dry and left it on the kitchen counter. She took the letter into the bedroom. After climbing into bed, she read it again and then a third time after glancing in the direction of the small picture that topped the bookcase in the dining room next to Bella's college graduation photo. Bella with her long, dark red curls and Destiny at age five, with huge blue eyes, an endearing smile, and a shock of slightly paler red curls that stood out around her head. Anyone who saw those pictures would assume the woman and child were related. *Funny. Ethan never asked or even paid attention to those pictures.*

Bella turned off the light, her mind whirling. Would Destiny want to be contacted? All the possible answers to that question reverberated in her brain. Yes, of course. Maybe. No. Definitely not. She doesn't even care. After all, it had been more than twenty years since Bella had last held Destiny. Maybe she didn't even live at home now.

After lying in bed for more than an hour, too keyed up to sleep, Bella wrapped up in her favorite terry robe and padded into the small guest room she used as an office. She flipped on the desk lamp and powered up her laptop.

She Googled the Denver address, hoping to find a phone number. Vanessa Harris's name came up with the address. *The woman who didn't even know how to hold a newborn.* She'd seemed reluctant to touch Destiny when her husband placed the baby in her arms.

She punched in Vanessa Harris in the search bar. A telephone number and the same address confirmed that Destiny must be living with her mother. Bella jotted down the phone number on Mr. Harris's letter. She closed her eyes. What to say? *I'll just speak to her from my heart.* Maybe she'll be curious enough to want to write me back.

She opened a blank Word file, poised her fingers over the keys, and then began to type.

Dear Destiny,

Your father sent me a letter on your twenty-first birthday that I only just now have received. It went to my mother's house, but I haven't lived there in many years. He gave me permission to contact you.

I remember your parents from the day they came to take you home from the hospital. Your father cried when he saw you. I'll never forget that. It made me feel like you were going to a loving home, one where you would be cherished.

Your folks probably told you about your adoption, and how very much they wanted you. I'm so grateful to your father that he said I could reach out to you. I've wanted to for a long time, but I didn't know where you were. Now that you're over twenty-one, deciding whether or not we meet is up to you.

May I call you? I'd love to hear your voice and find out how you're doing these days. Please know that I won't intrude if you don't want me to, but I would be so happy if we could have just one phone call. I've printed my mailing and email addresses, and cell phone number on the bottom of this letter so you'll know how to reach me.

Your birth mother, Isabella Campbell

Bella reread her letter several times until her tears prevented her from seeing what she had written. She printed off the letter, signed, then sealed the envelope and placed a stamp in the upper right corner, her fingers trembling. Unsure whether Vanessa Harris would welcome the arrival of her letter, she used only her initials, BC, above the return address.

Bella closed down her laptop and shut off the desk lamp before walking back into her bedroom. The clock face glowed in the early morning darkness. *Three-fifteen.* Getting up to make it to work on time was going to come around really soon. Bella slid under the covers, praying that she could now sleep.

Four hours later, she woke to the usual litany of bad news when the clock radio clicked on. She groaned, debated going back to sleep and begging Mitchell's forgiveness for being late, and decided against it. A shower would revive her, help her face the day. She rolled over and snatched a glance at the letter lying on her bedside table. Her words came back to her. *Will you reply, Destiny? Tell me we can talk, maybe even meet? I'd be so grateful.*

Bella climbed out of bed and headed for the shower. She would mail the letter and talk to Zoe. She would know how long Bella should wait for an answer. If she received one.

Chapter 2

DESTINY SHOVED THE BACK DOOR OPEN AND DROPPED her books on the kitchen counter. "Mom? You home?" *Oh, that's right. She's at her club meeting.* Destiny blew several tendrils of hair off her face and strolled into the living room. The mail pushed through the mail slot lay scattered near the front door. She picked up the pieces and returned to the kitchen. As she scanned the envelopes, one caught her eye. It was addressed to her, but not from her dad's wife, who was much more likely to write Destiny than her dad. He usually just called or texted her.

Destiny slid into one of the chairs and stared at the return address. Some place in Washington state. She opened the envelope and read the letter, her pulse climbing with each sentence. *Oh my God!*

The letter fluttered to the table. Destiny's hands trembled.

She had to talk to someone. Not her mom. She'd freak. Her dad? But he was at his office, probably in some big meeting where he couldn't be disturbed. And no way was Destiny going to ask his secretary to take *this* message. *Noah. I'll call him.*

Destiny pressed a hand to each of her cheeks, willing her heart to stop racing at the thought of talking to her birth mom, the woman who'd given her away when Destiny was a baby, practically the day after she'd been born. Destiny had often wondered what her real mom was like. Her dad had always answered her questions, even when her mom left the room after complaining that Destiny asked too many questions. Over the years, being adopted wasn't all that different from some of her friends' situations. Some had two dads or two moms, and stepbrothers and sisters, even if they weren't really related to them. But what would have made that woman she'd never known give her up? *If I had a baby, I'd never do that.*

Destiny gulped down a glass of water and picked up her phone. "Noah? Can you talk?" she asked when she overheard strident screeching and other background noises at the garage where he worked.

"Yeah. Let me go outside." When he spoke again, the background noise was muted. "What's the deal? Aren't you at the bookstore today? You never call me from work."

"I'm home. I got a letter. From my birth mom. I'm in shock."

"Hmm."

"You still there, Noah? What do you think—is that cool or, like, creepy?"

"What did it say? Something bad that you can't talk to your mom about? Not that you talk to her about much of anything these days."

She resented Noah's dismissive tone, even if he was right.

Destiny and her mom hadn't been on the same wavelength for months now, maybe even years. Ever since Dad left, actually. Something Dad kept telling her to change. Something she couldn't seem to do. "She wants to talk to me. Gave me her address and phone numbers." She huffed out a breath and coughed to clear her throat. "Can't you just imagine what my mom would say about *that*?"

Noah laughed. "Not a pretty picture." He paused then asked, "Where does she live? Maybe you could just go see her."

"She lives in Washington state. No way could I ask my mom for the money to see her."

"What about your dad? He's always sending you dough. You could ask him."

"He's the reason she wrote. He gave her permission to contact me. Something about my being twenty-one. Maybe she means that I'm of age and Dad said it was okay."

"Why don't you ask her to come here? She's probably got money. What does she do?"

"No idea. She didn't say. Maybe she's married and has kids."

"Well, you'll never find out if you don't ask her. I gotta get back to work, Des. If you want to talk more, how about after you're off tomorrow?"

"Okay." Destiny clicked off just before she heard her mother's car pull into the driveway. She tucked the letter into the envelope and shoved it into her backpack. Now was not the time to mention this. Not until she decided what to do. She headed for the stairs.

"Destiny, honey. Could you grab this bag?" her mother called to her.

She turned around, dropped her backpack near the stairs and returned to the kitchen. "You got groceries? I thought you were at your club meeting this afternoon."

"I was, but I thought I'd get something special to make for when your cousins come over this weekend. Did you forget? We're going to celebrate Aiden's birthday here, since his folks are in Germany with David, during his R&R."

"Oh. Right. But I have to work tomorrow. Want me to bake his cake tonight?"

"Would you, dear? That would be nice." Her mom gave her a quick hug before turning her attention to stowing the canned goods and paper products in the pantry. "I bought some balloons, too. I thought we could decorate the patio with them, even though Aiden is sixteen. Wait till you see the ones I got. They're not for little kids." Her mother chuckled.

Destiny emptied the second bag of groceries, placing the cake mix on the counter. She stepped away from the kitchen, intent on going to her room. "Let me put my books away and I'll come back down and get busy with his cake."

"Thank you, honey."

Destiny trotted up the stairs, her backpack in her arms. The letter seemed to burn a hole in her chest before she dropped the backpack onto her desk. She shut her door, pulled out the letter, and read it again. She imagined herself calling Isabella. The woman's name made her think of someone from Italy. Did she have an accent? Maybe she should write and invite her to come to Denver, like Noah had suggested. But what if Isabella wouldn't come? What if she didn't have the money? Or her family wouldn't let her?

Destiny flopped down on her bed and read the letter again. If only she knew more about this Isabella Campbell. *She must be married. Campbell isn't an Italian name.* Destiny clambered off her bed and opened her laptop. *I'll Google her.* Maybe find out something about her, before calling or texting.

Destiny slid into the chair in front of her desk and pounded the keyboard. Her birth mom didn't have a Facebook account.

Maybe she's too old to use social media. Too bad. Hmm. She found a Google entry for an Isabella Campbell, who worked at the Evergreen Public Library and another mention of her as a senior staff member on the library's website. That seemed to fit. The address on the envelope was from Evergreen. But Destiny found no information about Isabella being married or having children. She tried to remember what her dad had told her. *I'll have to call him.* Destiny knew Isabella Campbell wasn't as old as her folks. Hadn't Dad said once that she was a single mother when she gave Destiny up?

Her mother knocked on her door and opened it. "Des? Can you come down soon? I turned on the oven so it's ready for the cake, and dinner will be ready soon."

Destiny closed her laptop and turned toward the door, covering the letter with one hand, feeling vaguely guilty. "Okay. I'll be right down." She shoved the letter into the top drawer of her desk and followed her mother downstairs.

Bella's brain whirled. She'd slept little the last three nights, excited about having received the letter from Mr. Harris and then about mailing Destiny. How could she concentrate at work when all she could think about was how Destiny might react to her letter? *Maybe I should go to Denver.* If only she'd had the money to hire an investigator sixteen years earlier when she had stopped hearing from the Harrises, she would have more answers. But she'd been living hand-to-mouth then, working and going to college part-time, desperate to prove that she could survive without her parents' help.

She pulled Mr. Harris's letter from her purse, reading and

rereading the words during her afternoon break. Today her work involved back-office chores, entering new books into the computer and double-checking the special events calendar she'd promised Zoe she would update.

I'll talk with Zoe. She's always so practical. But Zoe was in the throes of being newly engaged, giddy on happiness that caused everyone who saw her to smile in remembrance, or in hope that something similar might happen to them. *That's how I feel, wishful, wistful.* But not with Ethan, Bella thought ruefully. That ship had already sailed.

She shook her head to rid herself of thoughts about Ethan. *Destiny. I'll concentrate on her.* But in doing so, Bella's brain fixed on her late father's hateful words and her mother's refusal to even hold Destiny. But she had allowed her parents to convince her that the child deserved a complete family, a mother and a father, not a scared teen mom.

Bella pushed out a breath as she scanned the computer screen, its words blurring for a moment. Her mother had spent most of Bella's pregnancy telling her it was all for the best, for the baby, for Bella. Her mother never said it was best for their family, though she probably thought it. Her father had never forgiven her for the pregnancy that wasn't supposed to happen. He'd died still sending her accusatory glances whenever he deigned to look at her that last year she lived at home.

Bella clung to the possibility that Destiny had asked to meet her birth mother. Maybe that was why Mr. Harris sent the letter.

A door slammed down the hall and seconds later, someone knocked on her door. Bella glanced at the wall clock. Almost time for lunch.

Mitchell poked his head around the doorframe. "I'd like you to come to my office, to discuss that recommendation you made."

"Which one?"

"Expanding the story time offerings." His mouth turned downward as if the idea was distasteful.

"Before or after lunch?"

"After's good enough." He left before she could reply. Bella walked down the hall to the front of the library, where Zoe, her black hair hanging in a thick braid down her back, was chatting with the woman at the checkout desk.

"Time for lunch. Can you go now?"

Zoe smiled at her. "You bet. Just let me grab my purse. Hey, what's with the long face? Did you talk to Mitchell already? He didn't like your proposal?"

"I'm not sure yet. He asked me to see him after lunch. I was hoping you and I could strategize and convince him."

"Good plan. I'm up for a taco salad today. How about you?"

"Sounds good."

After they found a table in the corner of the restaurant, Bella looked at Zoe. She suspected her friend had never associated with wild teens when she was in high school. Not like Bella when she'd taken advantage of her tutoring assignment with a star football player to go to parties her parents never knew about. Zoe had confided in Bella that her parents had always supported her, encouraging her to follow her dreams. They were ecstatic about the upcoming wedding, and had already spoken with Tör's parents.

Bella's parents had refused to let her do anything that last year she lived at home. Except for her tutoring sessions, all with elementary students, and babysitting, she spent the entire year at home in her room, studying. But she'd also used the time to plan how she would use the money she'd earned to live on her own.

"There's something else I need to talk to you about, Zoe." Tears she'd been holding back burned her lids as she reached for a napkin. "When I got home from the conference, there was a letter waiting for me. From the adoptive father of my baby."

"You have a baby?"

"She was born right before my senior year in high school. No one here knows."

"Oh, wow." Zoe reached over and patted Bella's hand. "And you didn't keep her?"

"My folks refused to let me. They insisted on adoption. The couple took her when she was three days old. I'll never forget that day."

"What did the letter say?" Zoe handed Bella a tissue.

Bella blotted her eyes, certain she'd removed all the mascara she'd so carefully applied that morning. She sniffed and wiped her nose.

"Now that she's twenty-one, he gave me permission to contact her. I haven't known where she was or what happened to her since she was five years old."

"Why not?"

"Maybe they moved. They lived in Portland when Destiny was born. The contract specified that I could send letters at Christmas and on her birthday, and they would send me pictures every year." She blinked at Zoe and wiped her eyes. "I've never told anyone. You're the only one who knows."

"You're not ashamed, are you?" Zoe inclined her head. "I'd like to think you knew I would understand, and that's why you're telling me now."

"It is. And I hoped you'd help me figure out what to do."

"What do you want to do?"

"I wrote her. Mailed the letter the day after I got home. I was hoping she would call me, but what I'd really like is to see her. I know where she lives. After I got the letter, I Googled her address. Her dad lives in Austin, I think. At least, that was where his letter came from. But the address he gave me was for her mother. Where Destiny's living, too."

"Do you think it's wise to see her without first having heard back?"

"You're probably right. But I so want to hear her voice, to see her. To know what happened to her."

"If you just mailed the letter a couple days ago, she probably hasn't even received it. What do you think she'll do?"

"I'm hoping she'll pick up the phone and call me. I gave her my cell, along with my email address. But last night I had this nightmare that her mother intercepted the letter and tore it up." Bella wiped her face again. "Shades of what *my* mother would have done. I'm surprised she even forwarded Mr. Harris's letter to me."

Zoe nodded. "Her mom didn't want you to stay in touch?"

"I was the one who insisted on that. I refused to go along with the adoption if that wasn't part of the deal. Mr. Harris was okay with it. I'm not sure about his wife. If my folks could have waved a magic wand and made my baby disappear, they would have."

"Is that why your mom never visits you here?"

The corners of Bella's mouth slid upward in the tiniest of grins. "You remember that? Let's just say my dad never forgave me for getting pregnant and my mom refused to help me. The day I graduated, I left home and never went back, except for my dad's funeral. I attended it, but I refused to go back to the house. I guess Mr. Harris still had that address. Why my mother even forwarded his letter to me, I don't know. Knowing her, she as easily could have thrown it away."

Bella visualized her mom's home as it had been the day she left, then wondered if it still was white with burgundy shutters on the front windows. A home where she didn't feel loved, where her dad made it clear she wasn't lovable.

Zoe patted Bella's hand again.

"When I left Portland, I thought I left all that behind. All the bad stuff."

"Your daughter could be married now."

"And she could also have a different last name, but I don't think so. Why would she be living with her mother if she's married?"

"Maybe her husband is in the service and he's overseas."

"I keep imagining seeing her in person. But would I even recognize her? The last picture I have is when she was five. I usually hide her photos whenever someone comes over. Maybe I should just try to call her first."

"What did she look like then?"

"Cute as can be. With red hair, like mine." Bella smiled. "I like to think she still looks like me."

"You mentioned letters you and the Harrises were supposed to share. I've never heard of that. I thought when a kid is adopted, the real mother is out of the picture."

"We agreed to a semi-open adoption. Not an open adoption where I could visit, or a closed one, which is what you're thinking of. That used to be the case ages ago." Bella sipped her tea. "But their letters and photographs stopped."

"Maybe something changed, like Destiny needing medical information, and that's why her father wrote you."

"Oh." Bella wiped her eyes. "Never thought of that. But then why wouldn't he just ask me for the information? I was thinking last night, when I couldn't sleep, that maybe she wouldn't want anything to do with me."

"That would be her loss," her friend said, gently.

Bella straightened her shoulders. "I need to find a number so I can talk to her dad in Austin. After all, he gave me permission to contact her. His address on the envelope was badly smeared, but maybe if I find him, I could ask about that. You know. If a medical issue is the reason. Even if she doesn't want me in her life."

"That sounds like a plan." Zoe sat quietly for a minute then sighed and worried her lip for a moment. "Sorry, but we need to get back on track. Plan how to convince Mitchell about what you want to do."

Bella nodded. "I'm sure he'll procrastinate, saying what I proposed will cost too much money, but I have an idea how we could get some extra books for the older kids." She smiled. "I want to talk to Henry. You know how he loves our Preschool Story Land."

"And you love him. He's like a cuddly old grandpa. And it doesn't hurt that he owns the bookstore with the best selection of children's books in Evergreen."

Bella nodded. "Can I help it if he and I have always had a special connection?"

"I called him yesterday to ask what picture books he might be placing on his sale table, but he hasn't called me back."

"Then let's see if we can cut a deal. In person. Before we go back to the library. You can check the sale table and I'll pitch my idea to him."

"What if he can't help us? Will you go to one of the franchises?" Zoe looked skeptical.

Bella snorted. "No way. You know we always support the independents."

"But most have gone out of business. That one down by the lake did, last year. Remember?"

Bella looked up from the list of books she'd just printed off, slipped in her purse to share with Zoe, and was now holding in one hand. "I suppose we could ask at The Bibliophile."

Zoe laughed out loud. "You have to be kidding. That old lady is Mitchell's ex. Probably still thinks we're taking turns boffing him, like she implied after she came in last year to yell at Mitchell. But if you want to see her, let me come, too. I'd love to flash my new ring in her face and *dare* her to accuse me again."

Bella nodded. "Let's go. Given the time, we'll probably find a parking place close to the park. I'm always amazed how close Books and More is to all the downtown businesses, and yet so few people come into the store whenever we visit Henry."

"Maybe he doesn't carry enough business books." Zoe giggled. "I've always thought his best collections were for kids."

"Has he added YA titles, too? I seem to recall seeing some new ones the last time we visited the store. That was at least a month ago. He was puttering around in the back, kind of humming to himself. Showed me a first edition he'd found at an estate sale. He's always going to them, looking for finds. I'm keeping my fingers crossed that he'll have extra copies of *Harry Potter* and might even donate them. So I can assure Mitchell we won't have to buy them."

"And in return, we'll advertise his gift and his shop. Right?" Zoe opened the door and held it for Bella.

"You are so smart, Zoe. He'll probably jump at the chance."

"Do you want to start with the *Harry Potter* series for this older kids' story time?"

"Of course. I'm planning some great activities centering around the first book. You know, make a closet like Harry lives in. The kids could take turns lying down in it. Then maybe play a version of Quidditch. I picked up some great ideas at the conference. Even if we can't really fly." She smiled. "And after that, the *Diary of a Wimpy Kid* series. Maybe Lemony Snicket after that. We could ask the kids what *they* want to read. I'm sure they'll have lots of ideas."

Zoe nodded. "You are so organized, always thinking at least two steps ahead. I know you'll convince Mitchell. Let's go talk to Henry and see what he can provide."

Chapter 3

BELLA AND ZOE ENTERED *BOOKS AND MORE*. ZOE detoured to check out the sale table finds and held up a picture book to show Bella.

"Great! I'm going to see if Henry's upstairs." Bella headed for the stairs near the back of the store. She heard coughing, the sound becoming more pronounced as she approached Henry's office. He was bent over his desk, holding his abdomen.

"Henry, are you sick?"

The older man's usually ruddy face was pasty white. He slumped back into his seat before more coughing consumed him.

"You *are*. How long have you been like this? Where's Earl? He should be helping you."

Henry waved a shaky hand in the air. "I sent him home.

He's sick, too. Probably gave it to me." He clumsily reached for the glass of water on his desk. Bella helped him bring it to his lips. After a sip, Henry gave her a smile. "My sweet Bella. Zoe said you went to some big conference. I'll bet you showed off our library a lot better than ol' Mitchell ever could." He pulled out a handkerchief and covered his mouth when another spell of coughing overtook him. "Sorry about that. I can't seem to stop coughing."

Bella pushed a lock of white hair off the man's wrinkled forehead. "You don't feel like you have a fever, but you don't look good, Henry. Have you been to the doctor?"

He shook his head and another spasm of coughing ensued. "No time."

"Didn't you say you had pneumonia a couple of years back?" She looked up and waved Zoe into the small office. "Do you remember when Henry had pneumonia?"

Zoe nodded. "Right after we started the Preschool Story Land for the little kids. After Mrs. Blair retired and you took it over. Remember? Mitchell was going to shut it down when he couldn't find a volunteer."

Bella patted the elderly man's back. "Henry, didn't the doctor say you were at greater risk for pneumonia again, after you had it that last time?"

The old man slumped back into his chair. "Maybe I should get some cough drops."

"What's your doctor's number? Zoe and I will take you."

Henry aimed a watery gaze first at Zoe and then Bella. "You two remind me of my dear wife. She was always fussin' at me to do this or do that, always trying to make me do something. For my own good, she'd say, when it was really to make herself feel better." He descended into another bout of coughing, longer than the previous ones.

Bella looked at Zoe, alarmed. Under her breath, Bella murmured, "Let's get him to the hospital. If he doesn't need to be there, we'll take him home."

Zoe nodded. "Henry, honey. Did I tell you I'm engaged now? See the ring Tör gave me?" She supported Henry under one arm as Bella lifted him by his other arm. "We're going to take you to get some help. Do you want your jacket? Here. Take it anyway." She draped his jacket across his shoulders.

The two women ignored the old man's protestations as they slowly descended the stairs.

"Here's my key. Go ahead and unlock the car, Zoe. I'm going to leave a note for Earl." Bella settled Henry in a chair next to the cash register on the main floor of the bookstore. "Stay right there." She quickly checked to see if any customers were in the little reading nooks scattered throughout the store, saw none, and returned to the front, where she penned a note to Earl. "Where are your keys, Henry? We need to lock the store."

He handed her a key. "Gotta change the Open sign, so people will know we'll be back," he muttered, as if to himself. Before they left, he flipped the little sign. Bella shut off the lights, closed and locked the door, and slowly walked Henry to her car. Zoe helped Henry inside. He closed his eyes and leaned into the seat as if exhausted. Bella and Zoe exchanged worried looks.

"Come on, Henry. We're here." With one on either side, Bella and Zoe walked Henry into the emergency room.

He began another extended coughing jag that got the attention of the nurse behind the admitting desk. She ushered him into a room. "Are you relatives, his daughters, perhaps?"

Bella shook her head. "No, just good friends. I'll ask him about family." She turned to the old bookstore owner. He'd been so dear to them, to her, and Henry was looking weaker by the minute. "Henry, do you have any relatives we should call?"

Henry looked confused for a moment, then muttered. "Gavin. In Spokane. My nephew."

Zoe asked, "What's Gavin's last name?"

"He's probably too busy. Big business man. Has his own shop. Sells fancy cars." Another fit of coughing stopped him from elaborating.

"That doesn't matter," Bella declared. "His last name, Henry? We'll call him."

"Cambridge. Haven't seen him in a coon's age."

"Well, you're going to see him soon," Bella muttered under her breath.

The nurse ushered her and Zoe out when a doctor entered the room.

Zoe followed Bella to a quiet corner in the waiting room.

Bella pulled out her smart phone. "Gavin Cambridge. Never heard of him. Has Henry ever mentioned him?"

"You calling up the address app?"

Bella nodded. "Doesn't sound like a really common name, and Spokane isn't as big as Seattle. Maybe we'll get lucky." She scrolled down the screen. "Two entries. One looks like a home number. The other one is for some car dealership. BMW. Didn't Henry say his nephew sold cars? Maybe that's his business."

"I'll call the house number. You call the business. Whoever gets him first buys margaritas at our next girls' night out."

Bella smiled. "I thought you said you weren't coming to our next one, now that you and Tör are heavy into wedding plans. I didn't see him when we came in."

"He's off today. And he never said I couldn't meet with my pals. Especially when he's watching the Sounders with the guys. He knows I'm really not into soccer—what he calls football." Zoe frowned after punching in the number that had shown on Bella's phone. "All I'm getting is ringing. Oops. Answering machine. Man's voice. Just said 'Sorry I missed you. Leave a message.' Not even a name. Your turn, Bella."

A quietly professional female announced, "Spokane BMW-Nissan Dealership. This is Darla. How may I help you?"

Bella nodded and pointed to her phone. "May I speak with Mr. Cambridge, please?"

The voice stated, "Let me switch you to Mr. Cambridge's assistant." The phone clicked over to classical music.

"This is Hortense. How may I help you?"

"I'd like to speak to Mr. Cambridge."

"I'm sorry, but he's in a staff meeting and can't be disturbed."

"Well, you're going to have to disturb him. I need to speak with him. It's urgent. And personal. An urgent *family* matter."

"Give me the message and I'll get it to him," the prissily firm female voice on the other end of the phone ordered.

"No. This is personal, a matter of life and death," Bella waited as elevator music again replaced the woman's voice. "Another gatekeeper," she muttered to Zoe, who nodded sympathetically.

"Hello?" A man's voice sounded loudly in her phone. "Who is this?"

"Gavin Cambridge?" Bella asked after she settled her phone into a position farther from her ear.

A softer baritone voice that reminded Bella of soothing syrup replied, "Yes. What's this about? My secretary said it was urgent."

"It is. Your uncle's in the hospital. He asked me to call you."

"Henry? What's the matter with him? Did he have a heart attack?" The man's voice rose slightly.

At least he sounds concerned. "No. But we think he may have pneumonia."

"You think? You don't know? What did the doctor say? Let me speak with him," he ordered in a manner that suggested to Bella that he often ordered people around. *Another Ethan? Do all men assume they can just* demand *and everyone else complies?*

"The doctor's with him now. Look, we know it's serious. And Henry needs your help. Earl is sick, too. We had to close the bookstore. I'm afraid unless he knows someone he trusts is looking after it—and he mentioned you—Henry won't listen to the doctors or rest like he should. If you could please come here and take charge of things until he's out of the hospital, Henry would be grateful."

Silence followed for a long beat before Gavin said, "I thought he was going to shut that place down."

Bella hoped her alarm at that news wasn't transmitted in her terse reply. "Well, he didn't. His bookstore is alive and well and so was Henry, until he got sick." Zoe gestured at Bella to lower her voice, but her anxiety about Henry had turned to anger that his nephew didn't seem all that interested in his uncle's welfare. "Listen, Henry is terribly ill. If he were *my* uncle, I'd want to get here right away. And he asked for you." *Sort of.* "I'm sure you wouldn't want it on your conscience if he … if he *died* without you seeing him." Her voice rasped as tears threatened and her heart clutched at the thought of losing Henry Quackenbush, one of her favorite people.

He'd been an enthusiastic supporter of everything she and Zoe had done at the library to enhance their children's section. For years, he'd happily flirted with her and Zoe whenever they met. He'd encouraged her to stick to her guns about increasing the frequency of the Preschool Story Land for the toddlers and preschoolers to weekly sessions after she'd taken over Mrs. Blair's monthly offerings. The idea that Henry's nephew *doesn't even care, for heaven's sake* was beyond her.

The silence on the phone was almost palpable in its heaviness. "Who is this again?" the man repeated. "Are you a nurse?"

"No. I'm a friend. A dear friend. We found your uncle coughing his guts out in his office. Alone. And Earl is sick, too."

"Earl who?"

"His assistant in the store. Henry needs you," Bella insisted.

The man sighed into the phone. "Tell Henry I'll see him as soon as I can."

"When will that be?" Bella pressed, imagining the man wanting to put off having to leave what Henry had called his fancy car business.

"Soon. Didn't I say soon?" he practically growled right before he hung up.

Bella stared at her phone, stunned.

Zoe jiggled Bella's elbow and whispered, "The doctor's here."

The man standing in front of them in a long white coat nodded. "Thank you for bringing Henry in. He has pneumonia and we've admitted him. He's too sick to go home, even though he wanted to. We convinced him otherwise."

"How'd you do that?" Bella asked. "He fought coming with us to the E.R."

"When he couldn't catch his breath and we had to give him oxygen."

"Oh." *That's bad. Good. Bad that he needs oxygen, good that he's getting it.* "Will you tell him we called his nephew?"

"Any idea when he'll be here?"

Bella shook her head. "He wasn't specific. Lives in Spokane. Maybe he'll fly."

"Thank you, doctor." Zoe grasped Bella's arm and led her out of the waiting room. "Come on. We'll come back tomorrow. During visiting hours. Henry'll probably feel better after they give him some medicine and he's had a chance to rest."

Gavin Cambridge raked a hand through his hair. He didn't need this. Not now. With two of his best salesmen out sick and two others disciplined after they'd practically come to blows last night, Gavin wasn't eager to leave his dealership in the hands of even his most experienced employee. Zeke had never handled conflict well and was less than eager to keep the other salespeople in line. But that woman with the sexy timbre when she first spoke, that *officious* woman who'd insisted that he drop everything to take care of Henry's bookstore ... Her tone implied that he didn't care whether his uncle lived or died. *She didn't sound so sexy when she climbed on her high horse, demanding to know* when *I'd arrive in Evergreen.* Well, actually, she did. Even then. *Why am I even thinking things like this?*

And what did she know about anything? She wasn't a doctor or even a nurse. Just a friend. What kind of friend, exactly? Was Henry holding out on him? Was he seeing someone, after twelve years as a widower? Gavin would have to pin old Henry down about his love life. The old man had assured Gavin's mother that he wasn't interested in getting married again. But maybe that was just his grief talking after Aunt Ina's death. Old Henry had always had an eye for the ladies, something Gavin liked to think he'd inherited, until he'd pulled in his horns post-Eileen. *Good riddance to* that *one.*

He picked up the phone and called the hospital, but learned only that the doctor was with another patient and that Henry was resting comfortably. A wave of guilt washed over Gavin.

It had been years since he'd been to Seattle. Years, too, since Henry had been to Spokane, not since Gavin's mother died. And now his elderly relative, a man who'd always been so kind to him, was in the hospital. Gavin strode out of his office and stopped in front of Hortense's desk.

"Well?" she asked, sounding like she wanted to rest her hands on her hips or waggle an accusatory finger in his face. She did neither, for which Gavin was grateful.

"My uncle's in the hospital. I need to see him. Call Zeke and tell him he's in charge while I'm gone."

Hortense sighed dramatically. "He's not going to like having to make decisions *or* that you're gone."

"Can't be helped." Gavin flexed his jaw muscle, imagining what Zeke might say to him when he returned. Probably complain about how he'd lost out on making salesman of the month because he had to attend to administrative duties that interfered with working the customers. "If Farley and Irving get into it again, cut whatever checks they've earned this month and have Zeke fire their sorry asses. I'm tired of the two of them giving this place a bad name with their lack of professionalism. Irving, especially, knows better."

"Yes, sir." Hortense gave him a smart salute and grinned. "I can tell Zeke that?"

"Only if you have to, but yes, you have my permission. And make him do it, if they get out of line."

"You want me to call the airport and see about getting you a flight?"

Gavin considered the idea for less than ten seconds. "No, I'll drive. I have no idea how long I'll be there. I'm hoping a week or less."

"Your uncle lives in Seattle, doesn't he?" Hortense asked, while Gavin retrieved his suit coat from the back of the door, smoothed the front of his shirt and loosened his tie. The drive was going to be a long one.

"Evergreen. Near Seattle. The old man's an avid trout fisherman. Took me with him every chance I could get away from chores. I hated to clean the catch, so most times, we'd use barbless hooks." Gavin smiled in remembrance. "Maybe I'll check out that dealership in Bellevue that's not doing so well, the one the Western regional franchise manager mentioned in his last email. See if they're up for new ownership."

"Meaning you, right?"

Gavin gave his secretary a tight smile. "How'd you guess, Hortie? You still reading minds?"

"Just yours, boss. Hope your uncle gets better fast. Are you going to stop by your place before you leave?"

"Just long enough to pack a suitcase."

"Be sure to bring a couple of extra suits with you if you're going to visit that dealership. No sense looking scruffy."

Gavin nodded as he slipped his laptop into its case.

"Something tells me it's going to get lively around here while the cat's away. You know, the mice playing and all that." Hortense sniffed.

"Not with you here. I'll call you after I see Henry and know more about his condition."

Hortense waved him out the door and Gavin trotted around the building to his car. If he grabbed some food at a drive-through and ate on the road, he might just make it to Evergreen before nine.

Bella dropped Zoe off at the library to retrieve her car and headed home. She couldn't do anything more for Henry tonight, but she would visit him tomorrow and confirm whether his nephew had shown up. She nibbled her lower lip, rehashing her conversation with the man. If *she'd* been called about *her* uncle, she would have dropped everything to rush to his side. Hadn't she made it clear to the man that Henry might die? The thought caused her lungs to scream for air.

She ate dinner half-heartedly and tried to put Henry out of her mind. He really wasn't her responsibility. For now at least, she would focus on her own family, such as it was. The daughter she'd recently learned about, anyway.

Call Mr. Harris. Her mind made up about reaching out to him, Bella went online. She was relieved that she was able to find a phone number for the Austin address, but was surprised that it was an office. She called the number, listened to the answering machine message, confirmed that Mr. Harris worked there, some kind of vice president. She'd call him tomorrow. She needed to settle her nerves before speaking with him, anticipating that he would be surprised to hear from her after so many years.

Throughout most of the night, Bella tossed and turned, unable to settle down. She imagined Mr. Harris being glad Bella had called, eager to talk with her. But what if he wasn't happy? What if he'd sent her that letter simply to satisfy the contract, even if it had arrived years late and long after Destiny's twenty-first birthday? Bella's mind whirled. She wanted to think her daughter would be thrilled to talk to her, to ask questions only Bella could answer, even questions Bella didn't want to consider, but had vowed that she *would* answer. But then she imagined the daughter who'd disappeared from her life so long ago wanting nothing to do with her, telling her to leave her alone and never contact her again. *What to do?*

Bella woke earlier than usual the next morning, nervous about calling what she now thought of as The Number. Calling in the morning would likely find Mr. Harris at work but not so busy he wouldn't talk to her. How would Destiny react if Bella called her? Surely Mr. Harris would know. And if he said it was okay, perhaps, then, Bella wouldn't be so tied in knots about calling. Zoe had said to wait until Destiny contacted her. But what if she didn't? What if Bella's letter was lost in the mail?

Bella had just finished her shower and was preparing breakfast, thinking a cup of coffee and toast would settle her nerves, when the phone rang. She reached for her coffee mug and answered the phone, shocked at the number that appeared.

"Mom. Hi."

Silence greeted Bella's words, as if her mother was surprised to hear her voice, too.

Then, in that raspy, slightly disappointed tone used so often when Bella was a teen, her mother said, "I thought it was about time we talked. How long's it been since you called me? Months? A year, maybe?"

Bella imagined her mother checking the calendar. Perhaps she wrote down when Bella called, if only to complain when Bella reached out to her. "It's been a while. I'm sorry."

"I suppose you're going to say you've been busy."

"I have. Just got back from a big library conference."

"Hmm. Well, what else have you been doing? Don't you have some news about that man you're dating? When's he going to *do* something, make things permanent? Or have you dumped him, like the others before him?"

Bella pinched her little finger as a reminder not to sound peeved. "I broke up with him."

"Not again? When are you going to settle down, Bella? You're over thirty-five. There's no such thing as a perfect man. Surely you know that."

Bella's stomach clenched. *Not this again.* "Zoe just got engaged and she's older than me. To a man *perfect* for her."

"Good for her," her mother harrumphed. "What was wrong this time? He didn't try to hit you, did he? Like that other man you were seeing?"

"No, but we weren't right for each other." Bella forced herself to take another sip of coffee, so she wouldn't say something she'd regret.

"Well, it took you long enough to figure that out. How long were you hanging around with him, five years now, six?"

"More like two, but it doesn't matter. It's over. I'm not seeing Ethan anymore." Deliberately lightening her tone, Bella said, "I have a question for you."

"Oh?"

Bella pressed a fist into her belly. *I* will *stay calm.* "About that letter you forwarded."

"Oh. Is that why he broke up with you? I'll bet you never told him about your little mistake, did you?"

Bella had been expecting that. Was Mom never going to stop taunting her for her teenage indiscretion? *I will* not *reply to that.* Bella squeezed her eyes shut. "We broke up months ago. Long before you mailed that letter." She sucked in a quick breath. "Why did you hold it so long? The postmarks are months apart."

Bella debated with herself and then decided to go for it, stand up for herself, and force her mother to think of her as an adult.

"Or did you read the letter first? Maybe even had second thoughts about sending it on? Dad would have destroyed it, never let you send it." The photos she'd received after Destiny's first birthday had come to her little apartment near the airport and then to the Y when she'd moved to Evergreen. Mr. Harris must have lost those addresses. But the contract had contained her parents' address. Was that why he'd mailed the letter to Portland?

The silence that followed her questions weighed down the phone in Bella's hand, her gut burning and then her lungs before she took another breath.

Bella listened to the silence and sighed in quiet disappointment. "You don't have to answer, Mom. It really doesn't matter. The important thing is you *did* send it. Thank you for that," Bella offered, her voice softer. *I have to be more accepting that she's never going to change.* Something she'd fought against admitting to herself whenever she had words with her mother. Bella had to be strong, had to protect her heart against the cavalier way her mother talked to her, inferring Bella was still a child, that she was undeserving of an adult conversation.

Or was it that Bella always felt herself regressing to the terrified teen she'd been her junior year and then the resentful one the last year she'd lived at home, frustrated that her mother hadn't protected her from her father's hatefulness? Was it her dad who'd prevented her mom from looking for her? The one time Bella had dared to ask, her mother had refused to say.

"No, Bella, I didn't open it. I just wasn't sure I should send it on." Her mother sounded tired. "After all, it's been twenty years. That kid must be all grown up now. I figured you'd tell me what it said if you ever bothered to call. When you didn't, I decided I'd better check. Make sure you got it. That's really why I called. When *did* you get it, the letter, I mean? A week ago? More than that?"

Does it really matter? "You're right. Your granddaughter's twenty-one," Bella replied, her gut churning again, wanting her mother to acknowledge Destiny. "Haven't you ever wondered what she's like, what she looks like now, what she's doing with her life?"

As if having read Bella's mind, her mother retorted, her words clipped, "She's *not* my granddaughter. Not after you gave her away." But the abruptness of her mother's words couldn't quite hide a hint of longing that maybe she did wonder about her granddaughter when she asked, "What did the letter say?"

"Nothing much. Mr. Harris just gave me permission to contact her."

"Oh." More silence, this time tinged with anticipation. After the briefest of pauses, her mother asked, "Did you?"

"I wrote her a letter."

Bella thought she heard an exhalation of air. "I'm still waiting for a reply," she added. Somehow, she couldn't bring herself to say more, to say that she intended to contact Mr. Harris, that she might also call Destiny. She refused to be ridiculed for reaching out to the man. Not after her mother had made no effort to reach out to her after she'd left home, to explain her reasons for letting her go, even after Bella's dad died. *She doesn't deserve to know about her only grandchild.*

But what if Destiny asked about her grandmother? What would Bella tell her? What did she *want* to tell her? Bella made a silent vow to protect Destiny from her mother's snide remarks, her constant scolding, harping whenever she had the opportunity to cut someone else down. That wasn't going to happen if Bella had anything to say about it.

Before her mother could ask another question, Bella said, "I need to go, Mom."

"Is that all you're going to say? That you wrote her a letter?"

There it was, the first of what Bella suspected would be a probing for answers she didn't want to offer. "Good-bye, Mom." Bella set down the phone, relieved that the call was over, suspecting her mother had opened the envelope in spite of her denial.

Chapter 4

I HAVE TO CALL MR. HARRIS, BELLA THOUGHT, EVEN though her brief chat with her mother had upset her. Like always.

I'll get dressed first. She wanted to sound calm, professional, mature when she spoke to him. If she was dressed for work, she'd feel more in charge, though her racing pulse gave the lie to her plan.

Minutes later, she finished combing her hair and checked the clock on the kitchen wall. It was just after ten in Austin, hopefully not too much into Mr. Harris's workday that he wouldn't have time to talk with her.

If only her fingers would stop shaking.

"Mr. Harris' office. This is Mrs. Braxton. How may I help you?" The administrative assistant sounded slightly southern and ever so calm and collected. Not nearly as standoffish as that *other* secretary Bella had spoken to yesterday—Mr. Gavin Cambridge's gatekeeper. *This* woman was just doing her job. Admirably, but would she prevent Bella from getting through to Destiny's father?

"I'd like to speak with Mr. Harris." Bella hoped she sounded equally calm.

"Who may I say is calling?"

"Ms. Campbell. Bell—er, Isabella Campbell."

"And what may I say is the nature of your call, Ms. Campbell?"

"It's personal." *Oh, not good.* What would Mrs. Braxton think now? "Not bad personal. Just personal," she sputtered, feeling her neck heating up, hoping the cool and collected Mrs. Braxton wasn't imagining the worst kind of personal business Bella might have with the woman's boss.

"One moment, please."

Bella reached for her coffee mug, took a sip, then grimaced. She hated cold coffee. While she waited, she went to the sink and dumped out the mug before placing it in the dishwasher. She tossed her half-eaten toast in the garbage and wiped down the kitchen table. How long would it take for the woman to talk to Mr. Harris, to transfer the call? Maybe he wasn't inter—

"Ms. Campbell?"

Bella reached for the nearest chair and sat down. Mr. Harris's voice slid through the receiver, warming her like a cloak thrown over her shoulders. That same voice when he was trying to convince Bella how much he and his wife wanted her baby. The same voice, tear-soaked, when he'd held Destiny for the first time.

"Yes. It's me," she replied. "I, um, I called to thank you for sending me that letter about Destiny. My, er, your daughter. I only recently received it or I would have called you sooner.

To thank you." She was rambling, repeating herself. *I must sound so juvenile.*

Mr. Harris gave a relaxed chuckle. Was he leaning back in his seat, probably in a big office befitting a vice president for a big oil company, with an unobstructed view of downtown Austin? "Have you talked with Destiny?"

"Not yet. I wasn't sure if I should call her, so I wrote her a letter, but I haven't heard back. Actually, it's only been about a week. Perhaps she hasn't even received it." Bella gulped. "I was wondering if you thought she'd be okay with me calling her. I'd like to hear her voice, maybe even meet her, but I don't want to presume."

"She would probably accept a call from you. But she lives with her mother." He paused and his voice turned serious. "Her mother might not be accepting of a personal visit, at least not to the house, and especially not without warning."

Bella heard mumbling. Mr. Harris must have covered the phone with a hand. Perhaps he was talking with Mrs. Braxton again.

"I'm sorry, Ms. Campbell. May I call you Isabella?"

"Call me Bella. What everyone calls me."

"Oh, that's right. Now I remember. Since you've already sent a letter, why don't you call Des? Do you have the number?"

"Yes."

"Good. Would you like me to call her first, or text her? She seems to prefer texting, at least from me," his voice warm again. "Her mother refuses to do that."

"No. I think it would be better if I call her, without you letting her know. I don't want her to be mad at you if she isn't thrilled that I called."

"Oh, I think she'll be happy. Even though it's been a long time. And I owe you an apology. For not sending you regular updates, like we were supposed to. Vanessa felt it wasn't necessary after we moved. I should have stood my ground on that score."

It was her *doing, and not his?* "It's all right. I understand." Even though Bella didn't. "Thank you for taking my call. I hope Mrs. Braxton doesn't think it was inappropriate for me to ask to speak with you."

Mr. Harris' voice took on a soothing tone. "Not to worry. When she mentioned you said it was personal, I told her you were a distant relative. She has lots of cousins of the third- or fourth-removed variety."

"Oh. Well, good. Thank you again, Mr. Harris."

"Call me Nolan, Bella. After all, I suspect we both want the same thing."

"What's that?"

"For Destiny to be happy."

"Yes, of course. Would you like me to call you after I speak with her?"

"That won't be necessary. My daughter will probably text me the minute the two of you hang up."

Bella nodded, feeling his smile as if he was in the room with her. "I'm sure you're right. Good-bye, Mr. Harris. Nolan."

"What do you mean? I thought it was all arranged." Bella saw her new, sort-of approved plan to offer a Chapter Read-Along with Activities for the elementary children fading into obscurity before it had even begun.

Zoe frowned as she sat down in Bella's office. "Mitchell stopped me in the hall right after I arrived. I showed him the poster I made up last night, figuring Henry would be happy to give us the books after he gets out of the hospital. See this sketch?"—Zoe showed Bella what she'd come up with—"But Mitchell claimed not to like it. Said it was too soon. That we

43

should wait until the next school year. Talk to him. You're always more convincing than I am."

"I will, after I see Henry. If he agrees to give us some books, I'll tell Mitchell. Maybe that'll convince him."

"Good luck with that. I'll take the Preschool Story Land today so you can go to the hospital earlier than four. I called this morning. Visiting hours begin at two."

"Thanks, Zoe. You just saved me a call."

"I called the bookstore, too. Earl answered. He sounded under the weather, but a lot better than Henry." Zoe shook her head. "That man has to be at least as old as Henry. I asked if any *Harry Potters* were scheduled for the sale table and he said no. When I asked him if he could approve giveaways, he said he wasn't 'authorized.'" She air-quoted.

"Then I'll ask Henry when I see him."

"Do you think his nephew is here now?"

Bella grimaced, recalling that the man had hung up on her. "For Henry's sake, I hope so. But who knows? He didn't sound like it was high on his to-do list. I'll pick up a get-well bouquet. Henry's always saying flowers cheer him up."

"And it'll make it easier for him to say 'yes,' right Bella?" Zoe gave her a slightly lopsided grin.

"Mostly, I'll just tell him he needs to get well quickly, so he can come to our first meeting. I'll want to introduce him to all the parents, like we did when we took on the little kids' session, to encourage them to buy their books at his store."

"When do you want to start, assuming you can change Mitchell's mind?"

Bella straightened to her full five-foot-five. "Like we planned. But we'll have to get the books first. I was so hoping we could announce it in posters beginning next week and then in emails to the library patrons and at the little kids' Story Land. Several have big brothers and sisters. You and I should take the posters around to the teachers at all three elementary schools."

"Sounds good. I'll work on another sample poster tonight. Mitchell didn't like some of the colors, so I'll change them and bring a couple in for you to see."

"You're a love. No wonder Tör couldn't resist you."

Zoe laughed and pointed to the clock on the wall of Bella's office. "Listen, if you're going to see Henry, you'd better leave right around one-thirty."

Bella laughed. "Have fun with the babies today." She opened the drawer where she stored her purse. "If Mitchell asks where I am—"

"Not to worry. I'll tell him you're on your way to collect the books. Free ones."

When Bella wagged a finger at her, Zoe replied, "Well, you are. Sort of."

Bella tucked a bright bouquet of yellow and red flowers under her arm and shifted the strap of her purse higher on her shoulder as she entered the hospital. Before the elevator doors closed, a tall man entered. He punched the fourth floor button just as Bella was getting ready to do so. He glanced her way for an instant before backing into a corner and facing the door as he looked down at his phone. His chestnut brown hair contained streaks of gold that offset his sky-blue eyes in an angular face, his cheeks and chin covered in what she guessed to be two days' worth of reddish gold stubble. Lines radiated out from either side of his eyes, as if he'd been up too long, or perhaps had slept poorly the night before. But the man wore his gray suit pants well. His dress shirt clung to his chest and when he flexed an arm, his muscles pressed against the sleeve. *He must be at least six feet tall.* Bella's gaze slid to his belt buckle. It skimmed a slim waist. *I'll bet he has a six-*

pack. His shoulders were broad, his hips narrow. Something about the confidence with which he held himself reminded her of Ethan. *But he's a lot better looking than Ethan. Maybe he's a surfer dude from California.* But why would a surfer wear a suit? And why was she imagining what he might look like without clothes?

When the man took one step to the side, Bella pressed her hand against his arm to protect the flowers she carried.

"Sorry," he muttered before stepping away without glancing at her.

He's probably a new father come to see his wife and baby. Wasn't the maternity wing on the fourth floor, too? She was still musing on that possibility when the elevator stopped, the doors opened, and the man stepped out, looked in the direction of the nurse's station to his left, and headed that way.

Bella checked the room number on the nearest door and turned to her right until she reached Henry's room. His door was closed. She knocked and opened it.

"Henry?" Bella placed the bouquet on the table next to Henry's bed. The old man's hair seemed to blend into the white of the pillowcase against which his head rested. He opened his eyes and looked as if he wasn't sure who she was for a moment, then smiled.

"The lovely Miss Bella. How are you, my dear? I should have thanked you and Zoe for bringing me here. Those docs said I was about ready to check out last night."

Bella sucked in a gulp of air. "But you're feeling better now?"

"That I am. Just shove my nephew's things off the chair and have a seat. You came to the store yesterday. Or am I not remembering that correctly?"

She nodded. "He made it?" She draped a black sport jacket off the end of Henry's bed, lifted the heavy briefcase off the chair and onto the floor, and took a seat.

"Yes, last night and again this morning, before I sent him to the store to make sure Earl was there to open. No sense missing business just 'cause I'm not there." He smiled and then had a coughing spell.

Bella waited while Henry sipped some water. "I can confirm that Earl is there. Zoe talked to him this morning. Is your nephew going to help you at the store while you're here?"

Henry started to laugh and then began to cough. "He doesn't know a thing about bookstores, but he asked to look over the accounts for me. They're in his briefcase. We were going over them before the nurse kicked him out so I could rest. I 'spect he'll be back for his things soon enough."

"Then I'd better not keep you. I came to see how you were doing. These are for you. To cheer you up," she offered, holding up the flowers for him to admire. "Can I put them in this extra glass?"

"'Course. Now tell me why you and Zoe, my two favorite girls, came to the store yesterday."

Bella leaned forward to grasp Henry's gnarled hand and told him about her plans for the new Chapter Read-Along and Activities session for older children. "All we have to do is secure extra books for the children who don't have their own, which is where you come in. We're going to start with the *Harry Potter* series and were wondering if you'd be willing to donate six copies of the first book."

"I'll bet ol' Mitchell is still a tightwad, isn't he?" Henry smiled benignly in Bella's direction.

"How'd you guess?"

"'Cause I know his ex-wife. She's just as bad." His lips curved upward and he began to cough. When he caught a breath, he raised one arm off the bed. "Could you move me up a bit, so I can see you better? When I'm closer to upright,

I don't cough so much."

"Sure." Bella looked around for the button, found it and pressed. "Tell me when to stop."

"That's good." The man's pale blue eyes settled on her face. "Let me guess. So you came today to wrangle books for your pet project. Kinda like when you started the little kids' story hour."

"I came to see you, to wish you well, so you'll get better," she protested.

"'Course you did, but I'll bet you and your pal, Zoe, have to convince Mitchell to let you do what any good library should do so kids'll like reading. And after a sample during your Story Times, they'll come into my store and see all the great books we have just for them. Am I right?"

Bella felt her cheeks bloom as her eyes filled. "You are such a dear man, and nothing gets past you."

Henry began to cough again. Bella watched with alarm as the coughing spell continued far longer than she thought was normal. "Should I call the nurse, Henry?" She rose from the chair she'd taken.

He waved his arm in her direction and shook his head before his coughing finally stopped. "No need. She'll be in soon enough. Sit back down so we can do our business." He reached for the water glass.

Bella helped him position the straw then set the glass back on the table.

"Thank you, Bella. Now, for the books." His brow furrowed, as if he was doing mental inventory. "I have all the titles you need. As long as you take the books that look kind of ratty, with torn dust jackets, that sort of thing. We have a few of the *Potters* in that condition. The pages are fine, but the dust jackets look kind of sad. They show how long we've had some of those copies."

"Of course. We might not even use the dust jackets, and the kids will only be reading our copies during the hour. They won't be taking them home, so the books won't be damaged further."

"Okay then. Go ahead and talk to Earl. He'll get you the books. Half a dozen of each title, right?"

"Yes, but we only need the first volume of Harry now. And each time we start a new book, we'll be sure to let the parents know where they can get their personal copies."

Henry nodded. "Just like before." He began to cough again, his face turning red as he did so.

A nurse entered the room and reached for Henry's wrist. "Mr. Quackenbush, I think it's time your visitor let you rest."

"I'm leaving." Bella stood. "May I give you a kiss, Henry?" she asked, her eyes welling up again.

"Not sure I deserve it. What would I do without you and Zoe to brighten my day?"

Bella leaned over the bed and kissed Henry's forehead, refusing to accept that he might not get better. "Promise me you'll get well real soon, Henry."

The nurse briefly took Bella's place at the head of the bed, checked his pulse, and left.

Bella wiped her eyes and began to back toward the door. *He has to get better.* At her next visit, she would remind Henry how much Zoe wanted Henry at her wedding. Maybe that would give him an incentive to follow the doctor's orders.

Bella turned to leave just as the door opened with a rush and she ran smack into a man's hard body. It carried a faint scent of something woodsy and male. Bella fell back against Henry's bed, and her feet went out from under her. She slid to the floor and lay there for a moment, stunned, her skirt hiked up well above her knees. When she glanced upward, a man's shocked gaze bore down on her as he stared at the length of leg showing before he focused on her face.

"Oh! I'm so sorry. Let me help you up." He leaned down to grasp Bella's hand, his gaze still locked on her face.

Who is she? He recalled the woman in the elevator, the one whose figure he'd wanted to enjoy, but out of propriety, he'd tried to ignore. But now, he looked, couldn't help it. She was sprawled on Henry's floor as she grasped his hand. Her mass of red shoulder-length curls looked fetchingly mussed. *Great legs ... and that hair ...* She didn't look hurt, but the way she was grimacing in his direction as she stood up and brushed her skirt down, her cheeks nearly as red as her hair, prompted him to come out of his trance and belatedly apologize again.

"Are you okay? Need a doctor?" he asked.

"Do you make a habit of knocking people down when you enter a room?" Her voice sounded familiar, but he'd never met her before, and what was she doing in his uncle's room?

"Not usually. On the other hand, you weren't exactly watching where you were going," he countered. He wanted to say more until he spied the nurse staring at him from the doorway as if *she* wanted to knock *him* down.

"Are you all right, Miss?" she asked.

The woman with the red cheeks, now a pretty pink, nodded. She turned toward the bed. "I'll see you tomorrow, Henry. Please follow the doctor's orders."

Henry nodded and grinned. "Bring sweet Zoe with you next time. Seeing the two of you is better'n any medicine the docs give me."

The woman glared briefly at Gavin before easing past him

and walking out the door. He watched her leave, regretting he hadn't thought to introduce himself.

Gavin remained where he was, still staring at the door as if seeing past it into the hall where the woman had disappeared.

"You certainly know how to make an entrance, boy," Henry commented drily.

He turned toward his uncle, then eased into the chair near his bed. "Who was that woman?"

With a broad chuckle, Henry announced, "If I were a bettin' man, I'd say she's the one you're going to marry."

His uncle's words cleared the fog from Gavin's brain and he resumed his scan of his uncle's face. The man looked okay, though his voice was kind of scratchy. "Are you crazy? She looked like she wanted to kill me."

"Only because she wasn't thrilled to meet you that way."

"Since when have I said I plan to marry? I learned my lesson on that score." But the redhead looked like she'd be a handful—maybe a fun handful, if he could just get her to forget how they'd run into each other.

Henry snorted and then coughed. "Give me that water, son." He took the glass from Gavin and sipped. "Her name's Isabella Campbell. Bella runs the Evergreen library. She and her buddy over there, Zoe, are two of my best lady friends. And they need my help. Your help, now that I'm stuck here."

"How's that?"

"I promised them some books for their new project. Free books. You're gonna take them to her. Personally." His pale blue eyes twinkled. "An easy way to meet her. Introduce yourself. Or didn't my sister teach you any manners?"

"You know she did." The thought of making the redhead's acquaintance again held a certain appeal, but not if his uncle was going into major matchmaking mode, taking up where his mother had left off. She'd finally apologized, weeks before her death, when it was clear that he and Eileen had been a mistake in the wedded bliss department. Gavin shook his head.

"And don't go thinking Bella's at all like that she-devil, Eileen. She didn't deserve you and I told you so before you got married. Or don't you remember?"

Gavin clenched his jaw in hopes of avoiding the emergence of words admitting that he should have listened to his uncle. Gavin hadn't come to the hospital to confirm Henry's opinion of Eileen, nor was it a topic he wished to dwell on. Reluctantly, he said, "You were right."

"'Course I was."

"Back to my question. Which you didn't answer. Why her?"

Henry bit back a cough. "The way you were looking at her, like you'd been knocked upside the head by a two-by-four. Same way your sister said I looked when I met Ina. And felt, too. Plain as the nose on your face."

Gavin shook his head vigorously. "No one gave me a dope slap, but I would *be* a dope if I even considered another walk down the aisle. And I didn't come here to find a wife. I'm here to check on you after some woman told me you were sick and I had to take care of your store. I was surprised you were still running it. If I'm to keep it going while you're in the hospital, I won't have time to waltz around town delivering a bunch of free books to a couple of librarians," he said dismissively. "Why are you giving away books, anyway? Aren't you supposed to sell them?"

Henry nodded. "That was Bella."

Gavin started in his chair. The voice that had sounded so familiar. "*She* called me?"

Henry nodded.

Gavin frowned. A quick glance at his uncle's knowing

grin encouraged him to change the subject. "Tell me how the store's doing. What about that helper you had? Is he still around?"

"Earl? Doesn't leave the store. Never makes deliveries, like I want you to do."

"Why's that?"

"Doesn't do well in parts of town he doesn't know, and the library is two bus rides from downtown. Too far for him to go on his bike."

"No car?"

"No, and he hates the bus. Besides, I want him *in* the store, helping the customers. Just take those books to Bella and Zoe. They're expectin' them." Henry began to cough again, pressed one hand to his chest and fell back against his pillow.

Gavin was silent when a nurse and a doctor entered the room after a quick knock. He stepped outside for a moment and returned to the room after the two medical personnel departed.

"What'd they say, Henry?"

"I've got pneumonia."

"Old news. They said that when I was here this morning, right before I left to get some breakfast."

"Then why are you here now?"

"Forgot my jacket. And my briefcase."

"Well, that's all I know. No more news, like when I can leave." He sighed. "You're still going to help me with the tax filing before you head home?"

"I said I would, didn't I? And after that ..." Gavin wondered if he should mention his concerns about the store. Somehow, Gavin didn't think his uncle would be coming home this week or maybe even the next. Another issue he needed to take up with the doctor before he called Hortense.

Henry waved a hand dismissively. "You do that, but first

check in with Earl. He'll know the books the girls need. My library girls, that's what I call them, Bella and Zoe." He began to cough again and reached for the water glass.

"I'll be your errand boy just this once, but you have to do something for me." Gavin shrugged into his sport jacket and looked for his briefcase. He spied one corner of it poking out from under the bed. It must have slid under there when that woman hit the floor. He'd been up too long, at least forty hours. He needed some sleep before tackling anything more strenuous than taking a shower and changing clothes after his drive from Spokane.

"Since when are you telling me what to do, boy?"

"I want you to get well. So we can talk about the store. After you're home, Henry. When you feel better." Gavin smothered a yawn behind one hand.

"I intend to," Henry rasped before lapsing into another fit of coughing. "Now, go. Bella wants to start that new story hour soon. I don't want her havin' to hold up on that because she doesn't have the books she needs."

Gavin grabbed his uncle's hand to shake it and was surprised when the man pulled him closer to the bed for an impromptu hug, not something he did all that often. *Wonder what brought that on?*

As he left the hospital, he mentally repeated, *Evergreen Public Library. Isabella Campbell.* Henry's outrageous statement came to mind again, that Gavin had just met the woman he would marry. *Fat chance of that.* He'd learned, the hard way, that marriage was another word for misery.

Chapter 5

GAVIN OPENED THE CAR DOOR AND TOSSED HIS BRIEF-case, crammed with his uncle's paperwork, onto the passenger seat before climbing into his red BMW Z4. Maybe with the help of Henry's one employee, Gavin could keep his uncle out of trouble with the IRS while he figured out why Henry hadn't completed and submitted the forms. Gavin's mother was always comparing her husband's I'll-get-it-done-eventually approach to her brother's I'll-be-the-first-to-file attitude.

Henry's pale countenance and the nearly-constant coughing told Gavin the man was likely to remain in the hospital for several days at least. Gavin's late mother, who'd died from cancer, would expect him to do what he could to help her brother. Gavin knew pneumonia could kill, too. Those little oxygen tubes running into Henry's nose were worrisome.

He'd already emailed Hortense that he wasn't sure he'd be able to leave by the end of the week.

Gavin sighed. Had he not received that call from the saucy redhead who claimed to be a friend of Henry's, he wouldn't even be here.

How long he would stay depended on his uncle's recovery. Maybe if Henry came home quickly, Gavin would visit that dealership he'd been meaning to check out, over the bridge near Redmond.

That woman he'd bumped into, Bella, claimed she wasn't hurt when she'd landed on her ass onto Henry's hospital room floor. Her shoulder-length red curls, and those hazel eyes with a ring of emerald, had pulled him in, made him want to get closer, to touch her in a way that soothed, maybe even excited. Henry hadn't said, but she must have been the one who'd brought the flowers. She had to be single, or Henry wouldn't have made that crack about marriage.

And what if she *was* available? Why should he care? Except that he did.

He'd sworn off women after his divorce, stomping his awareness of pretty women into nothingness, but his attraction to Bella had generated a response he hadn't felt since the night he'd met his ex-wife and been suckered into falling for her. Mistake number one, which led to mistake number two, marrying her.

His ex-wife's impending wedding to some poor schmuck had finally halted her calls to Gavin for assistance, and her insistence on being the center of a man's attention. *Thank you, God, and whoever you've hooked your claws into this time, Eileen.* For an instant, he felt a wave of sympathy for the new man in Eileen's life. He was glad to no longer be the first person she sought out for help. Glad she'd stopped showing up on his doorstep, begging him to help her out of a jam, asking for money when she'd run through hers.

Gavin had promised his uncle he would deliver the books. He wondered if his reaction to the woman would be as strong when he handed over those books she needed. He'd stick to business, deliver the damn books, and get the hell out of the library. He was here to help Henry, ride herd on his store until his uncle was able to get back to work, after which he'd hightail it back to Spokane.

Gavin started the car, eased out of the parking place, and drove to Henry's bookstore. Time to talk to the old guy who was holding down the fort. That morning, Earl had said something about a special event they'd been invited to participate in at the library. Probably related to the free books Henry had mentioned, the books Earl knew about. Free advertising seemed the least they could do if Henry was giving away books he should have insisted on getting paid for. Gavin suspected the woman and her friend had snookered Uncle Henry, let him think they liked him, let him flirt with them just to get freebies. Gavin's jaw tightened. He'd put a stop to that. No store could stay in business giving away merchandise.

Henry had said the librarian had a list of books they wanted. Didn't they know books were expensive? And since when did little kids read books almost as big as they were? Gavin grunted to himself. He'd read books when he was a kid, but none like those *Harry Potter* tomes that had hit the best-seller lists. Not that he hadn't been intrigued by wizards when he was a kid. He'd read the *Narnia* books. The *Oz* books, too. Before his interest turned to cars and girls.

His interest in cars had led to his business degree and, ultimately, his ownership of a BMW franchise. His interest in girls had led to numerous women before he'd fallen for Eileen. Gavin ground his back teeth. Other women had been fun; she'd been fun, too, before she'd turned into a disaster on two legs, practically the day after they'd returned from their honeymoon. A disaster in stilettos, a demanding disaster he could never satisfy except in bed. Probably the only reason she'd stayed with him before she suggested a divorce he'd agreed to with relief.

He parked his car behind the brick building that housed Henry's bookstore. *Not the best part of town.* Would his wheels be in danger here in the alley? But it was still daylight and he didn't intend to stay long.

He banged in through the back door of the bookstore. The old man—what *was* his name? Started with an E. *Edward?* No. *Earl?* That's it—was perched on a stool next to the cash register, his head in a book. *Of course.* Hadn't he said he read everything they carried?

"Earl, I'm back," Gavin announced, not wanting to startle the old coot into a heart attack.

"Good. I saved this for you. That list for the librarians. Zoe called. Maybe you could talk to them. If Henry doesn't get back to them by next week, they'll come marching in here, smart as you please, Monday morning."

"Them? I thought you said just one called."

"There're two. Zoe's the one who gave me the list. Bella's the other one. Henry calls them 'sisters of his heart.' Bella's always nice. That Zoe girl is nice, too, but pushier. I don't want to have to deal with her, if you know what I mean. You do that and you'll stay on Henry's good side. Mine, too."

"An admirable goal," Gavin replied drily. He looked at the list. "Good God! Do they think these books grow on trees? We can't afford to give all these away."

"Not all at once. They'll probably start with the big ones, those *Harry Potters.* We have a few that are kind of beat up. Henry'll want to give them those. Zoe said if we provide six, she's sure the parents will want to buy the same ones for the 'little darlings.'" Earl smirked. "Not what I call those brats. Some of those kids have smart mouths. Not the kind of thing you have to put up with in *your* business, I'm guessin'."

"I wouldn't say that. Some of my customers can be kind of hard to take, too." Gavin leaned against the counter. "Is my car safe behind this building?"

"Sure. I park my bike there all the time. Never had any trouble."

Gavin considered Earl's reply. Who would want to steal that old thing? Henry probably parked there, too, but his uncle drove a twenty-year-old Corolla with rusty fenders. Not exactly in the same class as his almost-new Z4.

"Maybe I'll leave it in the city garage tomorrow." He clutched the list of books Earl handed him. "I'll study this list, figure out Henry's cost for being so generous. Then you can deliver them."

Earl shook his head and looked anxious before he blurted, "Don't do deliveries."

"Sorry, I forgot."

"Call the library and let 'em know you're coming. So you don't have to wait around."

"Good idea."

"Just ask for Zoe. Or Bella, the prettier one. Nicer. Not so pushy."

"Right. Whatever. Whoever."

"Let me get those books for you. How was Henry this afternoon? He was asleep when I called."

"Very sick. The doctors are keeping him until his lungs are clear and he doesn't need extra oxygen. A good thing you convinced him to go to the emergency room. I'm turning over the tax stuff to my accountant. Know why Henry hasn't filed?"

"Those women did the convincing." Earl cleared his throat

and slid off the stool on which he'd been perched. "He kept saying he would get to the taxes, but then he got sick. Missed some days when I figured he was home working on them. You know, where it would be nice and quiet. Until you found them when you were going through his desk, I had no idea they weren't done."

Gavin nodded. *Is Henry suffering from dementia, too?* He'd ask the doctor about that.

Earl gestured toward the front door. "Since you're headed home, do you mind if I leave, too? We can put a sign up. Let people know Henry's sick. What he would do if he was here." He waved one arm, as if encompassing the entire store. "We're not exactly overrun with customers today."

Gavin had noticed. *Is it always like this, so empty every afternoon?* If so, no wonder Henry complained that the big box stores were taking his business. "Sure. Go on home. I'll see you tomorrow."

Gavin accepted the stack of books that Earl handed over and departed through the back door. *Zoe.* If he gave her the books, he wouldn't have to confront the other woman. *Bella.* The way his body reacted when he thought of her confirmed that he was making the right choice to ask for Zoe. Three teenagers scattered from around his car as they made a dash for the end of the alley. Gavin walked around his car, looking for flat tires and scratches in case they'd keyed the doors. Seeing no damage, he tossed the books into the passenger seat, climbed in, and headed for Henry's house.

It was nearly closing time when Gavin called the library.

"Evergreen Public Library, this is Mr. Hargrove. How may I help you?"

Gavin felt like clearing his throat after hearing the man's gravelly voice. "I'd like to speak with Zoe. Sorry, I don't know her last name."

"That would be Zoe Patrick. She's already left for the day. How can I help you?"

"I have some books for her. For a new project."

"Speak to Bella. She's probably in charge of that. I'll transfer you."

The man clicked off before Gavin could object. He listened to the phone ring twice before Bella, her voice breathless, as if she'd just run in, answered. "This is Ms. Campbell."

"It's Gavin Cambridge, Henry's nephew. I have the books you wanted. How long will you be there?"

"That's so nice of him, but you don't have to do that. Zoe or I could come get them tomorrow. I'm sure you're busy."

Was she being sarcastic or just stating what she thought obvious? At least she sounded pleasant enough and she seemed to have put that unhappy incident at the hospital behind her. But he would disappoint his uncle, who'd been quite specific about making sure the books got to the right person. "Sorry, I'm under orders to deliver them personally. When do you close?"

"The library is open until seven this evening. I'll wait for you if you plan to come over now." Maybe she was checking her watch and that explained the elongated pause that followed. "It's already after six. Can you make it in the next few minutes?"

"I'm on my way. Thank you, Ms. Campbell." Gavin hung up, grabbed his suit coat with one hand, and scooped up the half-dozen copies of *Harry Potter and the Sorcerer's Stone* with the other.

Gavin sucked in a deep breath as he keyed the address of the library into his car's GPS system. In the late afternoon, his brief perusal of the accounting records of the bookstore made it obvious that old Henry had paid less than total attention to his expenses. Or maybe it was the steady decline in income that he hadn't noticed. Probably both.

Taking care of things while Henry was hospitalized was looking like a bigger job than Gavin had imagined.

The doctor hadn't been all that helpful when queried. "Hard to tell how long he'll be here. After all, he's coming hard up on eighty and pneumonia's not easy to shake at that age."

Maybe Henry's illness explained his lack of attention to running the bookstore. Earl had said Henry had been fighting a cold for weeks. Gavin suspected Earl thought of the store as a handy spot to hang out, and that his uncle viewed his business as a hobby, not like when Aunt Ina was alive. *That has to change. I either get this place running like it should, or we shut it down.* It was the least he could do for his only living relative.

If the bookstore went out of business, maybe the library would accept their inventory. Providing it to them would generate a nice tax deduction. Gavin snorted. As if Henry needed one. But it might make him feel good. He seemed to have a soft spot for those librarians, Bella and Zoe.

He hit the brakes harder than necessary as he approached a red light. Too bad Zoe, the woman he hadn't met, wasn't available. The prospect of seeing Bella again had his pulse racing. Was it because he *wanted* to see her, or that she represented danger he didn't want to deal with? The danger of a beautiful woman he was attracted to.

A challenge. That's all. One I can handle, he assured himself. Come to think of it, he wouldn't mind seeing her socially. A dinner date, maybe. He'd prove to himself and Henry that he wasn't interested in anything more than that.

He decided against asking if the library would entertain receiving a major contribution if the bookstore closed. The woman might take it the wrong way, think he wasn't supportive of his uncle's business. He'd wait until Henry was out of the hospital. After all, *Henry* should be the one to approve a decision as big as shutting down the store, a decision Gavin was going to push for, if his accountant supported Gavin's preliminary reading of the finances.

He parked in the only remaining spot to one side of the Evergreen Public Library. As he entered the building, he noted how busy it was with patrons of all ages in the front reading room, even a few minutes before closing time. A group of small children filed out of another room, accompanied by their parents. Most carried books or book bags. One little tyke was sobbing.

"But I wanted the other one, too, like the movie." He scrubbed one tear-stained cheek.

"We'll read the other one after we finish this one," his harried father assured him.

Gavin approached the checkout desk. "Can you point me in the direction of Ms. Campbell's office?"

The woman at the desk smiled. "Straight back past the first set of shelves and then into the hall to the right. Her office is the second door on the right."

"Thank you."

The woman's door was closed. Gavin knocked.

"Come in." The occupant of the office was faced away from the door, which explained why her voice seemed muffled. She was bent over and appeared to be picking up something off the floor. Before turning, she added, "I'll be right with you."

Gavin admired her ass, wondering for a moment if she'd bruised it earlier that day, and, as she straightened up, the length of beautiful leg that her skirt again revealed. His pulse picked up and sent his blood rushing straight south.

She turned around slowly, giving him ample time to check out the curves even her tastefully modest dress revealed. Its pale blue color contrasted prettily with her deeper, more intense hair color.

Her smile declined into a slight frown. "Oh. It's you." Her gaze slid from his face to the books he was holding. She motioned for him to set them onto the nearby table. "Thank you for bringing them. Please tell Henry you did your duty."

Gavin felt her gaze on him. She must have been thinking of Henry when she smiled and he spied a dimple in her left cheek. A dimple he wanted to touch right before he kissed her slightly pouty lips.

"Henry is such a dear man. Please. Have a seat." She slid into her chair and pulled out a form. "Let me give you a receipt. I'm sure Henry will want to declare this as a tax-deductible contribution."

The rim of emerald around the gold of her eyes seemed to widen when she looked back at Gavin. "Make it out to Books and More. The bookstore."

"Of course. I do hope Henry comes home soon. We insisted he go to the hospital. He's always been so nice to us. We prefer to feature the indie bookstores in town and he has such a wonderful children's collection. When we revamped how we were doing the story hour for the kids under five, he was so generous with the picture books we used to get things started."

The corners of Gavin's mouth curved downward. *He's giving away* other *books instead of charging for them?*

"I don't believe Henry ever mentioned you. Do you see him often?" She straightened in her seat and Gavin found himself noticing the curve of her breasts.

"I live in Spokane. Came as soon as you called."

"Yes, well." Her cheeks seemed to turn pink for some reason Gavin couldn't fathom. "I'm glad he has a relative here. I worry about him, that he's all alone. Except for Earl, of course. But I'm not sure Earl pays much attention to the store. Every time we visit Henry, Earl is reading a book. Great advertisement for books, but not such a great salesperson." Her smile ceased when her gaze again focused on Gavin's face.

Gavin preferred to see her smile, to see those hazel eyes shift to green. "Perhaps we should find a time to discuss all these giveaways. Over dinner, maybe?"

Her expression turned wary and the color in her cheeks declined.

"A business dinner. You do have them, don't you?" He pressed, unable to prevent himself from imagining what might occur after dinner. Henry's words flashed. If she agreed, Gavin risked giving Henry a reason to taunt him. Business dinners were something Gavin engaged in frequently. None thus far had led to marriage, and Ms. Campbell, the librarian, didn't have to know what Henry had announced.

She lifted her chin slightly as if challenging him. "I'm sure Zoe and I would be happy to meet with you here in the library, or perhaps at your uncle's store. There's no need to go to dinner to discuss what Henry, what Mr. Quackenbush, offered."

Gavin's stomach slid downward as it clutched. *Does she know what Henry said?* Gavin rose from his chair. "What I have to say isn't something I want Earl to overhear. As for meeting here"—he looked around her office—"I suspect you're likely to be interrupted from time to time. A dinner meeting would be better." He leaned over her desk, close enough to discern how her eye color seemed to flicker between gold and green again. "More relaxed, too. Are you free tomorrow?" He eased back slightly and nodded at the nameplate on her desk. "Ms. Campbell?"

Had his invitation flummoxed her? *Doesn't she go out with men?* Or was there some other reason she seemed to be hesitating? She didn't strike him as a lesbian, but he'd been wrong before.

She was staring down at her desk calendar. "My social calendar tomorrow is already filled."

Her words were clipped and too businesslike, it seemed to Gavin. *Maybe she's in a relationship already and the guy's possessive.* Even if it was just an after-work Friday *business* dinner. *Saturday evenings are reserved for dates.* He decided to meet her challenge. "Then how about Saturday?" That might tell him what he wanted to know.

She leaned back in her seat then stood up and reached for the coat hanging on a coat rack to one side of the office door. "I believe that would work."

Hmm. *If she is with someone, he must not be that important. Or maybe she doesn't plan to tell him.* "Great. I'll pick you up at seven. What's your address?"

"I'd prefer to meet you here. At the library," she replied primly.

"Why here? You think I'm some kind of pervert?"

"Let's just say I'm cautious about men I don't know."

"You know who I am. Talk to Henry. He'll vouch for me, and he'd pound me into the ground if he got wind that I had harmed even one beautiful hair on that gorgeous head of yours." He watched her left eyebrow arch and color flood her cheeks again. He gave her a smile that he hoped suggested simple appreciation. Nothing more.

She pressed her lips together. "I believe I will. Call him, I mean. And I'll meet you here at seven on Saturday," she restated. "For our business dinner."

"Glad we're both clear on that."

Bella's eyebrow rose again and her lips pressed together into a thin line. *She must have caught my sarcasm.* To prevent her from coming up with an excuse for cancelling their dinner date, Gavin strode out of Bella's office, pleased that he'd be seeing her again soon. Not soon enough, if he'd had his way, though it was only a business dinner, but he'd better warn Henry that the library lady was likely to call him, maybe even visit to ask after his nephew. *As long as he says nice things, I'm in like Flynn.* But what if Henry told stories about him, like when he'd gotten into trouble in high school? Did he still remember Gavin's juvenile escapades? What if Henry mentioned to Bella what he'd predicted to Gavin? Maybe telling her to call his uncle wasn't such a good idea.

Bella went home shortly after the smug Gavin Cambridge left her office. After a relaxing cup of tea, she called Zoe.

"We have the books for our first session. Delivered this evening. You did it!"

Zoe sneezed and answered nasally. "Not me. It was probably those flowers you took to Henry in the hospital. Did Earl bring them? If so, that would be a first."

"No. Henry's nephew brought them in. That guy we called when we took Henry to the hospital."

"I remember. Does he look like Henry? You know, sort of rounded in the middle and mostly bald on top?"

Bella felt her stomach change places with her heart. *Not bald at all, and definitely not rounded in the middle.* "Not exactly." She flashed on his lean body and how well he filled out that barely-wrinkled suit he'd worn, probably more hours than usual.

"Old, kind of halfway between our age and Henry's?"

"Closer to our age, I think."

"Come on, Bella. Don't make me beg. Tell me more."

"He's tall. I'm thinking at least six feet. Medium brown

hair, but the first time I saw him, I was sure he was a surfer. Lots of blond streaks."

"What do you mean the first time?"

"In the elevator. And then he bumped into me. Literally. In Henry's room."

"Not exactly the most graceful way to meet a man. Tell me more, girl. Is he handsome? Nice eyes?"

"Blue eyes, not pale. More like summer sky blue. And, he knows how to dress. That is, what he was wearing fit him *really* well."

Zoe started to laugh then began to cough. She blew her nose and asked, "Is he married, this nephew of Henry's? Any chance you're going to see him again? Is he going to help out at the store while Henry's out of commission?"

"He wants to meet over dinner to discuss the book give-aways. I don't think he's happy about them. Maybe he thinks we're taking advantage. Don't you still have copies of the receipts for those other donations Henry made? Maybe I should take them with me."

"Check the file drawer on the left-hand side of my desk. I think the donations file is in there. But why does young Mr. Quackenbush think we're taking advantage of his uncle?"

"His name is Gavin Cambridge, remember? I have no idea, but he wasn't all that enthusiastic about the donations, even though he brought us the first set. Henry probably insisted."

"Anything else I should know about Gavin Cambridge?"

"The way he was dressed tells me he's not hurting for money. And I think he was the one who drove out of the side lot in a fancy red sports car."

"Really? Now that I'm happy and engaged, it's time you were, too, Bella. Maybe this is the man for you."

That thought leapt around in Bella's stomach, reminding her of a flurry of busy butterflies. "I doubt that. He doesn't even live around here."

"Too bad. Long-distance romances are the pits."

"Right." *And a good thing.* Something she'd remind herself if she was tempted. He was attractive, but Bella wasn't sure she wanted to be tempted.

"He does sound yummy." Zoe sneezed and blew her nose. "When's this business dinner occurring?"

"He asked about tomorrow. I told him I was already booked."

"With what, Bella? Or were you planning to visit Henry again? Maybe his nephew will be there, too."

"Tomorrow, before work, I'm going to follow up that conversation I had with Mr. Harris and call Destiny. Since I have no idea how that call will go, I don't want to have to pretend to be pleasant in the company of a man I don't even know. I'd rather sulk in my office and then go home and cry myself to sleep if Destiny wants nothing to do with me."

"Oh, Bella. I doubt she'd do that. You still haven't heard from her? No letters or anything?"

"Not a word. Maybe she doesn't know what to say. Or maybe she never got the letter. I've been wondering if her mother might have seen it first and, you know, tossed it out."

"Just because your mother might do that, doesn't mean hers would act that way. Mine wouldn't." Zoe blew her nose again. "I hate these late spring colds."

Bella sighed. "You're right. I shouldn't assume all moms are like mine."

"Look, think of this business dinner as your chance to replace awful old Ethan with a guy worthy of you. Promise me you'll call me afterward and tell me what he really wants to know. And all the raunchy details, in case he has more than dinner in mind."

Bella's cheeks heated and those butterflies returned and

began to flutter in her stomach. "We're meeting at the library. I doubt we'll do anything but eat dinner while I convince him that we would never do a thing to hurt Henry. I'll bet we're the only people who regularly feature him in the library newsletter and the story times. Now he'll be featured in two different ones, for different ages. That has to translate into more sales for him, don't you think?"

"You don't have to convince me. Why don't you bring one of those sample posters we used when he gave us books the first time? So he can see we're advertising Books and More?"

"Thanks for reminding me."

"Oh, and good luck with that *and* finding out other things, personal things about him."

"Oh, Zoe. It's only been …" *How long has it been?* Bella glanced at the calendar. *Months. It's been months since Ethan and I called it quits. Since I called it quits.*

"Too many months, Bella. Look, I was just kidding about the nephew, but since he's paying, enjoy the dinner while you reassure him we love his uncle."

From Zoe's side of their conversation, Bella heard a doorbell and then a voice that sounded suspiciously like Tör.

"Did your honey just walk in?"

"Yep. Gotta go. He's bringing me chicken soup and more Kleenex." Zoe hung up.

Bella wandered into her bedroom and opened the closet. What should she wear for this Saturday business dinner? She pulled out one dress after the other, undecided. It wasn't a date, so she wouldn't wear the shimmery pale green one. But it was a Saturday dinner and she guessed Henry's nephew would select a nice place.

He hadn't said where. Would he drive to Seattle? That would mean they'd be in the car at least a half hour each way. She'd have to come up with casual questions to ask him, to get him to tell her about himself. But maybe she wouldn't have to. Tomorrow, she would call Henry if she didn't have time to visit him. Perhaps that would be the best way to learn about the man, most especially, how trustworthy he was. He'd seemed almost insistent in his request that they have a business meeting. Maybe he really was worried about the bookstore and wanted her take on how it was doing. As if she knew—though it was never as busy as she thought it should be whenever she and Zoe paid Henry a visit.

Bella looked through her closet again and pulled out her favorite get-dressed-up-but-not-too-much outfit. Her little black dress. She would select accessories that were more than she'd wear at the office, but not really date-worthy. Perhaps a scarf instead of a necklace. The green one that Zoe said brought out the green in her eyes. And she'd wear her hair down. With dangly earrings that would only be seen if she brushed her hair back. Her wardrobe decision made, Bella returned to the kitchen for a late dinner.

Chapter 6

BELLA CLIMBED OUT OF THE SHOWER, DRIED HER HAIR and wrapped herself in her favorite terry bathrobe before sitting down at the kitchen table. She picked up her phone and dialed.

"'Ullo?" The voice sounded sleep-tinged.

"Is this Destiny Camp—er, Destiny Harris?"

"Yeah." Silence ensued for a long beat. "Who's this?"

"My name is Isabella Campbell." She gulped and cleared her throat to stem the panic that her daughter might hang up on hearing Bella's next words. "Your birth mother."

"What?" The voice, louder this time, no longer sounded sleepy.

"Your birth mother," Bella repeated. "I wrote you a letter. Did you get it? I spoke with your father. He said it was okay to call you."

"Oh." The voice sounded more alert. "How'd you get this number?"

"I Googled your address in Denver, the one your father gave me."

"Oh." Long silence.

Bella decided to try again. "You can call me Bella. What I go by. Your dad said I should call you after I wrote you. Even though … To let you know … to verify that … I just wanted to touch base with you. That's all." Bella's heart pounded in her chest and her lungs seemed bereft of sufficient air. *Maybe she doesn't want to talk to me, doesn't want anything to do with me.*

When no reply occurred, she said, "I'd really like to see you, meet with you … Perhaps you'd be more comfortable if I came to your house?"

"No! You can't do that! My mom won't … she wouldn't … She might even call the cops on you." Destiny's tone sounded desperate, even as she lowered her voice to barely above a murmur.

Bella hadn't thought Mrs. Harris was the freaking-out kind of woman when she'd met her during those pre-adoption sessions. The woman had seemed calm, serious. But, thinking back on those meetings, Bella recalled the woman's husband had done most of the talking. He'd smiled all the time. Maybe Mrs. Harris had been more nervous than she let on.

"Then how about a neutral place? A hotel or a restaurant." She had to reassure the girl. "I don't want to make trouble, Destiny. I don't want to hurt you *or* your … Mrs. Harris." *Why can't I just* say *the word, that she's your mother?* But she knew why. "Or maybe we could just talk first. It's been such a long time." Bella sucked in a breath, wishing she didn't feel so unsure how to direct the conversation. "I'll bet you have questions." She'd read of other adoptees asking lots of questions. "Whatever you want to know, I'll answer."

"Just a minute."

The girl must have put down the phone. Bella heard muffled voices, the words unclear. Then a door slammed and she heard rustling and another door closing.

"Okay. Now we can talk. My mom went downstairs."

Bella sought to reassure her. "What would you like to know? Whatever it is, just ask. I'll answer," she repeated. *Even if it hurts.* "Or maybe I could ask you a question."

"Like what?"

"Well, have you ever wondered about me? Who I am, where I live, that sort of thing?"

"Not so much. My folks said you were really young when you had me."

"Sixteen when I got pregnant. Seventeen when you were born."

"Why did you wait so long to write me?"

Destiny's question felt like an accusation, but at least it told Bella she'd received the letter. Was she hurting, thinking Bella didn't want her, had tried to forget about her until now?

"I didn't know for sure where you were, not until I got your dad's letter." Bella gulped for air and reached for her water glass, wishing it was filled, so she could moisten her parched throat. "We all signed a contract when I agreed to the adoption. I was supposed to receive letters and pictures at least once a year and I sent you letters, too, on your birthday and at Christmas. Until your fifth birthday. That was the last letter I received."

Had Destiny's parents never shown her those letters Bella had written? Did she dare ask? And if that was the case, would asking damage Destiny's relationship with her adoptive mother? "Did you know about my letters?"

"I'm not sure. My dad might have read them to me when I was little. But I don't remember. The summer before I was six, we moved. I remember that."

"Maybe that's why the letters stopped. I never heard, and … I have other letters, the ones I wrote to you every year after that, but never mailed, after the first one came back. If you want, I could send them to you. So you'll know I never forgot about you."

Destiny was silent, as if considering Bella's words.

"How old was I when you gave me away?"

Bella's heart clutched. *I never gave you away. It wasn't what I wanted.* Destiny's question sent her mind reeling backward to those weeks when she'd tried to ignore what her body was telling her, to the terrible scenes with her parents after they found out and those conversations she'd been forced to have with the adoption worker. Well, okay, it had been her decision, finally, but she'd made it under duress, after her father had demanded, threatened her, after her mother kept harping on how Bella would be alone, and poor, unable to finish school if she kept the baby, that she couldn't live at home if she kept the baby, how Bella would have to go on welfare. Back then, she had no idea how she could make it on her own if they kicked her out.

Her parents had railed against Taylor and his family, who refused to believe he was the father. He'd denied it at first, made all kinds of accusations about who she must have slept with, and only after being threatened by his father did he admit that he had slept with her, too. "Just like the other guys on the team," he'd sneered. Basically calling her a whore.

In Bella's mind, sleeping with Taylor was confirmation that he loved her for more than her tutoring. He'd paid her compliments during their tutoring sessions, told her she was pretty, like she was his girlfriend, even if they'd never gone on dates that didn't include helping him with his homework assignments. Only later did Bella realize what Taylor had stolen from her. He'd laughed in disbelief at her news, broken her heart, and claimed that she couldn't be pregnant. They'd always used protection. Bella had to be lying. Then he'd said it had to be another guy's baby. That accusation had hurt the most.

How was she to know back then that condoms weren't one-hundred percent guaranteed? She'd wanted to believe she couldn't get pregnant when Taylor said they'd be careful. At sixteen, she'd been so stupid, and then crushed—first by Taylor's denials and then by her parents' reaction when they refused to let her keep the baby who won her over with those first tentative feather-like tickles that soon became more obvious thumps, especially at night when she lay in bed and tried to imagine what the baby looked like and how much she wanted to be its mother. A scary thought, but one she looked forward to, even in the face of her father's refusal to let her keep the child.

Destiny deserved an answer. Bella replied, "You were three days old, but I didn't give you away, Destiny. I never wanted that. I couldn't bear to let you go, but you deserved a family who could take care of you, and back then … You deserved better than I could provide."

"You mean you were forced? It wasn't your decision?" She sounded surprised, maybe even hurt.

How do I tell her? "It was my decision. The lady at the adoption agency said I had to choose." *Yes, I felt forced.* But she didn't want Destiny to think that her birth mother was weak. It had taken all of Bella's emotional strength to say good-bye to the baby who'd bumped her throughout the last several weeks of her pregnancy, bumps Bella took to mean the baby was talking to her. She'd sit in study hall, trying to hide her enlarging belly in the loose clothes her mother insisted she wear, tapping her tummy, letting the baby know she was saying hello back, was telling her how much Bella wanted her, hoping she would understand when it was time for Bella to let her go.

She'd refused to go back to the adoption agency, the only battle she won against her parents' insistence. They then placed ads in the paper seeking adoptive couples and introduced three different couples to her. She'd rejected the first two, unwilling to even consider them. But late in the summer, a month before the baby was due, she was introduced to the Harrises. Bella had liked Mr. Harris right away, sensing that he would be a wonderful father. She'd been less sure of Mrs. Harris, but Bella's father had amped up the pressure that she agree this time or *he* would take the baby to the adoption agency. She shuddered at her memories of those shouting matches, those nights when she locked herself in her room, sobbing.

"I chose your parents. I had a say in that," Bella added.

"How?"

"When I talked to the adoption lady, she told me about three kinds of adoption—closed, semi-open, and open. When I met your folks, your dad offered a semi-open adoption. I really wanted an open one, but they wouldn't agree to it." Nor had her parents. *They wanted nothing to do with you after you were born. They just wanted you gone.* "That means—"

Destiny interrupted. "Probably not what my mom would have preferred. She's not open at all. If she had her way, I'll bet she wouldn't want me to know about you at all." Her tone was dismissive.

"She was probably nervous about me," Bella said. "I was only sixteen when I got pregnant. She probably thought I wasn't a very good person." Like her own father. *Destiny probably thinks I was out of control. That I was wild.*

But Bella hadn't been. She'd never really dated. Tutoring Taylor had given her an opportunity to imagine what it might be like to date him, one of the high school football players. *All* the girls knew him, even the ones like her, the ones who rarely dated, who studied all the time and got good grades. She'd been thrilled when Taylor had said he loved her, not just because she was helping him stay on the team. He was her only lover until after she'd started at City College, after she left Portland.

"Were you raped?" Destiny asked.

"No."

"Oh, then you *wanted* to get pregnant?"

"No."

Her parents were horrified when she could no longer hide the baby bump that had been growing for more than four months before she admitted she was pregnant. Taylor had already dumped her by then. He'd asked for another tutor and the coach had approved the change. When Bella's father had demanded a meeting with his parents, Taylor's dad had threatened to call the cops to escort him out of the house, calling him the father of a slut, not someone his precious son wanted anything to do with. The kids at school knew better and some of them kidded him about knocking up the nerd, what they'd called her because she'd been his tutor in History and English. He'd gone all red-faced and denied sleeping with her, said that she wasn't pretty enough for him. Yet another way he'd slapped her down.

"What happened?" Destiny asked.

Such a simple question, but not an answer easily provided. Bella sucked in her breath, reliving the hurt of that long-ago time. "I had a boyfriend, a football player. I was tutoring him so he wouldn't have to quit the team. And he used condoms. He was my first, and I thought he loved me. He said he did. But when I told him I was pregnant, he said it was someone else's, that I was …" She remembered his words. "Even though

I never had sex with anyone but Taylor." She pressed her lips together. She hadn't intended to name him. Not even Zoe knew that detail.

"Where does he live, my birth father?"

Her voice flat, Bella said, "I have no idea." *And I don't care to know.* Bella hoped she hadn't sounded cold, but Taylor wasn't someone she cared to think about.

After a brief silence, Destiny changed the subject. "What's semi-open adoption?" She was asking for facts, something Bella could provide without risking more tears that burned the backs of her lids and reminded her how much the people she loved had let her down. Still, acid churned in her stomach, making her nauseous.

"With semi-open adoption, the birth mother gets to read the letters adoptive parents write. You know, like why they want to adopt a child and what their family is like, if they have other children, their ages, what the parents do for a living. That sort of thing."

"What made you pick *my* folks?"

"It's been a long time," Bella sighed. "Your dad was so kind to me, so accepting." She couldn't help smiling, remembering him. "He was so eager to become a father." She'd liked that about him. He'd seemed so different from *her* father, who was so judgmental, so hateful. "Your father was very nice back then. And when we talked a few days ago."

"Where did you meet my mom and dad?"

"At my house. Where I lived with my folks. Twice. Your father told me I was giving them a gift, one your parents could never repay." Bella remembered how the man had stared at her stomach at their first meeting, as if he was seeing the baby curled inside. "They came to the hospital, too. He cried when he held you for the first time. Then he thanked me. More than once." Bella couldn't halt the tears that slid down her cheeks even as she struggled to sound normal. As if it was yesterday, her heart clutched and she recalled looking out the window after the Harrises left with baby Destiny. Outside, the sky looked heavy, as if it was going to rain, a late summer shower perfectly reflecting Bella's sadness. Her belly was empty, her arms were empty, but her heart was filled to overflowing with grief at the loss of her baby. She remembered seeing the Harrises emerge from the front entrance of the hospital. Mr. Harris opened the back door and placed the baby there, probably in a car seat. Mrs. Harris went around to the other side, opened the door and climbed in. Then, as if in slow motion, the car left the hospital parking area. Bella was still weeping when Nurse Kara entered and pulled her gently into her arms. "You did what was best for the baby, Bella. Remember that, won't you?"

Bella hadn't felt that way then. Instead, it was the worst kind of sorrow, the kind she was certain would never leave her. But now, perhaps, she had another chance to get to know Destiny, even though she'd missed out on raising her.

"What about my mom?" Destiny demanded.

"I don't remember if she said anything when she held you. I watched them drive away from the window of my room. It was the longest day of my life." She paused and wiped her eyes.

"You said my dad thanked you. My mom didn't?"

"I don't remember. I'm sure she felt the same," Bella replied.

"Did my mom send you letters along with my pictures?"

"I believe the first note was from both of your ... parents." That word continued to stick in her throat, something she didn't want to acknowledge. I'm *your parent, Destiny. Your mother. For always.* "It doesn't matter who sent them. I kept them all." She thought of the small frame that had pride of place on the dining room bookcase.

Destiny's voice intruded. "My name's really different. Not like any of my friends."

"You can blame me for that. I was the one who named you. Letting you be adopted was an opportunity I was giving you to live a good life. That's how I saw it. So you wouldn't be saddled with an unwed mother on welfare." How she'd thought of herself back then, certain she'd become one if her dad kicked her out of the house.

"I was hoping your parents would keep your name. That day at the hospital, your dad said they would, but I wasn't sure. I mean, when the adoption was finalized, they could have changed it." She listened to the silence that followed her declaration, willing Destiny to see that Bella had never given her away. Far from it. She'd kept her in her heart all these years, wanting so badly to see her, to talk to her, to help Destiny understand that she'd always been loved and wanted. Even after Bella feared her child might have died and the Harrises didn't want her to know.

But the bitterness in Destiny's next words shook Bella to the core. "Right. You gave me a mother who refuses to let me live my own life. Thanks a bunch."

"I didn't know that's how she would be, Destiny. Doesn't your father intercede for you?" Or was Destiny's father like Bella's? She'd never considered the possibility until now. What she remembered most clearly was Mr. Harris weeping silently as he gently lifted the green and yellow bundle out of Bella's arms in her hospital room and crooning, "Oh, you beautiful child. Look, Vanessa. She's so pretty, so perfect. She just opened her eyes. Blue, like you said they would be." He'd handed Destiny to his wife, who at first had seemed reluctant to take her.

The grown-up Destiny jarred Bella back into the present,

with words laced with bitterness. "They're divorced. He's having a baby with his new wife—even though he's really old."

Bella struggled to remember what the couple had looked like. "I think they were in their thirties when I met them."

"Close enough. Mom's in her mid-fifties now and Dad's older than that."

"Many adoptive parents are older than some birthparents—because they usually try for a long time before they decide to adopt."

"You mean they go for second-best," Destiny declared.

"I didn't mean that. Please, Destiny. Don't think that. They wanted you. Very much. They were eager to care for and love a child. Don't you see? Their hearts were open to a child and they had the means, too."

"Because they had more money than you."

"I was a senior in high school the month after you were born! My dad threatened to kick me out if I didn't do what they said. I couldn't have cared for you like the Harrises could. I'm sorry you don't see that." Bella wanted to say more, but was afraid her daughter would hang up.

Destiny was silent for an extra-long beat. "I have more questions, but I have to go. Before my mom comes back up to find out why I'm taking so long. I don't want be late for school."

"You're in college?"

"My senior year. I'm graduating this spring."

"Good for you. Maybe we could talk again. Or write letters or email. What would work for you?"

"Calls would be better. Or texts. I don't want my mom knowing. She wouldn't understand. Probably wouldn't like it. Please don't call this number again. I have a cell."

"Okay. Tell me when I can call you. Or maybe you'd like to call me. I'm a librarian. I don't usually have to be at work before ten except on Wednesdays. That's when I go in early, but then I'm done after about four. And I'm one hour behind you."

They exchanged email addresses and cell phone numbers, and Bella gave Destiny her number at the library, too.

"I'm usually in class in the afternoon, or working at the bookstore. Could I call you in the evening? It wouldn't be so late where you live."

Bella nodded. "Sure."

"You're probably married now, right? Since you're in your thirties?" A question Bella was surprised to hear. Bella hadn't expected Destiny to care about her personal life.

"I'm thirty-seven. Not married or engaged. Not even dating." The image of Gavin Cambridge floated, unbidden, into view in her mind's eye.

"You don't *want* to get married?"

Her pulse sped up again. "I haven't found the right man." She'd thought Ethan was that person, but he wasn't. "I love kids, would like to have one of my own." But would Destiny take that the wrong way? "You said you're in college now. What's your major?"

Destiny snorted. "Marketing, but what I like best is English. I'm taking a night class in children's lit. My mom would think it's worthless if she knew, but I love it."

Bella heard a muffled knock on the door and someone calling Destiny. Her mother. Mrs. Harris.

Bella heard Destiny reply, "In a minute, Mom." Into the phone she declared, "I have to go. I'll call you back. Maybe in a couple of days."

"Please do. Thank you for talking to me, Destiny." Bella listened to the dial tone, unwilling to acknowledge that the electronic link to her daughter was now broken. Wrong. Not broken, simply delayed until their next talk. Their conversation had gone longer than she expected, had covered more than she anticipated, but at least it hadn't ended badly. And Destiny wanted to talk again.

Bella wanted a picture of Destiny, a recent one. She would ask the next time they talked. She regretted that the man who had been so kind to her no longer lived with her daughter. And Destiny resented the mother Bella had imagined loving her, caring for her, getting close to her. But didn't all mothers and daughters have their moments of conflict?

She thought of her own mother, recalling that she'd come to the hospital every day of Bella's confinement, often standing at the window, looking out over the parking lot. Only on the second day had Bella's mother asked to hold her granddaughter, but Bella had clutched the baby tighter. When little Destiny began to fuss, Bella took her back, almost stating that she'd just breastfed her, something she knew her mother wouldn't approve of. Somehow, Bella couldn't bring herself to share Destiny with the baby's grandmother. Finally, she had grudgingly said, "You can look at her while I walk her." And when her mother reminded Bella what her father had said about forgetting about the baby, Bella's anger had erupted. "I don't care what he said." His words still burned in her brain, even as a wave of guilt flooded her. She was certain her mother agreed with him.

After her father's death, they'd begun to talk more, but never about those conflict-ridden days before Destiny's birth and after, when Bella usually retreated to her room, coming out only for meals. She used her hours at home to plan how she would survive after she finished high school. She'd saved every penny of her babysitting money, thanking her lucky stars that one of her babysitting families was rich and always paid her a lot more than the other couples. That and tutoring during her senior year at the nearby elementary school. She'd refused when her principal had asked her to help a basketball player. She'd told him pointedly that she'd never tutor a sports star, that he had to be crazy to think she would.

After months of planning, she'd left home on graduation night after asking a friend to drive her to the tiny apartment she'd rented a week earlier, a place where she stashed some of her clothes. She'd called home after moving in, glad neither of her parents had attended the celebration, and left a message that she wouldn't be back. The next day when her mother had come home early from work, Bella was collecting the rest of her clothes. She'd refused to tell her mother where she now lived. She'd worked all senior year to develop a backbone, determined to live independently, not dependent, like her mother, on her controlling father.

"Besides, Dad can't stand the sight of me," she'd declared after handing her mother the house key, ending the discussion that was fast becoming a shouting match. "I'm leaving so he can't kick me out. Like he threatened."

"But that was before you gave up the baby."

"I don't care. I won't stay here another minute." She'd stomped out of the house over to her friend's car, her stubbornness preventing her from admitting how scared she was to be cutting all ties with her parents, with her mother at least.

The next day, she'd begun her day job as a waitress in a hole-in-the-wall café not far from the Portland airport. She worked nights in a warehouse, too, and saved every penny so she could go to college. Two years later, she left Portland and hitchhiked north along the interstate. The friendly cop who picked her up outside Seattle warned her about the dangers of hitchhiking before letting her out in Evergreen when she said she knew someone there. It was a lie, but it seemed like a quiet little town, a nice place, and it had a college she'd looked up online. That's what she was looking for, after leaving Portland

and all it represented.

She'd considered it a blessing that the cop let her off across the street from the entrance to City College. After securing a room at the YWCA, she'd lucked into a job at the college and begun taking night classes.

Now she owned her own home, she had a good job and she harbored a hope that some day she would have a family of her own, a husband who loved her, and children to cherish. A gift her own parents had denied her when they'd insisted she give up her baby almost twenty-two years earlier.

Bella finished dressing and grabbed her purse. She had just enough time to grab a quick breakfast before heading to work.

Chapter 7

DESTINY'S BRAIN WHIRLED AS SHE RODE THE BUS TO work. Her birth mom had called. Even though Destiny hadn't written her back. *And Isabella wants to see me.* In the flesh. Their recent conversation spun around in Destiny's brain. Did she hear her right, that Isabella had talked to Dad? *I'll have to call him.* Maybe he figured she was old enough to deal with her birth mother without any help from him. *Didn't Bella say Dad had sent her a letter?* Talking to Isabella was such a shock, bigger even than that letter Destiny had hidden in her closet so her mom wouldn't find it. A box of keepsakes was hidden under extra blankets and the quilt her grandmother had given Destiny when she was ten. She'd dreamed about her birth mother when she was younger, especially after a fight with her mom, wanting her *real* mom to come get her and take her home, away from her demanding *adoptive* mom. But, after all these years, what did Isabella Campbell really want?

Dad, no longer living with them, was always telling her they'd waited for years and that he and Mom had loved her from the first moment they saw her. Dad once told her that her birth mom had red hair when Destiny had asked why she didn't look like anyone else, something her mom didn't like to be reminded of. She always stood out in family reunion photos, making her feel like some kind of freak.

But Noah liked her hair. He'd noticed her right off that day she was working in the bookstore, because of how fiery it was in the sun, when he'd wandered in to see her. Even in the moonlight, he said her hair glowed. He'd kissed her for the first time in the dark, after she'd closed up the shop for the owner. Too bad he was definitely *not* the guy her mom wanted her to date.

Mom was always going on about how Noah wasn't in college, would probably never go to college, and wasn't good enough for her. *Right!* As if college was all that important. She was supposed to get her degree in marketing this spring, but Des still wasn't sure what she would do then. She'd always wanted to be an English major, but her mom had convinced her she'd never get a job. Marketing was sought-after by businesses. So Des had declared a marketing major, even if she had trouble staying interested in her courses. She'd added the night class because it was for English majors: children's literature. She loved it, but kept the books she was assigned to read and review in her locker on campus.

Destiny let out a little chortle as she looked out the window of the bus. Maybe she was more like her birth mom than she thought. More than just having red hair, assuming she remembered that correctly. Isabella worked in a library. That must mean she liked being around books, too. Was a love of books genetic?

Destiny sighed. She pulled the cord and stood up to exit the side door of the bus. Her stomach took a plunge when the bus stopped suddenly. Or was it the thought of talking to her birth mom again, maybe even seeing her in person? If only her dad still lived at home. He'd know what she should do. Her dad usually took Destiny's side when it came to arguments with her mom. But he lived in Austin now.

His new wife was having a baby any day. Des was sure it would be a boy. Her dad was so happy about the new baby, even though he was in his late fifties, awfully old to be a new father. When she told him he'd probably be mistaken for the kid's *grand*father, he had just laughed and said, "Whatever." Destiny never figured he'd be a parent to anyone but her, especially after the baby her folks adopted when Destiny was nine, Derek—who looked like her dad, with dark hair and deep brown eyes—died a year later. Des was sure Derek's death was one reason her parents had divorced a few years later.

She waited for the light to change then crossed the street and entered the bookstore. Time to do her job and stop thinking about how her life was suddenly a lot more complicated.

That evening, while she was working on her marketing class project, Destiny glanced at her phone when it pinged. Her pulse amped up. *Noah. Good. A break from studying.* She lay down on the bed, her phone pressed to her ear.

"We can't talk long," she warned. "My mom just got home and she's going to tell me to come down for dinner any minute."

"What's this big news you texted me?" her boyfriend asked.

Destiny imagined Noah, his black curls pulled back off his face in a ponytail, his long legs stretched out in front of him as he lounged in a chair at the garage that he hoped to own one day.

"I talked to my birth mom this morning. Can you believe it?"

"No shit. Does your ma know?"

"Of course not. If she'd picked up the phone, she would have freaked."

"Hmm. What's she like?"

"She sounded nice. Her name is Isabella. She said I could call her Bella. And she wants to meet me."

"I know you're adopted, but until you said she wrote you, you never talked about it."

"I never knew about her, really, where she was, or if she even cared. I've been with my folks my whole life."

"Are you going to meet her?"

"I haven't decided. She asked if we could talk again. I never got around to answering that letter she sent. Wasn't sure what to say, and then she called. I told her she should call my cell. And she said I can text her."

"You comin' over to see me tonight?"

"Probably not. I have an exam on Monday and a paper to write in the next two days. I'm really busy with my classes."

From his silence Destiny knew Noah was frowning, his handsome face made more interesting by the small white scar on his upper lip that stood out against his dark skin.

"Yeah yeah, so you can get your degree. You keep saying that, but you keep taking classes that have nothing to do with your major. When's your ma going to catch on?"

"As long as I pass my last marketing class, she won't find out. Probably won't care as long as I have my degree. Besides, my dad covers my college bills, and he just wants me to be happy." She pursed her lips. Her degree was important, especially for her mom. *Probably Dad, too. Then I'll look for a real job if I can't convince the bookstore to hire me full time.* "Could I call her while I'm at your place?"

"You could, but you said you weren't coming over."

"After I finish the paper, I will. I'll work on it at the library. But it might be late, after ten. How's that?"

"Whatever. I'll be here."

The phone clicked off just as her mother's voice sounded from outside Destiny's bedroom door.

"Honey, time for dinner." *How long has she been standing there?*

Destiny opened the door. Her mother was frowning. "You're planning to see Noah again?"

What else had she heard, or was she just guessing? "Were you listening to my *private* conversation, Mom?"

"You shouldn't be seeing that boy. He's not good for you."

"He's *perfect* for me. Black and beautiful and a fabulous lover!"

Her mother backed up and she paled. "You're sleeping with him?"

"What are you afraid of, Mom, that I'll get pregnant? Like my birth mom?" The words slipped out.

Her mother seemed to stumble as she approached the stairs. She barely prevented herself from falling by grabbing the banister. "What did you say?" she almost whispered, the whites of her eyes showing when she stared at Destiny.

"Isn't that how you got me—because some girl got pregnant and couldn't keep me? A teenager, younger than me?" Her pulse pounded as she acknowledged what she knew to be fact, more than what her father always said, that she'd been a gift. *Some gift.* Now she knew her birth mom had practically been *forced* to get rid of her. Destiny always assumed her birth mother had been unmarried, had wanted to believe that the woman *couldn't* take care of her, not that she didn't *want* to take care of her. Bella had been talked into giving up her baby.

Which probably meant Des' real grandparents hadn't wanted her. To them, she represented the kind of mistake that was hard to clean up. *At least Bella didn't abort me.* Destiny clumped down the stairs after her mother, regretting having mentioned Bella. Was her mom going to pick up on that, maybe even volunteer information about Destiny's adoption? It was a subject only her dad had seemed comfortable talking about.

Her mother led the way into the kitchen, her voice sounding forced. "Yes, that's what happened. But it's not important." She straightened her spine even as she took her seat at the head of the table. "What's important is what you're doing with your life *now*. And I don't like that you've taken up with that boy."

"His name is Noah, Mom. He works in a garage, and he's going to own it some day—even without a college degree," she added defensively. "We're going to live together, as soon as I find us a decent place." She hadn't wanted to say that either, or imply she didn't like where Noah lived. His folks' place was just around the corner from his apartment and they didn't like her. But her mind was so full of what Isabella had told her.

Now, her mother knew about her living-together plans. Not that it was going to stop Des from acting on them, but Noah had said they should just do it and not tell her mom until it was a done deal. Would her mother try to stop her? Noah would be mad that she'd shot off her mouth ahead of time. He was always telling her to stop baiting her mother, that doing so only made her mom hang on more desperately. Noah was probably right. He seemed to know what made her mother tick. Too bad he couldn't get *his* parents to be more welcoming when she was with Noah.

Destiny glanced at her mother. She was running one hand through her graying hair, finger-combing and then patting it into place, only to run her fingers through it again, dislodging the curls she'd patted behind her ear. A sign of her mother's nerves. What she did whenever Destiny's dad called.

"Does your father know?"

"About what? Noah and me? Why should I talk to him about my boyfriends? He doesn't even live here anymore." But she had that day she'd been on Skype. The two men had talked about business stuff before Des had insisted that Noah let her talk with her dad again. By herself.

Destiny plucked a cherry tomato out of the large salad her mom placed in front of her. "I'll bet *he* recognizes how smart Noah is. He got his GED when he was in jail—" Her mother gasped. "He's saving his money to go to night school so he can take business courses. He wants to build his garage into something really big." She mentally dared her mother to question Noah's actions. Des had no idea if Noah actually would go to night school. He'd only talked about it once. But she couldn't stop wanting her mother to react, to become angry, and to forbid Des from seeing Noah tonight, to show that she really cared.

Instead, her mother sat quietly, alternately glancing at Des and then looking away. What was she thinking?

Des rose from the table, her few bites of the dinner salad lying heavily in her stomach. "I have to go to the library, to study."

"And then you're going to Noah's place?" her mom murmured. "You'll be home late?"

"Maybe I'll just sleep over," Des replied. "His place is close to campus. So I can still make it to my first class on time."

"But this is your home, Des." Her mother stood up so suddenly, her chair toppled over and banged into the wall.

"Not for long," she retorted and ran up the stairs to get her books and her bus pass.

When she trotted back down the stairs, her mother was waiting for her, car keys in her hand. "Take the car—so you don't have to ride the bus."

Destiny accepted the keys, surprised at her mother's will-ingness to allow her to take the car.

Her voice turned cool again. "One more thing, Destiny."

"What?" she snapped, regretting that she sounded so harsh when she saw the hurt look on her mother's face.

"Have you been talking to your father about your birth mother? Have you tried to contact her?"

Destiny's pulse shot skyward. Did her mom know about Dad's letter, or was she just guessing? "Why would you think that?"

"Lots of children who've been adopted try to find out about … want to know about their birth parents. Is that what this is all about? Haven't we—your father and I—shared enough with you about … what we know … what happened?"

Destiny had to leave, before she said more than she wanted to. "I know what happened. Like I said before."

Her mother's lips pursed so tightly they seemed to disap-pear in her pale face.

"She had sex and got pregnant and then she gave me away." Destiny turned on her heel and walked out the kitchen door to the garage. But that wasn't all there was to it. First, her birth mom got rid of her; second, her dad moved away; and, third, Des could hardly stand to be with her mom anymore.

Vanessa Harris collapsed onto the bottom step after Destiny stomped out of the house. She gulped air like a landed fish, distraught that she and her daughter were increasingly at odds with each other. The closeness they'd shared before Nolan left them, left *her*, to build a new life and a new family, had evaporated. Especially in the past few months, Destiny had continued to pull away, distancing herself from Vanessa, closing herself off, no longer sharing information about her college classes, or her friends at Metro State. Especially after she started seeing that boy, Noah.

Vanessa shook her head. Maybe she shouldn't have insisted that Des pursue a marketing degree, something Vanessa had earned before she met Nolan. *Why* they had met. He'd hired her to provide the skills his company needed. Then they'd married and begun a family, or tried to. She recalled their many visits to the doctor, who had concluded the problem lay with her. Nolan hadn't blamed her, but she thought she saw regret in his gaze when they'd talked about options. She'd flatly rejected a surrogate, though Nolan had said any child resulting would have their genes, hers and his. And when it became clear she was never going to become pregnant, she finally agreed to adopt. She hoped for a baby who would look like at least one of them.

The adoption agencies they approached had said they might have to wait two or more years for a white child. But once she and Nolan made the decision, Vanessa was unwilling to wait that long. She had spotted the ads in the Portland paper. Four of the young women they called were unsuitable. But the Campbells had sounded nice. Mr. Campbell had assured her his daughter would not go back on her decision to give up the baby, although Vanessa had her doubts after meeting the girl. She'd answered Nolan's questions so sullenly, been tearful, too. And she'd insisted on a semi-open adoption, after the girl's mother said her daughter had selected them from among the other couples they had met. Nolan was ecstatic, she less so. "What kind of background does she have? Her folks look like working-class people. They keep saying she won't change her mind, but what kind of girl gets pregnant and then gives up her child?" she'd asked Nolan while they were driving home after that first meeting.

"A girl who wants more for her child than she can provide," he replied. "She's a junior in high school, Vanessa. She doesn't smoke, doesn't drink, claims she never took drugs, is healthy. And her mother says the pregnancy has been routine since she began prenatal care."

"But she wasn't even seen by a doctor until almost her fifth month, according to Mrs. Campbell." The girl had to have been careless of her baby's health if she hadn't seen a doctor until then.

"She was probably hiding her condition." Nolan seemed to sympathize with the girl. "You saw her father. He's not happy. Her mother said the girl hasn't missed an appointment, takes her prenatals like she should. And she wanted to meet us. Didn't Mrs. Campbell say we're tops on her list?"

Vanessa had clutched Nolan's hand then, hoping this would be the baby they were seeking, afraid to think the pregnant girl might reject them.

Their second meeting went better than the first, except that the girl continued to insist on maintaining contact with her child. Nolan agreed immediately, saying it was only fair that she have that opportunity. Vanessa wasn't so sure. She'd read of nightmarish situations, birth mothers who had refused to relinquish their babies at the last minute, changed their minds and convinced a judge they had been coerced, even shown up without warning years later, wresting the child from the only family he or she had ever known.

For weeks after those meetings with the birth mother, Vanessa woke before dawn, gasping for breath, imagining the worst. Nolan tried to reassure her. A semi-open adoption would reduce that risk precisely because the girl would have continuing contact, structured to occur no more than twice a year, according to the girl's father.

Vanessa had begged Nolan for a closed adoption. It was the only option she felt comfortable with. Two of the pregnant girls they met had agreed, but their babies were unsuitable to Vanessa. She didn't think of herself as a racist, but she didn't want a mixed race baby. Nolan finally convinced her to go with the semi-open option. He kept telling her that Ms. Campbell seemed like a very nice girl.

Vanessa had harrumphed. Nice girls didn't get pregnant when they were in high school. Maybe college, she admitted reluctantly, reminded of a friend who had done just that.

Now Destiny was talking—for the first time in years—about her birth mother. Had she begun searching for her? Had she found the letters the young woman had sent before they moved to Denver, the ones Vanessa kept hidden? She'd felt invaded each time those letters and cards arrived, at Christmas time and the ones dated a week in advance of Destiny's birthday, timed to arrive just before the big day.

When Nolan's big promotion occurred, Vanessa convinced him to stop sending the girl pictures of Destiny. After all, they were moving practically across the country. What was the point of continued, even occasional, contact? Nolan finally agreed.

Vanessa's gaze slid to the calendar on the far wall of the kitchen. Mid-May. Nolan's new wife, carrying *his* child, would give birth soon. Destiny planned to visit her dad and his new family after her graduation.

Maybe Destiny would be in a better mood when she returned. Maybe being separated from Noah for two weeks would help Destiny see that the boy wasn't right for her. Vanessa would talk to Nolan about Des's attitude. He always seemed to get through to her. Was it one of those father-daughter connections that people talked about? That mothers and daughters were too close, too hormonal, to understand each other? Or was it something she had created, by clinging so tightly to her daughter, especially after Nolan deserted her?

Vanessa knew she should give Destiny more freedom, but she feared losing her, too. She convinced Destiny how much easier it was to live at home while in college. No meals to fix, or worrisome roommates in shared apartments in those low-rent parts of town near the campus. And she persuaded Nolan not to buy his daughter a car after high school graduation. Des could use *her* car, even though Vanessa usually insisted that Destiny take the bus to campus and back.

Now Destiny was threatening to move in with that boy who worked at a garage, with grease constantly under his fingernails—who had been to jail, for God's sake! Vanessa wondered if Noah's mother had been another pregnant un-married teen. But Noah's parents were also raising the boy's two sisters, according to Destiny. Still, *how* could Destiny pick someone like that, who lived in what Vanessa thought of as the wrong side of town?

She stood up and went to the wall phone in the kitchen. She had to talk to Nolan, maybe get him to talk sense into Destiny. Vanessa knew she should be grateful that Nolan had provided her with a generous portion of the proceeds from the sale of the Denver business, enough that she didn't have to work, that he was covering Destiny's college expenses. Still, she resented that he'd found someone else, a young someone who was happy to have his child, even though he now looked like a gray-headed grandfather in the pictures he sent Destiny.

She picked up the phone and decided to call his private office number, even though Nolan had asked her not to after their last argument. When they were told Des' birth mom had picked them, the girl had refused to tell them what she was having. Vanessa had been secretly pleased it was a girl and Nolan had wept the first time he saw the tiny baby with her flyaway wisps of red hair that stood up off her head. He didn't care that she didn't look like either of them.

"Nolan Harris here," her ex-husband answered.

"It's me. Vanessa," she said, and mentally kicked herself. Of course, he knew who it was. "I want you to talk to Destiny."

"What about this time?"

"That boy she's seeing. I think she's sleeping with him. If she's to be believed, she *is* sleeping with him." Vanessa choked on her words and cleared her throat. "And, there's something else." How could she say it without weeping? "She's talking about her birth mother again. Just like when she was seven. Did you have anything to do with that? Didn't you say you were going to get in touch with the girl after Des' birthday last year? Please tell me you didn't do that."

She pulled a chair closer to the wall so she could sit down.

"I did. Isabella called me the other day, after she wrote Des a letter. Wanted to know if I thought it would be all right if she called her. I told her to go for it."

"But why, Nolan? You know Des is impulsive. She may even want to see the girl."

"Vanessa, get real. Des is twenty-one, a grown woman. Why shouldn't she get in touch with her birth mother if she wants? She can vote, join the military. And if Des only recently started asking, I doubt it was because of that letter I sent. Maybe it's time you showed her those letters you've been hoarding all these years."

Vanessa gasped into the phone, hoping Nolan hadn't heard.

"Do you still have them? And if you weren't planning to give them to Des someday, why did you keep them?"

He knows. Maybe Des found them. Or maybe he told Des about them. But he said he'd never do that, that it was *her* job to share them. What was Nolan saying now? Vanessa concentrated on his words.

"… and if she reads them, maybe she'll have the information she needs. She deserves to know where she came from."

His gentle reminder felt like a punch to her gut. He'd argued with her when they left Portland about continuing to send pictures and letters. But Vanessa had viewed their move to Denver as an escape from the agreement all parties had signed. Not sharing any more pictures had been Vanessa's way of protecting her family. Only now, somehow, it wasn't enough.

Her daughter hadn't said a word about a letter from that girl. Had she answered it? Des had never been much for letters, but maybe she'd gone on the Internet. She was smart about that sort of thing. "I deserve to know what you told her about that girl."

"That woman, Vanessa. She's no sixteen-year-old now. She's got to be in her late thirties. All I did was send Isabella a letter, per our agreement when the adoption was final, that she could contact Des directly once she was twenty-one. So she wouldn't have to go through us. And she was polite enough to contact me before going further. You can't keep our daughter in the dark forever. It's not right."

Vanessa choked back tears. "Okay, okay. But will you *please* talk to Destiny about this *boy* she's seeing? What if *she* gets pregnant? Like her birth mother? Only worse?"

"What would make it worse, Vanessa? Besides, *your* daughter wouldn't dare do such a thing." His sarcasm wasn't lost on her.

"He's all wrong for her, has been in jail, works in a car place."

"Are you talking about Noah?"

Vanessa almost dropped the phone. "You know about the

black kid?"

Nolan chuckled. "Of course I know about him. I talked to him the last time Destiny and I Skyped. That kid has all kinds of plans. Reminds me of when I was his age. Wants to run his own business."

"Oh, my God. And you *approve* of him?"

"I wasn't so sure until after I talked to him, but if Destiny likes him and he treats her right, leave them alone. The more you object, the more she's going to cling to him. Let her figure out for herself if he's the one she wants to spend time with. Is she home? Let me talk to her."

"She went to the library."

"Then I'll text her. Ask her to call me back. You're still okay with her coming down here to spend time with us after the baby comes?"

"I bought Destiny's ticket the other day. Just haven't given it to her yet. She's scheduled to leave the day after graduation. She's going to miss that you aren't there to see her."

"And you know I promised Erin our first month with the baby I'd be home with them. Destiny understands that. That's why she wants to come down after graduation." Nolan's voice seemed to gentle after a short pause. "You didn't even wait to see if she got decent grades before getting her ticket. Good for you, Vanessa."

"Do you promise to talk to her? I can't seem to get through to her about anything these days."

"I'll talk with her. Relax. Destiny's got a good head on her shoulders. She's not going to toss you aside just because she gets to know her birth mother. You raised her. That makes you her *real* mother. Maybe Des'll keep her birth mother's situation in mind and use extra protection."

How is it he reads my mind? If only Des would take extra care. But maybe she figured if her birth mother could do it, she could, too. These days, most girls kept their babies. Not like before, when at least some of them gave them to couples like her and Nolan.

"I can only hope," she replied. "Good-bye, Nolan."

"It's time for Destiny to try her wings, Vanessa. Letting her go means she'll come back to you. You'll see." He hung up.

Chapter 8

Destiny checked her phone when it rattled on the desk in the college library carrel. *Dad!*

She picked up the phone and spoke just above a whisper. "Hey, Dad. I can't talk here. I'm at the library. Studying."

He laughed softly. "Then call me back when you're free."

She scooted her chair back. "I can do it now, just not here." She picked up her purse, but left her books and notepad on the table. "Why did you call?" She opened the door to the back stairwell and sat down on the grated metal stairs.

"Just thought I'd check in. How've you been?"

She sighed. "Mom's on my case again."

"What about?"

"Everything, especially Noah, but she let me borrow the car to go to school tonight. Mostly because she didn't want me walking at night in Noah's neighborhood."

"How is he?"

"Good."

"Anything besides him on your mind, Des?"

He's fishing. I'll bet Mom called him. "I got a call from my birth mom." What would he say to that? "Or did you know about that already?"

"I knew she wanted to call you, not that she did."

"Because she called you?" *Good old Dad. Always playing it cool.*

"If you're asking did I ask her to call you, the answer is no. She asked if she should and I encouraged her. That's all. Bella wanting to talk with you is between you and her, sweetie."

"Why?"

"She's your birth mother and you have a right to get to know her, or at least as much as she'll tell you."

"She asked if I had questions."

"I figured she might. Did you take her up on that?"

"Uh-huh."

Her father made a sound deep in his throat, the way he always sounded, a cross between a laugh and a cough. "Good. It was part of the contract that we keep her informed about you. I'm sorry we didn't do that. I was going to give you her name when you came down here so you could touch base with her, if you wanted. If she hadn't already reached out. You're an adult now, Des. Not every adoptee wants to know about their past, but I saw no reason why you couldn't. Your choice. Not mine or your mother's."

"She said she wrote me letters every year and that you sent her pictures, but then they stopped. When I was pretty small."

"Your mother's doing. She may still have the letters Bella sent."

Anger rose in Destiny's chest. Her mom had letters and never told her? Before she could ask for details, her dad's voice intervened.

"Your mom says you're still planning to come see us after graduation."

"Yes, and I made a baby blanket. In green, since you don't know the sex."

"I'm sure it's beautiful. Erin will be touched that you were so thoughtful."

"Don't tell her, Dad. I want it to be a surprise. Or should I send it ahead, so she can use it when you bring the baby home from the hospital?"

"We're using a midwife, going to a birth center."

"Even so."

He laughed. "Sure. Send it on. We can thank you when you come down."

"I better go, Dad. Still have to review one more chapter and finish this paper."

"I hear you. Love you, honey."

Destiny returned to her library carrel, her thoughts on the letters her dad had mentioned. She refilled her water bottle and forced her mind back on the notes she'd written in the margins of her textbook. For the next several minutes, she added to the outline for her paper and then shoved her work into her backpack, too keyed up to stay focused.

How dare her mom keep those letters from her! She had no right.

Bella finished brushing her hair and slipped into her black dress. She had less than fifteen minutes before leaving for the library to meet Gavin. Nervous flutters combined with her imaginings that Gavin might have a reason other than his implied doubts about the wisdom of his uncle offering books for the new story reading group. *It's just a business dinner,* she kept repeating to herself, *even if he's a really handsome man.* Bella pursed her lips and adjusted the teal scarf loosely around her neck. *I'll show him the posters encouraging parents to purchase books at Henry's store.* In spite of the planning session she and Zoe had engaged in, Bella's mind kept skittering back to Gavin and his invitation to dinner. He seemed interested in her. But she'd refused to admit to Zoe that she'd entertained similar thoughts of getting to know him. Thoughts she needed to set aside. He was only here until Henry was better. And there was no future in a long-distance relationship.

Her conversation with Henry on Friday afternoon had been brief, interspersed with too many worrisome coughing spells. But Henry kept assuring her he was getting better. He told her Gavin had owned his car dealership for almost ten years, one of the youngest franchisees for BMW in the western states. He was thirty-eight, had graduated from the University of Washington, and had an MBA from Gonzaga University, too.

So he's educated. Odd that he should be so distrustful of a library. Or of her. She glared back at her image in the mirror as she adjusted one silver dangly earring, recalling that portion of their conversation. But it was Henry's little laugh followed by a statement that maybe Gavin was testing himself by asking her out that fed Bella's nervousness. Testing what, exactly? It wasn't something she chose to ask dear Henry and he hadn't elaborated.

The doorbell rang. *Oh no! I need to leave.* This was no time for a door-to-door salesperson asking her to buy something she didn't need.

Bella trotted to her front door, determined to send away whoever was delaying her departure. "I really don't have—"

Gavin stood at her front door, dressed in a black pinstriped suit, a pale blue shirt and a rep tie that implied he'd pledged a fraternity in college. The cut of his clothes suggested he hadn't bought them off the rack.

She sucked in a breath. A thought flashed that he looked good enough to eat. Correction: kiss. Maybe climb all over. "I—I thought we—weren't we meeting at the library?" she sputtered.

"My uncle said I was lacking in good taste if I didn't pick you up at your home. So I Googled your address." He gave her a mischievous half-grin then looked apologetic, sort of. "I probably should have called, but I wanted to get here before you left for the library."

"Oh." She stared at him as he stood on her porch, and ran her tongue over her lips.

"I've been going over the accounts at the bookstore. Financial records. They're a mess," he declared, not waiting for an invitation to enter.

"I thought Earl took care of them." Hadn't Henry implied that, the last time he'd given them free books? They were to tell Earl how many, and leave the receipt with him.

"If he is, he's not doing a good job." Gavin's left eyebrow rose at the same time he lifted a shoulder in the direction of her door in a silent question.

Bella pursed her lips. Sending him away would be rude. Hauling him into her bed was too forward … *Get real, girl. Dinner. Think dinner.* "Since you're here, come in. I'm almost ready." Bella stepped back, allowed him to enter, then closed the door and turned on her heel. "I'll just be a minute." She returned to her bedroom to retrieve her light summer coat. As she passed by the kitchen table, she snatched up the large manila envelope with the papers she planned to show him.

"Nice place you have here," he said, scanning her living

room. "Cozy."

"Thank you." She reached for the door, but he opened it for her. She flipped on the porch light and waited until he was out of the way so that she could lock the door.

He walked her in the direction of the fancy red car she'd seen in the library parking lot the day he delivered the *Harry Potter* books. "I thought that was your car. Is it really big enough for two?"

His left eyebrow rose again. "See for yourself." He helped her into the bucket seat.

She smoothed her hands over her coat, aware that her position in the seat caused the hem of her dress to ride up on her thigh.

"You never said where we're eating."

The smile he gave her seemed to light up the interior of his car. "I picked Danielli's. Hope you like steak. If not, it has other offerings, too."

Hmm. Bella had been there once before. Was this guy trying to impress her with his preferences, maybe with his money? "I don't see your briefcase. Isn't this a business meeting?" She brushed a hand down her leg and pulled at the hem of her dress, wishing it reached her knees, wishing she couldn't stop thinking how well he wore that suit.

"In the trunk." When he stopped at a red light, he glanced her way. "Tell me about yourself. How long have you worked at the library?"

"More than ten years in my current position." She pressed her hands closer to her belly, willing the butterfly quivers away. Unsuccessfully. "Just so you know, I have posters with me that show how we advertise your uncle's store. We prefer to involve the indies in our special activities. Mostly his store, especially, well … there are only two independent bookstores in town now. Henry's is our favorite."

He nodded. "What about your family? They live around here?"

"Just me. My mother lives in Portland." *And Destiny. In Denver.* Why was he asking about her family? This was supposed to be a business meeting. Why did he care how long she'd been working at the library? Was that part of *the test* Henry had mentioned? She decided to ask him questions. "Is Henry your only uncle?"

"My last surviving relative since my mom's death."

"No brothers and sisters?"

He shook his head. "What about you?"

"No."

"Seems we're like two peas in a pod then. The last of our particular lines." That intriguing grin appeared again.

She swept her tongue over her lips again, wishing she didn't feel so warm. "You're not married? No children?" she asked.

"Divorced. No kids." His grin disappeared into jaw-flexing tension.

"I'm guessing you had a bad experience."

"Let's just say I didn't contest the divorce."

She nodded, but before she could think of something else to ask him, Gavin pulled into the parking lot next to the building housing Danielli's. A valet accepted the keys from Gavin. Another valet opened Bella's door and helped her out of the low-slung car. "Thank you."

Gavin placed a hand at the small of Bella's back as they entered the restaurant. They were seated quickly, evidence that Gavin had made a reservation. *Good thing. He must have come here before,* she thought, after observing the friendly muted conversation between him and the wine steward, who displayed a bottle that Bella recognized as an award-winning vintage. *But he's from Spokane. Maybe he visits Henry more regularly than he implied.* That being the case, maybe she would see him more often, a dating relationship, she mused, aware of his blue eyes when he smiled at her. *But we don't* have *a relationship,* whispered white-robed Little Angel Bella, always parked on her right shoulder and ever so practical. *More's the pity,* Little Devil Bella retorted, what Bella had taken to calling her baser thoughts and dressed in red brighter than Bella's hair.

Through the salad course and the arrival of the entrées, their conversation was limited to comments relating to the food, but when their plates were removed, Gavin leaned back in his seat, sipped the wine in his glass, and said, "This is a business dinner, right?" He didn't wait for her to confirm. "You mentioned you advertise my uncle's place."

Bella nodded and pulled out several different posters from the large envelope. They all prominently featured Books and More. Devil Bella swore. Angel Bella sighed with relief.

He stared at each one for a long minute. "From what I've seen of the store's finances, I don't think this generates much income."

"But that can't be right. Several parents have told us how much they enjoy going to Henry's store to buy books for their children. More than just the ones we read with the little ones. Maybe Henry needs to do more advertising, other than what he does with us."

Gavin frowned. "May I keep these posters? I want to compare the dates you penned on the side with purchases of those titles you mentioned."

"Of course. Here. Take these, too. In case Henry didn't keep copies. Zoe and I always give him a receipt acknowledging his donations. So he can deduct his costs. It's the least we can do to help him out. He loves the library and what we do here, especially with the children." She wondered if she sounded desperate. Gavin's expression, so solemn and unchanging, told her nothing.

He gave her a half-grin. "You must like children."

"Of course I do," her cheeks beginning to burn. Why must she blush now? What was it about his smile, and the way his eyes seemed to twinkle at her, that her pulse began racing?

"You never said if you have children of your own."

She almost said no, but then she remembered what Zoe had said once, that honesty was a policy imperative in any social relationship, especially a romantic one. But why was she thinking she had such a relationship with Gavin Cambridge? He was Henry Quackenbush's nephew. Strictly a business relationship. Nothing more.

She took a quick sip of wine and cleared her throat. "One daughter. Grown."

He seemed surprised. "You don't look old enough to have a grown daughter."

What should she say to that? Her throat seemed to close for a moment, as she pondered explaining further. "She's never lived with me. She's been with her adoptive parents since she was three days old."

"Oh." His tone turned quiet, edged with what Bella wanted to think was sympathy. "That must have been hard. Giving her away, I mean."

She nodded. "I only recently made contact with her again." There, she'd said it and breathed a mental sigh of relief when Gavin seemed to accept her explanation without judgment.

He leaned forward and speared her with another intense gaze before focusing on his coffee cup. "Does she want contact with you, too?"

"I think so. I'm not sure." It was a question she'd been asking herself almost hourly since her first talk with Destiny. "We're both testing the waters, I guess."

Gavin studied her. "And you've never wanted other children?"

"Never had the opportunity." She hoped she sounded breezily casual. She folded her napkin into a small rectangle. "Isn't this supposed to be a business meeting?"

"You're right." He sat for a moment, looking serious, his gaze now on his hands, as tanned as his neck. When he looked up and returned Bella's gaze, he smiled, and her skin warmed as if by the summer sun. "Business. Right. What do you know about Earl?"

"Not very much. He's always at the store, almost never talks to us. But Henry seems to trust him. Do you suspect a problem, other than he isn't managing the books very well?"

"I'm not sure. He wasn't very forthcoming. When are you starting that new reading group, the one where you plan to use those *Harry Potter* books?"

"Mitchell finally approved the display posters on Friday, and Zoe and I are going to take them around to the different schools on Monday. We'll begin on Wednesday of this coming week. Why do you ask?"

"Mind if I stop in and see how it goes?"

"You're welcome to stay the entire time."

"I won't stay that long." His crooked grin suggested he wasn't entirely comfortable with her suggestion.

"But if you're there at the beginning, we'll thank Henry's store publicly. Usually he comes by so we can do that. Since he isn't able to make it ..."

"I'd like you to call me"—he reached into the chest pocket of his suit coat and pulled out a business card—"at the end of that first session and tell me how many parents say they plan to buy copies for their kids."

The glimpse of his silk-covered chest called to her. "I can do that." She looked at the embossed card with a picture of a car like Gavin's. "Do you always drive a company car?"

"That one's mine," he said. "No one ever said a franchise

owner couldn't drive his own car."

"I guess not."

Gavin glanced at his watch. "Time to take you home. It's getting late."

Their conversation on the ride home was relaxed, focusing mostly on why Gavin liked Spokane, and his plans to expand, perhaps with a franchise in a city other than Spokane. She was surprised when he took a slight detour and stopped at the park.

"Are you up for a little walk?" he said. "I need to stretch my legs."

"Sure." After all, it was a lovely night.

She joined him for a quiet stroll along the empty pathways that curled around the play equipment, now silent in the moonlight. When they returned to the car, he took her hand in his, then turned it over and kissed her palm before closing her fingers and leaning closer. She was certain he was going to kiss her, something she was sure she should avoid, though she didn't want to. She held her breath, Devil Bella cheering.

His eyes were almost midnight-blue in the light from the open car door as he studied her expression. Did he detect her uncertainty? "Hold that kiss, Bella. Consider it a down payment. Something I'll ask for later. When you're ready."

Bella's knees seemed to buckle as she slid into the car. She was thankful the rest of the ride was long enough for her bones to harden. Everything had changed. Clearly, business wasn't all that he was interested in.

Feeling daring, Bella asked when they returned to her house. "Would you like to come in for coffee?"

"Thanks. I'd like that."

Bella started the coffee maker and set two mugs on the dining room table as she motioned for Gavin to take a seat. But he remained next to the bookcase, staring at the picture frames that sat on top next to a house plant.

"Is this her?" he asked, pointing to Destiny's picture.

Bella nodded. "When she was five. I don't have more recent ones. Not yet, anyway."

"She looks a lot like you. Anyone could see that."

What I think, too. Bella cocked her head and stared at Gavin, his gaze still on Destiny's innocent five-year-old smile. Ethan had never seemed to notice that picture, never even asked. He probably thought the picture was of Bella as a small child. *Why* didn't *he ask?* Because she'd never told him about Destiny? It had to be because Ethan's focus had always been on Ethan.

Gavin's voice hauled her back to the present. "Does your daughter know you two look alike?"

"I'm not sure what her folks told her about me. But I was thinking I'd send her a picture and ask for one in return."

While she waited for the coffee to finish perking, she asked, "Would you like to see the others? When she was younger?"

She wasn't sure why she wanted Gavin to see them, only that she felt like sharing, perhaps because she'd never done so. Now that she'd found her, Destiny was no longer a secret Bella wanted to keep.

She opened the frame and pulled out six photos, laying them on the table, one after the other. "All at different ages. Probably taken on her birthday." In one, the child held a ball decorated in red stars and blue stripes in the lap of her white dress, her feet clad in white socks and black patent leather Mary Janes.

In one photo, Destiny's hair resembled a wild red cloud surrounding her head. The child looked as if she was about to cry, as if someone had taken a toy from her. In the background was a birthday cake with two unlit candles, one listing markedly to the side. Perhaps the child had tried to remove it and been stopped right before the photographer took the picture.

A still younger version of Destiny showed red wisps barely

covering her head. She was giving the photographer a gummy grin. The last picture included a teenage Bella holding a bundle in a yellow-and green-striped blanket. The baby's face was barely visible and it was impossible to see if she had any hair. But one tiny hand, clasping Bella's little finger, was visible in the photo.

Gavin stared at that picture, at Bella's expression. "You look proud of her, maybe of yourself, too, but so sad. So vulnerable." He touched the edge of the photo and then grasped Bella's hand and squeezed. "Am I right? That's how it was for you?" Gavin turned over the photo of mother and child. On the back was a date. "Her birthday?"

Bella nodded, her eyes burning as she fought against showing him how touched she was by his gentle words. He'd guessed how she'd felt when Mr. and Mrs. Harris had come for Destiny. Mrs. Harris was dressed formally, in a black suit, the neckline of a red silk blouse showing, and heels. Not the kind of clothes Bella imagined a mother would wear. Destiny's new mother stared solemnly at Bella and at the baby she cuddled in her arms.

Mr. Harris wore dark chinos and a casual shirt unbuttoned at the neck. His checked jacket with leather at the elbows was draped over one shoulder. He'd said Bella looked good before shifting his gaze to the bundle in her arms. Bella had dressed Destiny that morning in a tiny white onesie, on which she'd embroidered a bright red D weeks earlier. Her mother had brought a yellow and green receiving blanket the day before, and Bella had swaddled Destiny in it, not wanting her to go home in one of the hospital blankets.

Bella glanced at Gavin. He seemed to understand how she was feeling tonight after telling him about the daughter she'd kept a secret from everyone else in Evergreen.

The coffee maker stopped bubbling and Bella returned to

the kitchen, needing to steady herself.

"Have a seat." She filled his mug, and hers too, with the steaming brew.

"What's her name? You never said."

She plucked the pictures off the table, and slid them back into the frame, hoping she sounded casual, as if she shared the pictures, talked about her daughter, every day. "Destiny. She lives in Denver."

Gavin reached across the table and covered her hand with one of his. "You must have been very brave back then, when you had to give her up."

"I didn't have a choice. These pictures are all I have. I'm hoping she wants to get to know me. I didn't want to let her go ..." She hoped she sounded matter-of-fact. "My dad made it clear I had to. I think my mom suspected my pregnancy for weeks. Probably was hoping it wasn't true." The ire she'd felt at her mother's accusations, her late father's demands, still rankled. "I didn't tell them—hid it, actually—for months. By that time, I felt the baby moving and I couldn't imagine giving her up."

"What about the boy? The father?"

"Denied it was his." She couldn't bear to repeat what she'd told Destiny.

"You used an adoption agency?"

"No. It was a private adoption. We had a contract. According to Destiny, they moved sometime before she was six." She wiped an errant tear off her cheek. "I'd like to meet her. But that isn't something we've agreed to. Not yet, any-way. I'm hoping we'll talk again. She's in college now. Her last year."

"If it were me, I'd want to know my birth mother."

"Destiny and her other mother don't always see eye-to-eye. And I'm not sure Mrs. Harris would appreciate my reaching out to Destiny. I spoke to her dad and he was encouraging, but ... he doesn't live with them now. I always felt he understood me more than she did." She allowed the corners of her mouth to curve upward.

"How is it you so recently had contact?"

"Mr. Harris sent me a letter. After Destiny turned twenty-one." She glanced at Gavin, wondering if he saw her as somehow tainted, after having admitted she'd been a teenage mother. But he just looked sad, as though he felt some of the pain she'd shared at having to give up Destiny so long ago.

"I'm sorry I dumped all this on you."

His expression implied surprise. "Don't be. I'm honored you shared it. I had no idea." The corners of his mouth quirked upward. "Henry said you're wasting your time at the library, that you were born to be a mother. With a whole team of kids. What sport is your favorite? So I'll know what to tell him what's in your future."

Bella laughed. "Henry is such a dear. Reminds me of my grandfather. He's so kind, so caring. His children's selections are the best in town, one of the reasons we support his store. Tell him he's right, that I love children. As for having a team of them ... I'm not sure my house is big enough for more than one or two. And since I'm not married ..."

"Maybe that's in your future, too," he murmured, his neck pinker than before. "After all, you're young enough."

He's blushing? But why? Bella ducked her head and took a long sip of her coffee, stroking the mug with two fingers after she set it on the table. "I need to ask *you* something," hoping to change the direction of their conversation.

"Fire away."

"You seem to care a lot about your uncle. Are you suspicious of Earl? Think he's stealing from Henry?"

His eyes seemed to turn a darker blue. "I've been wondering about that. But I won't make an accusation without proof. I've already sent a copy of last year's financials to my accountant so he can take care of the taxes, which Henry hasn't paid. Now I'm going through the books myself. Something about the numbers doesn't add up. And Henry's too sick to help me figure them out."

"Maybe your accountant will know."

"I'll call him if I come across issues that suggest something untoward. I'm hoping it's a simple matter of inattention. And not recording everything. I want to make sure Henry's business is worth hanging on to. He loves the store. About as much as he loved his wife. They ran it together, you know."

"Henry was already a widower when I met him. I'd hate to think of him closing the store."

"But if the store's losing money and he's not up to running it, he needs to let it go." He drained his coffee mug and stood up. "If that happens, the library might receive his inventory, assuming I can't return the books to the publishers. Something else I need to figure out."

"If you need help at the store, let me know. One of the volunteers at the library might be willing. But Zoe and I would hate to see his store go under."

"I'll see if it can be saved. Before Henry gets out of the hospital."

Bella walked with Gavin to the front door.

He leaned closer, one finger tracing the curve of her left cheek, his gaze focusing on her lips. "May I take that down payment now? As a thank-you for a very pleasant evening," he murmured in her ear, just before the sensation of his lips on hers sent sizzles of desire into her middle. His mouth focused first on her top lip, then the lower one. His exploration was gentle and so softly insistent that Bella wanted to beg for more. But then he broke their connection and stepped back.

He opened the door and walked outside. Just before he folded himself into the car, he smiled and waved.

Bella waved back and stood where she was for a long minute, watching his car back out of the driveway and then turn down the road. *Oh my God. He kisses like a dream.* She debated telling Zoe what had just happened and decided to keep the kiss to herself. At least for a little while.

Chapter 9

BELLA GATHERED UP THE LETTERS SHE HAD WRITTEN each year, surprised that she needed two large envelopes to contain them. She added a note in the first envelope.

```
Dear Destiny,

Even though I wasn't sure why your
parents stopped sending me pic-
tures, I wrote these letters in the
hope that some day they would con-
tact me again. Perhaps you'd like
to see them, now that we've talk-
ed. I was so thrilled to hear your
voice the other day. And, I'd love
it if you would send me a recent
```

```
picture.
```

```
All my love, Bella
```

She stopped at the post office, praying that Destiny would be home when the mail arrived.

"Don't you want to put a return address on these, in case they get lost, so they can come back to you?" the postal clerk asked.

"Oh. Of course." Bella appended her address. Bella imagined Destiny reading the letters and being reassured that her birth mother loved her. Maybe their arrival would generate another call. Bella could only hope.

Vanessa gathered up the mail that had been placed in the box that the letter carrier used for bulky packages too large to fit into the slot near the front door. Two large envelopes caught her attention. The return address was unfamiliar. What had Destiny ordered? She glanced at the clock. Wasn't Destiny working at the bookstore tonight? If so, she wouldn't be home until after dinner.

Vanessa shook the envelopes. Clothes, maybe? Something shifted inside, but she couldn't tell what they contained. She turned on the stove and placed a pan of water on the burner. When steam was wafting into the air above the pan, she held the first envelope over the steam until the glue loosened under the flap. She tipped the package onto the table and several cards slid out, each of them addressed to Destiny, the return address containing the name "Isabella Campbell."

Vanessa's pulse picked up. She steamed open the second

envelope. More cards. One rattled as if it contained something other than a card. Destiny's birth mother had sent them? Had Nolan told her to do so? Vanessa stared at the letters and counted them. More than thirty cards. None of them postmarked. As the white and cream-colored envelopes, and two that were red, stared back at her, she imagined them to be snakes, slithering into her home, aimed at poisoning Destiny against Vanessa, asking her daughter to reach out to her birth mother. That girl hadn't known enough to protect herself from getting pregnant, had wanted to keep the baby against her parents' wishes.

The girl's father had worn a perpetual scowl on the two occasions when she and Nolan had visited, intent on convincing his daughter to let them adopt her baby. Mrs. Campbell had seemed nervous whenever they came to the house, offering them coffee and cookies before disappearing into another room whenever they sat down to talk with Isabella. Both parents had seemed relieved when the girl finally signed the papers that Nolan's attorney had drawn up.

If only Nolan hadn't convinced Vanessa to agree to that semi-open adoption. Perhaps if she'd had her way, no such letters would have found their way into her house. She glanced in the direction of the trash container just outside the kitchen door. If she hurried, she could get rid of those cards, which probably contained letters. But before she could do so, she heard a car pull into the driveway.

Damn! Maybe Destiny didn't have to work today after all. But hadn't she said she was going to see Noah again after work? Vanessa hurriedly gathered up the letters, stuffed them into the large envelopes, and resealed them. She clutched the packets to her breast as she climbed the stairs, entered her bedroom, and shoved the envelopes into the lowest drawer in the highboy, next to the others she'd kept for so many years. She would get rid of all the letters tomorrow. After Des went to class. Right before trash pickup. No one would be the wiser. Vanessa sat down on her bed and picked up the book she'd been reading every evening for the past week, not wanting to imagine Destiny with the boyfriend she dared her mother to accept. *Maybe they had a fight and that's why Des came home so early.*

The sound of the kitchen door slamming seemed to echo in Vanessa's chest as she listened for Destiny's feet on the stairs.

"You up, Mom?" she called out.

"Come on in, dear." She pressed one hand against her chest as she leaned against her bed pillows. She squeezed her eyes shut for an instant. *I will not ask her why she isn't with Noah. I will remain calm, like Nolan said.* "Did you get lots of studying done? Weren't you supposed to work at the bookstore tonight?"

"Not till tomorrow." Des flopped down on Vanessa's bed, reminding her of their mother-daughter talks after school in years gone by. She held a white card in her hand. "What's this?"

Oh, no. Did I forget one? Vanessa's heart changed places with her stomach and her pulse began to race.

"It was on the floor next to the kitchen table. Addressed to me."

"I'm sure it's nothing, dear."

Destiny ripped open the envelope and a card slid out. "From Bella. Looks like it was meant for a little kid." Destiny stared at Vanessa. "Me."

Vanessa was certain she looked guilty, like she felt.

"I talked to Dad the other day. He said you have letters from my birth mom. That you might still have them."

The air in Vanessa's lungs disappeared. She'd known a time would come when she would have to do something about those letters. Why had Nolan mentioned them? Why *didn't I toss them out when we moved?* Somehow, she hadn't expected Des to ask. She felt caught, like a rat in a trap of her own making …

Vanessa sighed and climbed off the bed. She approached the highboy, Nolan's dresser before the divorce. She opened the lowest drawer and pulled out a shoebox holding the letters she'd saved. For good measure, she also grabbed the two large envelopes. Clutching all three items to her chest, she turned and faced Destiny.

"Are you sure you want to see them?" Her voice trembled. "They're really nothing special. Just cards she sent for your birthday. And Christmas. These others—" she nodded at the large envelopes in her arms, "—just arrived. Probably little kid cards, like that one you just opened. Not something a young woman your age would want." Her heart was a hammer pounding against her ribs. What if Des became upset when she read what her birth mother had written? A real mother protected her child. Vanessa couldn't bear it if Des was hurt by words from that girl who had given her up, words she herself had refused to read when those letters had first arrived.

Deciding to take the high road, as if nothing Des' birth mother could possibly say was of any concern of hers, Vanessa suggested, "How about we read them together?" She took a seat next to Destiny.

Vanessa repeated her mental vow to stay calm, even as she imagined each of those letters to be bombs ready to explode, petrified that their reading would upset Destiny. Never mind what they would do to Vanessa and her relationship with her daughter.

"You know she couldn't take care of you, don't you? That she was only sixteen? Not even out of high school. She told us she wanted you to have a complete family, Des. That's why she chose us. These cards can't possibly be anything of value. I'm not even sure why I saved them. Or why she sent you these others." Vanessa's mind whirled at what her daughter might do after reading the cards.

Destiny frowned. "You're saying she wasn't good enough for me? I want to see them." Her voice rising, Destiny pulled the box and the large envelopes out of Vanessa's arms. "Dad said it's my *right*. She sent them to *me*, only you never told me. What are you afraid of, Mom? They're probably just cards. Dad said *you* didn't want to keep sending Bella my picture, even though you were supposed to. It was in that contract you guys signed."

Vanessa pressed her hands to her face. They felt like ice against the heat of her cheeks. Her pulse pounded like a runaway horse. "What else did Dad say?"

"Not much. I talked to her—" Destiny's face paled right before her cheeks and neck bloomed with color.

Vanessa groaned when Destiny confirmed her worst fear. "You did? When? Does she live here now?"

"She sent me a letter and then she called me. After she talked to Dad."

Incensed that she'd been in the dark for who knows how long, Vanessa lost her battle to remain in wise-mother mode. "How *dare* she talk to you without asking me first!"

"I'm twenty-one, Mom. She didn't *have* to ask permission. Not anymore. You agreed, you and Dad." She fumbled with the string that bound the box and set everything down for a moment. "What did Bella ever do to you that you refused to even send her a picture of me once a year?"

Vanessa wasn't prepared for this. All she'd wanted was to protect Destiny, but she didn't want Vanessa's protection, maybe didn't even want *her*. *Nolan put that girl up to this.* He'd never seen the harm in maintaining occasional contact with

Destiny's birth mother. Why couldn't he see how dangerous that was? *He* was to blame!

Destiny stacked the box on top of the two large envelopes. "No, Mom. I'll read them by myself." The slamming of her bedroom door a moment later punctuated Destiny's words.

Vanessa sobbed into her pillow. Now what was she going to do?

Destiny locked her bedroom door, certain her mother was going to rush in and grab the letters. She opened the box. It held envelopes with postmarks from when she was a little kid. She opened the first large envelope. A sheaf of letters slid onto her bed. She stacked the letters and forced herself to open them, one after the other. Most of the cards held little more than a few words, but all ended with, "All my love, Bella, your birth mom."

Bella. That's what she called herself when they'd talked. Not Mom. Not Isabella, her old-fashioned name. Destiny realized each pair of cards represented a year in her life gone. In some of the letters, she read of news Bella shared about herself. One of the early ones reported that she had graduated from high school, that she was working two jobs, had moved out of her parents' house, and that she was hoping to be able to go to college someday.

Destiny guessed Bella was ambitious, but poor. Not like Des. She'd been coasting through life. Had taken almost five years if she counted the two summers to finish college, even though two of her friends had finished in four. She was only working part-time, not because she had to—Dad was taking care of all her expenses—but because she loved being surrounded by books. Most of what she earned she spent on clothes, going out with her friends, or the latest DVDs.

The style of the cards on her bed reflected the age of the recipient. One for Destiny's sixth birthday included a small book—the kind a child would enjoy playing with, being read to, maybe even reading herself. Destiny set it aside. Extra credit for her night class could be had with written reviews of different children's books. She would review the little book, designed for an early reader, one of the Boxcar Children series titles she hadn't seen before.

The last card in the first envelope was for Christmas when she was nine. It bore the same inscription as before, but also reported that Bella had graduated from college, having worked full-time while going to school part-time for seven years. *Wow!* Des had thought taking five years to finish college was a long time, and she was going full time.

Destiny set the first pile of cards and letters aside and climbed into her favorite tank top and pajama bottoms. She slid her feet under the covers and pulled the second envelope closer. She lined up the cards and letters and opened the card that was slightly larger than the others, heavier, too. Inside was another envelope, taped closed. When she opened it a necklace fell into her hand.

The words of the letter seemed to burn her chest, branding her with the love it expressed.

Dear Destiny,

You're ten years old now, your first birthday with two digits. It seems only yesterday that I held you in my arms before handing you over to your parents. I saw this necklace earlier this summer when I took a weekend trip with friends. We wandered around the art fair, looking at the sculptures, the clay pottery, and the paintings. Then we saw the jewelers, all local artists. This necklace called to me and I thought of you. I think of it as my heart, which I'm giving to you. The key is yours, when you slip it into the side of the heart, it opens, just as my heart shall always be open to you. I hope you know that I love you, that I've loved you from the first moment I knew you were growing inside me. Wear it and know that you are loved. My hope for you—every single day—is that you have a happy life, one filled with wonderful dreams for the future and lots of play, too.

All my love, Bella

Destiny held up the silver heart. On the right edge of the heart was a tiny hole. The longest segment of the key fit into the hole and when Destiny pressed, the heart opened, revealing a space just large enough for the folded piece of paper that fell into her hand. On one side was printed "Destiny" and on the other "Bella." She rubbed a hand across her face to wipe away tears. If she needed proof that her birth mother loved her, this was it. But she hadn't known that Bella had sent it to her until now. Had she done so years earlier, Des would have insisted on wearing the necklace. But what would her mom think? It was probably not something she'd want Destiny to have.

She read the other letters through tears that caused the words to wobble on the page. The card celebrating her eighteenth birthday suggested she might want to purchase a favorite book as a keepsake. Bella must love books, probably why she worked in a library. How could she know that Des loved books, too?

Destiny placed the letters in a pile on her dresser. The silver heart, and the key attached to the necklace, sparkled in the light on her bedside table. She turned out the light and lay back against her pillows, staring into the darkness. She *had* to talk to Bella again. Her mind whirled at what she now knew. Her birth mom hadn't wanted to give her away. She'd told her that, but Destiny hadn't fully accepted those words at the time. It seemed too easy for a birth mom to say that. Now she knew for sure. She'd wondered about the woman who'd given her life whenever her dad talked about that day they'd taken her home. Destiny was now certain Bella still loved her, even if she hadn't heard from Destiny's family in years. If she didn't love her, why would Bella have called?

I'm going to see Dad soon. We'll talk then. Destiny wondered if she might change her return ticket and fly from Austin to Seattle before returning to Denver. She fell asleep imagining how she might change her itinerary without having to tell her mom.

The Wednesday after her business meeting with Gavin, Bella gathered the extra copies of the *Harry Potter* books for the new afternoon story time. Most of the ten to twelve elementary-age children who had signed up would read along with her. Bella's heart thumped in her chest when she caught sight of the eager attendees.

Many parents perched on the window seats. One of the boys she knew, Eli, approached her. "Ms. Bella. Hi. I'm glad you're going to read about Harry Potter. I really like these books."

She brushed her curls off her neck and smiled. "Did you bring your own copy or do you need to use one of these?"

"My own. My dad reminded me before I went to school."

Eli pointed to the books Bella was holding. "Want me to give them out to the kids who don't have their own?"

"Thank you, Eli. That's very nice of you." She looked up when Otis, the high school boy who worked in the library every afternoon, approached her. "Ms. Campbell. There's a call for you. In your office. Want me to say you're busy?"

"I'll take it." She thought of Gavin and her pulse picked up. Was he calling to say he wouldn't be arriving in time for the first session? She'd intended to introduce him so everyone could thank him for the extra books. "We still have time before everyone arrives. Why don't you ask the caller if he can give me a minute to arrange things here?"

"I'll tell her." The boy turned on his heel and walked purposefully toward Bella's office.

Bella handed Eli three more books and watched as he began dropping them onto the oversized pillows she'd placed around the room. "Could you tell the other children I'll be right back?"

He nodded and resumed his seat.

Bella walked to her office and picked up her phone. "This

is Ms. Campbell."

"It's Destiny. I sent you a text, but you never answered, so I decided to use your office number. Should I have waited until tonight to call?"

Bella's stomach slammed into her ribs on hearing her daughter's voice. She sounded tentative, almost regretting that she had called, not nearly as confrontational as her questions during their first phone call. Bella fumbled for her cell phone. There it was. A short text from Destiny. *Can we talk again?*

"It's fine. I'm glad you called." She gulped air. "But I'm leading a new story time in a few minutes. Could I call you back in about an hour?"

"It would be better if I call you. Same number as this or your cell?"

"This number is fine. I'll be finished no later than four-thirty. Five-thirty your time, right?"

"Okay. I call you back." The girl hung up.

Bella walked back to the children's reading room, her legs feeling wobbly, her pulse gradually slowing. She glanced around the room, aware that she was smiling broadly. The children probably thought she was happy they had arrived. She was, but oh, how good it felt that Destiny had reached out to her.

Bella took her seat. All but one of the pillows was now taken and the quiet chatter of the children told her they were eager for her to begin. She glanced at several of the parents who sat around the edges of the room. All the window seats were taken and two other parents had moved chairs near some of the tables. Roberta's mother, at a table removed from where the children had gathered, was peering intently at her laptop, paying no attention to her daughter, who sat close to Bella's chair, a *Harry Potter* book open. Roberta often got into disagreements with the other children. Bella concluded the girl was troubled. "Is everyone ready? How many of you will bring your own books next week?"

Several hands went up.

Bella nodded, prepared to begin, and saw that Gavin had entered the room and was standing quietly near the door. *Why do I keep reacting to his presence as if he* means *something to me?* He really didn't; but he did. She shouldn't think that way, but she did. She sighed. Devil Bella was winning out.

"Everyone, let's thank Mr. Cambridge, over by the door, for helping us today. He is helping Mr. Quackenbush at Books and More, our very favorite bookstore, that donated several copies of the book we'll be reading."

Gavin smiled and nodded, acknowledging the parents and children who looked his way and clapped.

"Parents, if your child doesn't yet have a personal copy, you can get one at Books and More, just like it says on the posters throughout the library. We'd love it if you would bring them next week, so that newcomers who don't have the book can also follow along." She paused and waited for the children to quiet. "Ready? We'll begin today on page one." Bella watched as the children opened their books.

"Do we have to start there?" Roberta's whine carried throughout the room, generating a frown from her mother. "I've already read this book."

"Then just follow along with the other boys and girls, Roberta. Some of the others may not know the story."

The girl frowned and began flipping pages back to the front of the book.

Bella began reading, aware that a part of her mind was focused on her daughter's upcoming phone call, another part on the gorgeous man still standing near the door. She wondered how long Gavin would stay, and whether she'd have time to ask him about Henry before he left. She turned another page and continued with the story until Eli interrupted her.

"I have a question, Ms. Bella." When she looked up, she saw that Eli's dad had come into the room and had taken a seat in the far corner. Toward the back of the children's reading room, Gavin was still watching the proceedings. Her pulse jumped again and then began to pound.

"What is it, Eli?" she asked, forcing herself to concentrate on the boy. He asked a question that two other children answered. Bella allowed the discussion to proceed longer than usual and set the book down. She tried not to look at Gavin, but her glances around the room seemed to be pulled to that corner of the library as she described how, over the next couple of weeks, they would be making a cupboard just like the one where Harry's muggle guardians made him sleep. Several of the children began to chatter excitedly.

She felt Gavin's gaze on her. The forest green dress with a slightly paler hue in the skirt that Zoe said brought out the color of her eyes now seemed almost too warm for being inside on this sunny spring day. Bella glanced up when another child's hand went up. "Yes, Nickie?"

"Can you stop for a minute, Ms. Bella? I have to … you know, and I don't want to miss a single word."

Bella nodded. "If anyone else needs to take a break, now's a good time." Three other children stood up and followed Nickie in the direction of the bathrooms.

Gavin approached her chair. "Didn't want to bother you, but I need to go. Promised Henry I'd look in on him this afternoon. I gather things are going well?"

Bella detected warmth when his fingers grazed her hand and sent a zing of awareness she tried to ignore.

"So far, it's going great. I'll repeat our thank-you when the session is over." She lifted her chin slightly. "So you know we're serious about advertising Henry's store."

"I never doubted you. And thanks. How many of these kids need their own copies?"

"I'm betting at least eight, maybe more. We handed out all six of the ones you provided and two more kids are sharing. I'll text you with that information later today."

He nodded. "See you around." He sauntered out, the casual jeans he wore showing off his tight buns and long legs.

Zoe, he's so gorgeous. Too bad you're not here to check him out. Bella waited as the children returned and settled on the pillows scattered in a large semi-circle around her chair. Bella began reading and did so almost without interruption through the rest of the hour. After closing the book, she checked the clock. Only ten minutes before Destiny was to call back. Bella took two more questions and then counted the hands that went up when she asked how many would be buying their own copies before next week.

She turned toward her office and walked quickly away from the children's reading room. The anxiety she'd felt during her pregnancy flooded back when she wondered what questions Destiny would ask this time.

Nearly an hour later, Bella was about to gather up her things and go home, having concluded that Destiny wasn't going to call after all, when the phone rang.

"Evergreen Public Library. This is Ms. Campbell. How may I help you?"

Destiny laughed. "Is that how you answer the phone when you're working?"

Bella leaned back into her seat with a quiet sigh, aware that her pulse was jumping again. "Thanks for calling me back."

"What's it like working in a library?"

"It's what I always wanted to do."

"I read all your letters. Even the ones my mom had from when I was little." Destiny breathed into the phone for a long beat. "Do you remember what you sent me for my tenth birthday?"

Bella's stomach clutched. "A heart necklace, with a key." *How could I forget?*

"I'm wearing it right now."

Tears burned the back of Bella's lids. "You like it?"

"Uh-huh. I'm at the student union right now, getting ready to go to my job. At a bookstore."

"Then you must like books, too."

"Yes."

Bella wiped her eyes. "Didn't you say you are graduating soon? I could send you a gift card to commemorate that milestone." Bella waited for Destiny to reply. Her family was wealthy. Perhaps she thought a gift card wasn't sufficient as a college graduation gift.

"You don't have to. I mean, it's the thought that counts, right?" The sounds of distant laughter from other voices almost covered Destiny's words.

"Do you have more questions, Destiny? Ones we never got to when we talked before?"

"I just wanted to call you back. So you'd know I got your cards and stuff." Another burst of laughter interrupted. "Would you send me a picture? I want to know what you look like."

"Of course. Perhaps your boyfriend could take your picture and email it to me? Didn't you say that you had a boyfriend?"

Destiny chuckled softly. "I'll ask him. He's betting I look like you. Since no one else in my family has red hair. It'd be nice to know I look like *someone*. My grandma was always asking my folks why they didn't go for someone whose baby would look like them."

"Your birth father had dark hair. Doesn't your Dad have brown hair?"

"You remember that?" Des rushed on. "He's mostly gray now. Do you look like anyone else in your family, your dad or mom?"

"My great-grandmother. She died the year after I was born, but when she came to see me in the hospital, my mom and grandma told me she predicted I'd look just like her." Bella laughed. "The pictures I have all show her with white hair, but they said it was red when she was younger. My mom has blonde hair and my dad's hair was dark, before he lost it all."

"What about your grandmother?"

"She was a strawberry blonde. Over the years, it darkened. She dyed it so her gray wouldn't show. She was kind of vain about the age thing."

"Does your grandmother know about me?"

"No. She died when I was fourteen." The grandmother who'd always been so loving. Bella imagined her being forgiving had she known of Bella's pregnancy. Maybe she'd have even taken her in, let her live with her that last year in high school when her dad watched her every minute, insisted on driving her to her tutoring lessons, even when they were just with elementary kids. She liked to think her grandmother would have stood up to her parents.

"You said you didn't give me away."

Bella sucked in her lower lip at those words. "No, I didn't. The words we use—even today to describe adoption—are so hurtful, most of them. Like 'birth mother' or 'biological parent'—as if that's all we are good for, to give you birth. And the way we describe the children, and the actions of women like me."

"What do you mean?"

"Adding 'adopted' to child, as if you're different from other children. Or 'foundling.' Like I dropped you off by the side of the road and your folks came along and picked up you, *found* you, and took you home. Or calling your parents 'adoptive,' as if they are somehow different from other parents." She paused before adding, "It's hard for me to think of Mr. and Mrs. Harris as your parents, even though they raised you." Bella wondered if she should have shared how she felt, but she couldn't seem to stop talking. "I don't really deserve to think of you as mine, just because I gave birth to you." She coughed and choked, surprised she was expressing her feelings so forthrightly to a girl she hadn't even met. *I need to ask Destiny how she feels.* "I'm sure your parents consider themselves your parents, no adjective preceding the word."

Destiny's silence suggested that she might be thinking about Bella's comments. "I guess you think a lot about words. Since you're a librarian. You like books, and books are filled with words."

Bella laughed softly. "You're right. Please don't think I resent your folks, Destiny. I'm so grateful to them for raising you. And I could never take the place of your ... mother—"

"It's hard for you to say that word, isn't it?"

She's so perceptive. Bella felt her cheeks beginning to burn and was glad Destiny couldn't see her. "Guilty as charged. I'm guessing she might be upset, maybe even thinks I *want* to replace her. Which I don't, can't. I have no right, really." She listened to the background noises issuing from the phone and decided to inject lightness into the conversation. "What would you like to call me, Destiny? Librarian, maybe? Or that weird person who called you the other day?"

Destiny was quiet for so long Bella wasn't sure their call was still connected.

The girl's voice seemed almost pensive when she replied. "I like the name you signed on all those cards. Bella."

She smiled, relieved. "Good. I'm fine with that."

"Is it okay, for now, if I think of you as a friend?"

Bella wiped her eyes, determined not to weep that her daughter seemed so accepting. "I'd love that. I'm honored you think so."

Destiny's voice took on a more businesslike tone. "I have to go. To get to my job at the bookstore."

"Of course. How long have you worked there?"

"Two years. My mom thinks it's a waste of time. It doesn't have a thing to do with my major, but I love books."

Bella hoped Destiny heard her smile her response. "Maybe it's in our genes, yours and mine. I'll email you a picture, so you can see what I look like. May I call you the next time, Destiny? Or do you still prefer to touch base with me when you're not so busy?"

"Let me call you. I'll text you first. If you don't mind."

Maybe she doesn't want others to know about us. "I understand."

"It was good to talk to you again." After a slight pause, she added, "Bella."

Bella remained in her seat, holding the phone long after Destiny hung up. She pulled out her cell phone and scanned the pictures stored there. She found one of her and Zoe and Tör, taken when they'd shared a boat ride on Lake Geneva last Christmas. She attached it to a text message: *Here's a picture of me. The other woman is Zoe, my best friend, and her fiancé. I look forward to seeing a picture of you. Bella.*

Chapter 10

TWO DAYS LATER, BELLA ENTERED HENRY Quackenbush's hospital room. He looked paler than before, and his cough sounded worse. He seemed to have shrunk in the bed, which shook when he coughed.

He halfheartedly raised a hand off the sheet and waited for her to take a seat. "Hello there, Bella, dear. Gavin got you the books?"

"Yes. And our first session went really well. How are *you* feeling?" The nurse had told Bella not to extend her visit past a few minutes.

"Can't seem to shake this cough. But Gavin seems to be takin' care of things at the store. Least, he said he was." Another harsh round of coughing racked Henry's frame.

"I'm sure he is. Along with Earl."

"Do me a favor, Bella."

"Anything, Henry. Whatever you want."

"Tell Gavin to come see me. I was asleep last time he showed up and he refused to wake me. I gotta talk to him." He paused and seemed to gather himself. "You know he isn't from around here?"

Bella nodded and patted his gnarled hand, the prominent veins curvy blue trails under his skin. "I'll give him the message."

"He works too much. Maybe you could show him around. I want him to get to know our little town."

Bella's heart shifted against her lungs as she imagined where she'd like to take Gavin. "He's not moving here?"

"Don't really know, but that'd be nice. He said something about checking out a local dealership. If he was to stick around, it might help me out some." Henry glanced at Bella from beneath his bushy brows, his lids at half-mast, and quirked a brief grin. "You know, with the store and all."

"Oh."

"Will you do that, Bella? Show him around?"

"I'll ask him." Would he have the time? Something about the way Gavin had looked at her during dinner implied he'd say 'yes.' Little Devil Bella certainly was interested in getting to know *him*. How he'd talked to Bella about Destiny was soothing, like he cared that she wanted to get to know her daughter. The man had a big heart, the way he seemed to care about people. The way he cared about Henry, even though her first impression had suggested otherwise. He *had* dropped everything after Bella, a perfect stranger, had called him.

Henry nodded and closed his eyes. "Thank you, Bella."

She watched Henry's chest rise and fall, his skin leached of the color that normally brightened his cheeks. She felt a chilling wave of dread that Henry might die. She felt burning in her fingers and looked down. Three fingers on her left hand were turning white, two on her right hand, too, and burning, as if she was holding them against a flame. *Just like when Dad used to yell at me.* Her doctor called it Raynaud's Syndrome, a response to stress or extreme cold. She'd thought it a gift from the baby that her fingers stopped turning white during her pregnancy, even when her dad yelled at her. And after she'd left home, she rarely experienced an attack.

Thinking that Henry wasn't going to make it brought back those feelings of desperate hopelessness. He wasn't a relative, but something about the old man drew her in, made her will him to live. Thank goodness his nephew was here, the nephew who gave heavenly kisses, the nephew she couldn't seem to ban from her dreams. But Bella doubted Gavin would stay after Henry came home, even if she showed him around.

She imagined red-draped Devil Bella perched on her left shoulder. *That* Bella thrilled at the thought of seeing Gavin again, but white-robed Angel Bella shook a finger at her, reminding her that men—*have you forgotten about Ethan, that creep?*—couldn't be trusted to think of others more than themselves.

Bella shrugged her shoulders and dislodged the two Bellas. Zoe had said that Bella shouldn't paint all men with the same brush that colored Ethan, but somehow, she couldn't help herself. *Face it, he's soured you on* all *men.* All except Gavin. Bella was practically salivating over the man. *You hardly know him,* Angel Bella protested. *But you'd like to,* Little Devil Bella crooned in her ear, climbing back up on her shoulder.

Bella stood up to leave and patted Henry's hand once more. "I'll call him right away, Henry. Please get well," she whispered before planting a kiss on his forehead and patting his grizzled cheek, his unshaven whiskers soft against her palm.

As she rode the elevator to the main floor, she willed the tips of her fingers to stop burning and tingling, a sure sign blood was starting to flow again.

Bella drove directly to Books and More. When she opened the door, Earl looked up from his usual spot near the cash register. "Hey, Bella."

"Hi. Is Mr. Cambridge here? Gavin?"

Earl pointed toward the stairs. "Henry's office." He pulled down his ever-present Mariner's cap, its brim practically hiding his entire face.

"Have you had many customers this week?" she asked, recalling the issue Gavin had raised during their business dinner.

"A bunch more'n usual. Most of 'em wanting those books you got from us."

Her heart warmed at the news. "The *Harry Potter* series? Not just the first volume?"

"That'd be them." Earl didn't look up as she walked past him toward the stairs leading to Henry's upstairs office with the circular window that looked out onto the street.

Bella climbed the stairs, looking past the shelves. She spotted three people in the store near the nonfiction corner on the first floor. All seemed to be browsing. *Let's hope you people buy something.* She walked in the direction of Henry's office and heard the clicks of someone working a keyboard.

"Knock, knock."

Gavin's expression was a study in concentration as he hunched over his laptop. He glanced up and gave her a smile that warmed her to her toes. Then he leaned back in his chair and rubbed the back of his neck with one hand. "You're a perfect excuse to take a break."

"I've never been called an excuse before." But the idea had merit, she concluded, privately acknowledging that Henry's request was *her* excuse to see Gavin again. "I've come from the hospital. Have they called you? Henry wants you to stop in."

"Was he awake? Last two times I've been there he was

asleep. I didn't want to disturb him." Gavin tiredly ran a hand through his blond-streaked hair, squeezed the bridge of his nose and rubbed his eyes. "How was he?"

Bella took a seat in the tiny office, her knees almost touching Gavin's. "I'm not a nurse, but he didn't look good. And he's still coughing. I'm worried. It's been almost two weeks and he seems no better."

Gavin nodded. "That's what the doctor said when I spoke to him."

"What about the store? Are sales better? Did the parents come in to pick up books?"

"According to Earl, lots of them. I checked the shelves myself. It seems several full sets have been purchased, but the sales reports don't match the money in the till."

"Maybe Earl doesn't write down all the sales."

"That's what I'm thinking. I've asked him to use the computer system. He claims it's too hard to learn."

"Maybe you need more help in the store. Earl doesn't seem to do much more than sit next to the cash register. Have you thought about hiring a high schooler or a college kid looking for part-time work? Especially after you leave and Henry comes back?"

"We can't afford to pay someone and I doubt we'd get any volunteers. I watched Earl the other day and he wasn't all that thrilled to be interrupted when a couple of people came in and asked where the sale table was."

"I was wondering where you moved it. Henry usually sets it up center front on the main floor."

Gavin shook his head. "Earl must have taken it down. He claims we don't need one, that our prices were low enough."

"But Henry's always had a sale table. Zoe and I make a point of checking it whenever we come in."

Gavin frowned. "I'll talk to Earl again. Today, I've spent

most of my time going through last years' accounts, trying to get things to balance. Not a pretty picture."

"What about your accountant? Has he found anything out of the ordinary?"

"Not that he's said. The tax forms are done. I cut a check to cover the penalty for late filing. All I need now is Henry's signature."

"You can get that when you talk to him." Bella stood up.

Gavin gave her a lopsided grin. "Wanna bet another dinner that he wants me to take it over? Every time I've seen him, he's made noises about that. Even though I know nothing about selling books. Not even books about cars."

"Maybe he's worried about Earl. That you'll fire him. They were buddies in Vietnam, you know. That's how they met."

"Really? When I asked about Earl, Henry just said he's a friend who helps him out. But I can't find any paystubs for him, so maybe that's all he is. A friend who hangs out here. All Henry wanted to talk about was his two favorite library ladies. You and—what's your friend's name?"

"Zoe. He's always teasing us, saying he wished he was younger so he could marry us two old single ladies, but Zoe's already engaged. Not available." She waved a hand as if dismissing Henry's jokes.

Gavin chuckled. "But you are. Available, I mean."

Bella felt her neck warming. "Yes."

Gavin was giving her another one of those wry grins. "Henry's way too old for you."

She nodded, intent on not repeating Devil Bella's taunt in her left ear. *But not for you, Mr. so-hot Cambridge.*

"Do me a favor before you leave the store." Gavin's eyes sparked at her.

"Anything." Well, maybe not anything. Bella's cheeks and neck heated at the naughty thoughts she was entertaining.

"Ask Earl about the sale table. Then call me back with what he said."

"Consider it done." She left his office and the clickety-clack of his laptop followed her out.

She reached the bottom of the stairs in time to see a customer leave with a book in hand. "Another sale, Earl?"

"Yep."

"Where's the sale table? Gavin said he set one up and that I'm interested in seeing what he selected."

Earl gave her a full-face frown. "I cleared it out. Put those books back where they belong."

"But it moves the inventory and Henry's always had a sale table. You are recording all sales, aren't you, Earl? So Henry will know you're taking good care of the store when he gets back?"

He seemed to squirm in his seat. "*If* he comes back. I hear he's not doing so good."

"And if he doesn't, maybe Gavin will take over the store."

That comment brought another grimace and a mutter Earl probably hadn't meant for her to hear. "More like sell it."

Bella's heart did another skip. *He would do that?* He'd made similar noises at dinner, but she hadn't taken him seriously. Surely Gavin would talk to Henry first. Bella stepped closer. "Would *you* like to run the store, Earl? Is that why you don't seem to like Gavin?"

Earl's dark eyes, shadowed under the brim of his hat, reminded Bella of ebonies, as hard as the stones and maybe as unfeeling. He chose not to answer.

She decided to press him. "A sale table is a great idea, Earl. Henry's always had one. Will you please set it up again?" Bella left the building and trotted to her car. She called Gavin on her cell.

"I asked Earl about the sale table. He doesn't appreciate

you being here."

Gavin's laughter came through loudly. "He's made that obvious. Refuses to answer my questions and he doesn't like that I keep asking. I'm leaving for the hospital in a couple minutes."

"Will you let me know what the doctor says?"

"Count on it. Henry'll be happy you asked."

A knock sounded on Bella's door and Mitchell announced he was heading home. "Are you staying much longer?"

"I have more calls to make about our new story hour for one of the radio stations. Their DJ asked if Zoe and I might do an interview about it."

"Oh? That'll be good advertising. Be sure to mention the other activities we have here, like that book club those blue-hairs attend."

You should be more respectful, Mitchell. Those ladies are old enough to be your mother. "I'll mention it. By the way, our first reading with the *Harry Potter* books went really well. Thank you for approving it." He had been grudging at best, but at least Mitchell hadn't stood in the way.

"Glad to hear it." He headed in the direction of the check-out desk.

Bella turned her focus back to the proposed interview. The DJ had asked her to come up with questions she especially wanted to answer about the library. Her stomach rumbled, reminding her how long it had been since she'd eaten lunch. She wanted to finish the list of questions, more than could be answered in ten short minutes in case the DJ didn't like some of the topics she wanted to touch on. She added a question about other activities, for people older than sixty, and was about to close her laptop and call it a day when another knock sounded and her door opened.

Not Mitchell again. Did he forget something? She looked up when the scent of something delicious wafted in her direction.

Gavin stood in the doorway of Bella's office and took in the way certain strands of Bella's hair shone in the light. He held up a large bag. "I called the library. The guy who answered said you were working late. Figured you'd stop if I brought you something to munch on. Or have you already eaten?"

"You must read minds in addition to account books. Whatever is in that bag smells heavenly." She motioned him to the table in the corner of her office.

"Glad you think so." But he hoped Henry couldn't—read minds, that is. The old man had gone on and on about how nice Bella was, had tried to talk about her more than the store. Especially when Gavin waved the profit-and-loss statement he'd created and how the financial records showed Henry was barely making ends meet. His uncle had growled at him and insisted the store was doing just fine, that it would do better after he was on his feet again. The only good thing about meeting with Henry was his statement that he always maintained a sale table. And Earl knew where the books were stored that he'd want set out there.

Gavin pulled out the little boxes he'd picked up at the Italian restaurant two blocks from the library. "Hope you like lasagna. I got two kinds. This one has meat, the other is eggplant, in case you prefer vegetarian."

"How about a little of both?" She disappeared from the office briefly and returned with two mugs of coffee, two plates, forks, knives, and spoons.

"Good idea." He cut up the lasagna and slid portions onto the plates she placed on the table.

They ate in silence for several minutes, during which Gavin observed Bella whenever her gaze wasn't focused on him. Was it the hot coffee, the food he'd brought, or something else that had heightened the color in her cheeks? He liked the effect, wondered if she blushed more than others because she was a redhead.

While he was taking a final sip of his coffee, Bella cleared her throat. "Henry asked me to show you around Evergreen. Do you want to, or is that just his way of saying he wants you to stick around? Even though you have a business in Spokane and intend to go back to it."

That old rascal. He's playing matchmaker. Not that Gavin objected, as long as it didn't lead to anything more permanent than a good time while he was stuck here, holding down Henry's tottering fort of a bookstore. But, it had been Gavin's idea to bring Bella dinner tonight. Their second dinner. The BMW dealership he'd been meaning to visit came to mind.

"How far is Bellevue from Evergreen?"

"Next town over. You know someone there?"

"Not someone. A business I want to check out."

"Busman's holiday?" she asked.

"You could say that." He didn't want to reveal the reason for his interest until he was sure he wanted to step up his research on why it was doing so poorly.

"When will you have time to … um … do that?" Bella's cheeks had darkened further. Her eyes, mostly a brilliant shade of green with gold sparks, seemed to mirror his own feelings. Particularly when her hand brushed his as she reached for his empty plate.

"Next week, assuming I can get through the rest of the financials." He rose and gathered up the empty food boxes, needing to keep busy so she wouldn't see how she affected him. "Where shall we dump these?"

"The kitchen. Follow me." She led the way into a tiny area near the back of the library, her hips moving seductively in her skirt, causing his groin to fill.

When they returned to her office, Bella checked her calendar and nodded her head. "I'm off on Monday next week, but the bookstore is open on Mondays."

"I want to make some changes and I was going to close it Monday afternoon anyway. If that works for you, maybe you could show me around for an hour or so and then help me at the store. Since you know the kinds of books that sell."

"What kind of help?"

"I want to go through some books in the storage area. And decide if we should send them back to the publishers."

"I'd be happy to help with that." She made a note on her calendar for Monday. "Thanks for dinner tonight. It was fun."

"Yes, it was," he murmured as he helped her on with her coat. Her scent, a subtle combination of something floral he couldn't quite pin down, wafted back to him. *I shouldn't do this,* he warned himself, but he couldn't seem to stop the impulse to turn her around to face him. To kiss her. He'd intended the kiss to be brief, but it became prolonged when she responded with a little sound that suggested she wanted more. He pulled her closer, aware of how she seemed to melt against him, her softness contrasting with what was fast becoming painfully hard.

Reluctantly, he eased away from her and turned toward the door.

"I'll pick you up for lunch on Monday," he rasped, hoping she didn't notice that his throat had gone dry. *Since when does a woman do that to me? It was just a kiss,* but somehow it was more than a meeting of two sets of lips, his eager for more and hers so compliant.

Bella slept poorly that night, reliving her impromptu dinner with Gavin. Their kiss. As unexpected as the first and just as shattering of her intention *not* to kiss him again. *Think of him only as Henry's nephew,* she kept repeating to herself. But she couldn't seem to stop wanting more of those trembles she'd felt deep inside whenever he'd glanced at her during their impromptu dinner. His eyes seemed to be sending her challenges that heated not only her cheeks but the rest of her. His comment that he wanted to check a nearby dealership left her confused. Maybe he *was* thinking of moving here, though he hadn't exactly said that. Henry had seemed wistful, as if he wanted Gavin to stay, but didn't believe he would.

The sun was not yet up when Bella climbed out of bed, concluding there was no point trying to sleep when she was too pent up. She had to stop thinking about Gavin and concentrate on something else. She padded into her spare bedroom and booted up her laptop.

Oh, good. Destiny got back to me. But it was just a short note, asking Bella her opinion about when her daughter should approach her boss about working full time.

How nice that she'd asked Bella's opinion. It made her feel like a real mom. Did she ask her other mother's opinion, too? *I want to see her!* Was it too soon to suggest such a meeting? After all, they'd only talked a couple of times. She decided to text Destiny. *Maybe I'll invite her to come for a visit.* She sat down in front of the computer and began her message.

… I'll pay for your airfare if you'd like to come. Perhaps after you

finish your classes this term? Would you prefer that I speak to your mother first? I'd be honored if she would come with you ...

Bella wondered how Destiny's mom would feel about such an invitation. Even if the woman chose not to accept, perhaps it would tell Destiny's parents that Bella's invitation was completely aboveboard. She added a few more words, hit the send button and went into the bathroom to shower and get ready for work.

When Bella arrived at the library, Zoe was staffing the main desk. She smiled as Bella walked in. "Lunch together today?"

Bella nodded and continued to her office to complete the order of new books she'd told Mitchell she would handle. She finished the order and set it aside, then looked over the calendar.

"You ready?" Zoe poked her head into the office.

"Sure." She followed Zoe from the lobby and into the sunshine. Late spring flowers nodded as they walked down the block to their favorite sandwich shop. After ordering, Bella took a seat in a corner booth.

Zoe slipped into the seat opposite. "Something's on your mind. What gives?"

"That nephew of Henry's. He *really* knows how to kiss, but I don't know if I should trust him. Or get close to him. Even though parts of me want to." She swallowed a bite of sandwich and took a quick sip of her tea.

Zoe snorted. "I can guess which parts, girlfriend."

"Henry asked me to show Gavin around town and Gavin mentioned a car dealership in Bellevue that he wants to visit. He already has a business in Spokane. I can't imagine him moving here when all his business and professional ties are back there."

"But what if they aren't? Maybe he wants to be closer

to Henry, especially since he's been so sick. If Gavin opens another dealership, he would probably travel back and forth between the two to keep an eye on both of them." She paused. "Are you worried you might be jumping into another relationship too soon?"

Bella nodded. Little Devil Bella whispered, *And Gavin is really nice. Hot, too.* "I told him about Destiny. He seemed very understanding of my situation, my reasons for having to give her up."

"You've never done that before, have you? Did Ethan know?"

"Just you. I wanted to tell Ethan." She sighed. "Just never got around to it. And he never asked."

"Gavin took it well?"

"He was very kind." She sighed. "I sent Destiny an invitation. To come here. I want to meet her. But how can I possibly concentrate on her when all this other stuff is going on?"

Zoe chuckled. "Like Henry being sick and Gavin tying you in romantic knots." She gave a full-throated laugh. "I say go for it, Bella. Let everything play out. Sometimes that's the best way. Let the complications simplify themselves."

Bella took another bite of her sandwich. "Maybe you're right." The thought of seeing Gavin again on Monday excited her and she felt her cheeks heat. Hoping Zoe wouldn't notice, Bella added, "I sent Destiny a picture, too, since she asked. I'm hoping she sends me one."

"What if she doesn't want to meet?"

"That's a risk I have to take. She did say she thought of me as a friend. I figured that was a good place to start. And if that's all we'll ever be, friends from afar, well ... I'm keeping my fingers crossed that she'll agree to a visit." Her muted phone rattled on the table, signaling the arrival of a message.

"Hey, look. From Destiny." She opened the message and

scrolled down to the attachment. "She sent a picture."

Bella stared at the photo. Destiny stood next to a young man with bushy black curls, smiling at the camera. She wore a black T-shirt and black jeans. A silver belt rode low on the girl's slim hips and stood out against the dark fabric. Silver studs gleamed on one ear and three long earrings dangled from her other ear, peeking out from among the young woman's red waves that draped over one shoulder.

"Wow! She looks a lot like you, Bella. Who's that guy she's hanging onto?"

"That's probably Noah, her boyfriend. I don't think her mom is all that thrilled about their relationship."

"What do you know about him?"

"Not much."

"Well, she replied to your request for a photo. Maybe she'll come see you, too."

"I've never stopped wondering about her. And now that I see what she looks like … It's like I'm seeing myself when I was her age—except that after I had her, I hacked off my hair. Before Taylor, Dad was always saying how much he loved my red hair. After the baby was born, I dyed it black and wore it in spikes for a couple of years. I was so rebellious my senior year. To get back at my folks, I suppose. But I don't want Destiny to make the same mistakes I made. It worries me that she seems at odds with her mom."

"What about her dad?"

"She didn't say much, only that he doesn't live with them anymore. Her folks are divorced. How ironic is that? I wanted my baby to have a complete family and what I gave her was a couple who got divorced."

"Hey, how could you have predicted that?"

"I know. I keep reminding myself that I couldn't have taken care of her when she was a baby." Bella stroked her finger down the picture of Destiny. "Maybe if she decides to meet me, I'll tell her I was wrong to let Taylor take advantage. He knew I had a crush on him, like most of the rest of the girls in school. She needs to use birth control if she sleeps with Noah, so she doesn't get pregnant like I did."

"Most girls keep their babies now."

"I know. If that happens, I hope her mother doesn't desert her like mine did."

"I thought it was your dad who made you go to the adoption agency and give her up."

"But my mom didn't stop him, even though she told me she wasn't so sure going to the adoption agency was the right thing to do. But after my dad had a huge fight with her, she wouldn't take my side. Refused to stand up to him. I'll never forgive her for not helping me."

Zoe shook her head. "She probably knew how hard it was for you to let your baby go." Zoe must have seen the tears gathering behind Bella's lashes. Zoe patted her hand. "Anyway—time to go back to work. Why don't you take the rest of your sandwich?" Zoe wrapped it and handed it to Bella with an encouraging smile.

"Are you going to introduce Destiny to Gavin?"

Bella's cheeks burned at the thought. "I don't know. He might not even be here, assuming she agrees to come." She sighed, wondering if the kindness Gavin had shown when Bella had explained about Destiny would extend to the girl herself.

"If Destiny does visit, I want to introduce her to Henry. She asked my opinion about her work in a bookstore. Maybe she's thinking she'd like to run one herself. Henry could tell her what it's like."

"And, if he needs help, she might be willing to provide it." Zoe smiled.

That was a happy thought, Bella considered as she walked back to the library.

Chapter 11

DESTINY FINISHED HER EXAM AND TURNED IN HER BLUE book. She returned to her seat and jotted down her thoughts on a spare piece of paper, trying to decide what to say and how to talk to her mom about Bella. She decided to call her dad and talk to him first. Maybe she should invite Bella to Denver, even though Destiny preferred to go to Seattle. Going to see her dad's new baby was the perfect excuse to leave town after she finished her spring quarter courses. If she flew from Austin to Seattle, she wouldn't even have to tell her mom why her trip took longer than two weeks.

Going to see Bella felt good. Des had printed off Bella's picture and folded it into her wallet. *I do look a lot like her.* Bella had texted that Destiny looked just like her when she was Destiny's age.

Now she knew she looked like *someone* who was really

related to her, not just a relative by adoption. If she had her picture taken with Bella, people would know right off who her real mother was. But she felt a twinge of guilt at that thought. Bella hadn't raised her. Her real mom was driving her batty with her constant questions about where she was going, who she was seeing, why she wasn't coming home every night, and on and on and on. Ever since she'd blurted out that she'd talked with Bella, her mom had been like a cat in a room full of rocking chairs. She never said Bella's name, referring to her only as 'that girl,' which wasn't very nice. *I shouldn't have told her about the calls.* She should have asked her dad to talk to Mom first, even though she was sure he would say Des needed to take responsibility for such a conversation.

Destiny really needed to talk to her mom, to explain why she wanted to meet Bella face-to-face. Maybe she would tell her Bella had invited *both* of them to come see her. But she couldn't imagine her mom agreeing to that. And if she didn't, would she prevent Destiny from seeing Bella?

Destiny gathered her belongings and walked to the bus stop. Tonight. During dinner. They would talk. A discussion between two adults, which she was now, at least according to her dad. She would be calm, soft-spoken, and logical. What her dad reminded her about whenever he listened to her complaints about her mother. Mom really did love her, really did want what was best for her, even if her questions made Des crazy.

She took a seat in the back of the bus. When she stepped out of the side door, she straightened her shoulders and walked home, determined not to get upset, no matter what her mom said.

"I have a question for you," Destiny began while she toyed with her salad and watched her mother blot her lips with her napkin.

"What's that, dear?"

"Tell me what it was like, when you got me." Dad had said it was a happy time. If Des began there, maybe her mom would be willing to talk, be more positive.

Her mother looked up at her, her gaze wary, as if surmising already that Destiny was leading up to something. "You already know. I'm sure we've told you that story more than once."

"I want to hear it again. From you. It's important. Or didn't you want me? Was it really all Dad's doing?"

"Whatever gave you that idea?" Her mom's lips pursed. "I couldn't have children, so after we tried for ten years, we decided to adopt. And we chose you."

"But it didn't really work that way, did it? You couldn't just go in and pick from a bunch of babies, like you were at the grocery store, selecting apples." Des laughed softly, hoping the ridiculous nature of the comparison would make her mother laugh, or at least stop frowning.

But her mom didn't smile. "The pregnant girl picked us. Some other families were in the running, according to her father, but we won her over," she said, her voice softening. "Really, Des. You know this already." Her mom peered at her again, and twirled a finger around one of the gray strands that accented her dark blond strands.

"So my birth mom was the one to pick, not you and Dad," she repeated. "What did you tell her that made her want you for my parents?"

"Our introductory letter probably convinced her, and the pictures we showed her. We wrote the letter when we were trying through an agency. Figured we might as well show it to her, too. Your dad has always been a good provider. We paid her hospital bill, you know. I suppose she liked that we lived in a good neighborhood, and that I planned to stay home full time. We made a point of mentioning that." Her mother leaned back in her chair, no longer fiddling with her hair, seeming more relaxed.

Destiny nodded encouragingly. "And that was when you met her? After she narrowed her pick down to you and those other couples?"

"I suppose so." Her mother's lips thinned. "What is this about, Destiny?"

She knew she wasn't going to hear any more details. "I got an invitation from my birth mom. Her name's Isabella." Dad had said to just tell Mom, not beat around the bush. So there it was. "Says I can call her Bella. It's a pretty name, don't you think? I looked it up. In Italian, it means beautiful. Was she?" Destiny thought Bella was.

Her mom crossed her arms over her chest, the image of defensiveness. "I never really noticed," she said, her voice clipped.

"She wants to meet me. She lives near Seattle and—"

"That girl wants *you* to come see her?"

"Us, Mom. She invited you, too."

Her mother's eyes widened, suggesting she was shocked. But was it the invitation or that Bella had invited both of them?

"Whatever for?" Her mother shook her head. "No. Out of the question. You have to finish school and get your degree. And you're already scheduled to go to Austin to see your dad and that new child. How can you *possibly* think we have time to traipse all the way out to Seattle? I suppose she wants me to pay for that, too. Nothing doing."

Destiny pressed her back against the chair, wishing she wasn't the only one sitting at the table across from her mother, who was staring—no, glaring—at her. "Mom, it's not like that. She said *she'd* pay. For both of us. And she said she was happy for you to come. She didn't say where we'd be staying. Maybe at her house. But I could ask her to put us up in a hotel if you want. But if you—"

"How can she possibly afford to pay? She didn't even graduate from high school."

Destiny rose from her chair. "That was *years* ago. She finished college and she's a librarian now. She probably has plenty of money."

"What's the *real* reason that girl wants you to come out there, Des? Did you put her up to this … this invitation?" Her mom said the word like it was distasteful, tainted.

"Dad says you're afraid I'll choose Bella and not you. But I don't even know her. And the only way I'll get to know her is to meet her."

Her mom's anger, her unwillingness to even consider the idea of a visit, triggered a knee-jerk reaction in Destiny. Why they never seemed to *talk* without one or the other stomping off or leaving the house. Usually Des.

"I'll bet you weren't very nice to her back then and that's why you won't come. What makes you think—"

"Nice to her? You mean when she let us adopt you? That girl was *desperate* to leave the hospital, to get on with her life. Of course we were nice to her. We gave you a home, have loved you all these years, given you everything you wanted—"

"No, you haven't. You don't like Noah, even though I like him. I *love* him. You were so nasty to Dad that he divorced you. I can imagine how you must have been with Bella. You won't even say her name. Dad keeps telling me I was her gift to you, but you've never liked that I don't look like you or anyone else in our family." Destiny panted as the words spilled out. "Did you know I look just like Bella? Is that why you're always so nasty to me? Because you remember what she looked like? Want to see her picture? I have one now."

She fumbled with her phone, brought up the picture, and pointed it toward her mother who stood up.

"Are you afraid I'm going to do what she did? Get pregnant? Maybe with Noah's baby?" She couldn't tell her mom that Noah had refused to have sex with her until she'd gone on the patch. And he *always* used a condom. Kept reminding her that a baby wasn't something he wanted right now, and that she shouldn't, either. Now her mom was crying. *Maybe I went too far, said too much.* Des took two steps toward her mom, wishing she had been nicer, not so accusing.

Her mother eased away from the table. "I can't deal with this right now, Destiny. You have no idea how I felt back then, how much I love you, have loved you from the first time we saw you."

"Were you at the hospital when I was born?"

"Right after. We saw you in the nursery that first night. Sleeping."

Destiny remained where she was. "When did you take me home?"

"Back then, babies usually stayed in the hospital for a few days. We took you home as soon as they would let us. The adoption wasn't final for another month and I worried every day that she was going to change her mind." She seemed to gasp out the words, as if reliving her worries of so long ago. "That we'd get a call from the lawyer and have to start all over again." She sucked in a loud breath. "But we didn't."

"Bella said she named me. Did you know she watched you take me away?"

"I wanted to change your name, but your father promised her we would keep it. So we added your middle name. That's what I felt, what you were to us. A joy." Her mom mopped her eyes and wiped her nose before meeting Destiny's gaze.

"We were thrilled to have you, sweetheart, and you seemed to be happy with us, too. Until the last few years, when nothing I do or say meets with your approval." She sniffed again and squared her shoulders. "Can't you just accept that I'm not—that I don't want you to meet that woman?" She halted her nervous pacing, seeming to consider another alternative. "But if you insist, why don't you invite her to come here? If you *have* to meet her, I'd feel better if she came here."

"To our house?" Destiny was incredulous. *Wow!* That was a surprise.

"Not *here*. Perhaps at some other place. A restaurant or maybe a hotel."

Stunned, Destiny said nothing. She finally nodded. "I'll ask her." Almost as an afterthought, she said, "Thanks, Mom," before she headed upstairs to text Bella. *OMG!*

"You encouraged her, didn't you? Don't deny it," Vanessa hissed when she reached Nolan the next morning.

"Encouraged what, Vanessa?" He sighed, suspecting she was calling about yet another confrontation with Destiny.

"Des has been in touch with that girl, that woman, the one—"

"Isabella Campbell? Why don't you just say her name, Vanessa? She's a woman, just like you. Our daughter's birth mother."

"But what if ... what if?" Vanessa wept, unable to stop the fear that seemed to cloak her in despair at the thought of Destiny wanting to meet, maybe even live near or *with,* Isabella.

"Destiny's not going to throw you over for her birth mom. That's what you're afraid of, isn't it? What you've *always* been afraid of. *You're* her mother. *You* raised her. Our daughter isn't going to suddenly decide she wants nothing to do with you." He halted his conversation and seemed to be mumbling to someone in his office.

Vanessa now questioned why she had called him, knowing he would be busy. He had asked her, more than once, not to call him at the office. But she hated to have to call him at home and risk having to speak to his wife.

"I can't talk now. I've got an important meeting coming up in the next few minutes."

"Don't hang up, Nolan. Please. Destiny's birth mother wants her—me, too—to come to Seattle. Did you put Des up to that?"

"She wants *both* of you to come out? I'd say that woman has a lot more charity than you. I can see her inviting Des, but you, too? Give her credit for reaching out. Why don't you accept the invitation? See for yourself that Isabella doesn't have two heads. She probably just wants to let Des know who she is, maybe answer any questions she has about why she couldn't keep her. It's a good thing, Vanessa. Maybe it'll clear the air between you and Des, which is long overdue."

Nolan had always sympathized with that girl, Isabella. Vanessa listened to the dial tone and shook her head. She sat down on the couch in the home she'd won in the divorce settlement. All because Nolan wanted out, refused to stay married to her any longer. She'd suspected he was having an affair when he announced he wanted a divorce, but she'd never had proof. At least he hadn't cheated on her with the woman he was now married to.

The man she'd been married to, who loved children, was having a baby with his new wife, a woman able to give him what Vanessa couldn't. A child who shared his DNA. Vanessa hadn't been so sure about adoption when they'd first talked about it, but Nolan had encouraged her, telling her that if they had a child, maybe her fertility problems would be resolved. She'd prayed that would be the case, even though their research into the matter told her it wasn't very likely. Nevertheless, she'd gone along with what he wanted, and when Destiny lay in her arms, she'd been happy to be a mother. Now her daughter was demanding to meet her birth mother. *Why* had Nolan upset the applecart by sending that letter to Isabella? If only he'd left well enough alone.

Vanessa wandered toward the wall covered with numerous photos, most of them showing three smiling faces, a couple of them with little Derek in Vanessa's arms. More recent pictures no longer included Nolan. The photo he'd sent home with Destiny after his marriage to Erin sat in Des's room. Vanessa had denied its inclusion on what she had always called their family wall. But Des was right. In the two photos taken at the family reunions when she was ten and again shortly before her fifteenth birthday—only a month before Nolan made his escape—Des's bright red hair had stood out in the picture, setting her daughter apart from the rest of the Harris and Coleman clans.

Vanessa's mother had wanted to know why they hadn't tried for a child whose parents had dark hair and dark eyes, like Nolan's. She'd tried to explain that it was the birth mother who chose them. Besides, how were they to know that the child would have red hair? The birth mother's parents weren't so endowed and, according to the girl's father, neither was the birth father, that boy who'd signed away his rights so quickly. Bella had shown them his picture when they'd asked. Even after the baby was born, Vanessa had hoped Destiny's hair wouldn't stay red. Those feathery wisps that covered the top of the baby's head had looked to Vanessa to be more blonde than red. Only after the baby's hair began coming in fully was it obvious she was going to be a true redhead, the first in the family, as if that mattered. But it had, at least to her. Destiny had complained that her cousins teased her, said she didn't look like anyone else, even the oldest members. Vanessa knew Destiny was hurt by their remarks.

Vanessa felt her heart lurch as she remembered how joyfully she'd accepted the little bundle that was Destiny when Nolan handed the baby to her. What had caused such a rift between her daughter and herself? Had it begun when Vanessa discovered that Destiny was dating Noah? If only she'd been clairvoyant, able to see into the future so that she could have somehow prevented their meeting.

Or was it during Destiny's junior year in high school when she'd begun wearing all black clothes, insisting on dating boys Vanessa didn't approve of? Des had seemed to want to pick fights with her that year, especially after Nolan left. He'd said Vanessa needed to trust Destiny, but her fear had prevented her from loosening up, letting Destiny have the freedom she craved. She sighed. It was probably her fault that Destiny had welcomed her birth mother's call, a woman who wasn't trying to keep her safe, who might even encourage Des to take the chances Vanessa was so afraid of.

At least Nolan had held off getting Destiny her own car. But would she find herself an apartment after she finished college and make good on her threat to move in with Noah?

Vanessa wandered into the kitchen. Cooking always made her feel better. Maybe she would bake a cake for dessert. Destiny had always liked Vanessa's desserts, until she'd decided she was getting fat and had stopped eating them.

Vanessa's conversation with Nolan had been singularly unhelpful. She was alone in her distrust of Destiny's birth mom.

If only Vanessa knew other adoptive mothers, could ask their opinion, get their advice about what to do. But she didn't know other women in her situation. She would have to come up with a decision, a way to broach the subject with Destiny on her own. Without losing her temper or collapsing into tearful recriminations. She needed to apologize for not offering to show Destiny those letters she'd finally turned over. She was wrong about wanting to throw them out, reluctantly relieved that Des's arrival had prevented her from doing so. But would Des accept her apology? It seemed she wasn't very accepting of anything Vanessa said these days.

"Ms. Harris," the professor called Destiny's name, bringing her abruptly out of a fog. She shouldn't have sat near the front of the room.

"Yes?"

"What was your reply to the ethical question I posed?" Soft twitters sounded from behind Destiny when she hesitated to reply. "Perhaps you need to get a good night's sleep before venturing to class again."

She knew her face had to be beet red. "Sorry." She waited until the professor called on another student. She hated the business ethics class, the last in her major that she had to pass if she was to graduate. When the class broke up into small groups, she made a break for the exit, not caring that her lack of participation might lower her grade.

Yesterday's conversation with her mother still weighed on her. She'd called her dad and talked with him again, but he kept saying she needed to clear the air with her mother.

However, every time she'd picked a time to do so, something interfered. Noah's phone calls or texts, extra assignments she'd decided to tackle instead—all excuses not to confront her mother—and the meetings her mother announced she was going to. Funny thing about those meetings. They weren't something her mother had been attending earlier in the year. Suddenly, she seemed a lot busier at the women's club. Maybe Mom was avoiding her, too.

The bell rang, announcing her next class.

Two hours later Destiny dialed Bella's number. It was noon in Seattle, or wherever that little town was where Bella lived.

"Evergreen Public Library. How may I help you?" a woman's voice answered.

The voice sounded vaguely like Bella, but not quite. Destiny double-checked the number. "Is that you, Bella?" *Maybe I should have called her cell.*

"I'm sorry. Ms. Campbell isn't here. May I take a message?"

"Oh. When could I call back?"

"Why don't you try after two? May I ask who's calling?"

"I'll just call back."

It was nearly nine when Destiny arrived home from her shift at the bookstore. She went to her room, checked the time, reached for her phone, and dialed Bella's cell phone.

"This is Bella."

She'd picked up on the first ring, her voice sounding so calm. *Not at all like Mom.*

"Hi. It's Destiny."

"Was that you who tried to reach me at the library today?" She seemed to be smiling.

Destiny's heart shifted into her throat. "Maybe I shouldn't try to call you during the day when you're working."

"It's okay. Usually I'm there. My best friend and I went to see someone at the hospital. What was it you wanted to talk with me about?"

"Well, I ... um." Now that she was going to tell her, Destiny suddenly felt anxious. What if Bella had changed her mind about meeting her? "I talked to my mom. About us coming to see you, I mean. All the way to Seattle. She's not so hot for the idea. So I was wondering if you'd come here instead." Destiny bit down on her lower lip to settle her nerves, even though one foot bumped against the frame of the bed, causing the mattress to shake. "I'm not sure our house is the best place to meet, but if you were at a hotel, maybe, or a restaurant?"

Destiny hated the hesitation in her voice. What if Bella refused to come to Denver?

"I'm happy to come see you. I'm not sure I can do that this month, but perhaps in June. Would that work for you? The timing of it, anyway?"

Destiny blew out a breath of air. *She wants to see me, too. Here.* She lifted a fist into the air in triumph. "I think so. Maybe. I'm going to Austin to see my dad and his new baby right after finals, but maybe you could come after I get back, or even before."

"Why don't you send me the best dates and I'll see about arranging a flight after that? Is your mother okay with my visiting you, meeting you?"

"She's ... she's not quite as sure about it as I am, but that's okay. She suggested you come here. My dad thinks it's cool that you want to meet me."

Destiny hoped her enthusiasm when mentioning her dad would offset her mother's hesitation. Disagreement, actually, but Bella didn't need to know that, especially since her coming to Denver was almost a month away. Destiny would work on Mom, get her to see it was a good thing. She would make a real effort to be nice to her so she would relax.

"So," she said, injecting additional cheeriness into her tone. "I'll text you when I'm going to be home. Thanks, Bella."

"Thank *you*," Bella replied. "I'm looking forward to meeting you."

"Me, too." Destiny hung up and rolled over on her bed, giving herself an impromptu hug in the process.

After deciding that she wanted Noah with her if her mom didn't want to meet Bella, Destiny went to her desk, relaxed enough to be able to concentrate on the book review she needed to write for her children's lit class tomorrow evening. On her desk calendar, she stared for a long minute at the days in June that she'd blocked off for her trip to Austin. June thirteenth through the twentieth. She circled the first ten days in June and fourteen days after her return from Austin. Then she texted Bella.

I'm in Austin June thirteenth through the twentieth. You could come in the first ten days of the month or after I get back. Let me know if any of those days work for you. Des.

She went to bed, happy that she'd called Bella. Only three weeks remained before she might actually meet her birth mom. In person.

Chapter 12

A WEEK LATER THAN ORIGINALLY PLANNED, GAVIN pulled into Bella's driveway and parked the car, glad that his uncle had finally been released from the hospital. The past nearly four weeks had been a slog filled with emotional pitfalls. His visits to the hospital had been a real downer, not helped by the rainy days that were more numerous than he was used to. Not until Henry seemed to rally did Gavin's own mood brighten. But he continued to worry about the store's finances, a subject he intended to bring up with Henry now that he was home.

Then there was Earl. The old man's mood remained frosty. Only after Gavin's "come to Jesus" meeting had the man stopped fighting him about the sale table. And in the last week, sales had taken a decided upward turn. Gavin had given Earl a counter to verify that more people were coming into the store, but when he asked Earl to keep track of the number of people he sold books to, the man's mouth had turned down.

"This ain't no movie theater. The customers won't like it."

"We need the information, Earl."

"Henry never asked me to do that."

"Well, I'm asking you. Telling you." Gavin felt his molars grind as he debated whether to say more. When it looked like Earl wasn't going to budge, and customers approached with their arms laden with books, Gavin took refuge in the office. He'd talk to Earl again. Later.

Gavin's encounters with Bella continued to inject sun into his otherwise dreary existence, but they'd been too infrequent and not nearly long enough for his taste. He chose not to mention their dates to Henry, fearing his uncle would ratchet up his matchmaking efforts. Bella was easy to look at, had a pleasing sense of humor, and she'd responded to his kisses as though she was parched and his caresses were a longed-for drink of water. He would enjoy his time with her as long as it lasted. *Why worry about something that isn't going to matter once I go home?*

Zeke had finally settled things with the two salesmen who'd gotten into a fight. The other two salesmen who'd been out sick were back and challenging the others to outpace them in a race for the monthly sales bonuses. Thank goodness that was one business he didn't have worry about.

Today had dawned bright and sunny, perfect for welcoming Henry home. Gavin had planned to pick up Bella, but he didn't want to leave Henry. Then his uncle proclaimed, in a grouchy tone, that he didn't need a nursemaid.

"Okay. Then I'll see you later."

"You going back to the store?"

"No."

"Well, wherever you're headed, have a good time." Henry

winked broadly, as if he knew what Gavin had in mind.

He walked to Bella's front door. Today he was going to check out that Bellevue dealership. If it looked like it could be turned around and his profits in Spokane exceeded the last two months' numbers, he'd get serious about offering to take the floundering dealership in hand. Perhaps Zeke would entertain a move to the cooler, wetter part of the state. Or, maybe Gavin would stay here until the status of Henry's store improved to the point it was no longer in danger of folding.

His pulse picked up at the sight of Bella as she opened the door. She was another reason he toyed with the idea of sticking around. "You ready?" he asked, as she tripped down the stairs of her porch in a pair of white skinny jeans and a teal blouse, its arm ruffles fluttering in the light spring breeze. How she managed not to topple off those stilettos she was wearing he couldn't guess. But he loved how they elongated her legs.

Bella brushed a curl behind her ear that had escaped the ponytail. To Gavin, she looked like a teenager with womanly curves. "All ready. I'm to be navigator today?" she asked before giving him a saucy grin. "Or can I drive?"

"Not a chance. This baby is a *man's* wheels."

Her giggle warmed his heart and set his pulse galloping as Bella settled herself in the passenger seat and he backed out onto the street.

"But I will change seats with you right before we get where we're going."

"I thought I was just going to show you around."

"That, too. In fact, you're in charge for the first half hour or so. Tell me where to go." He imagined what he'd like to show *her,* and where, and his groin swelled. He glanced her way and was relieved to see that her gaze was focused on the road. "Later we'll take care of some other business."

"Because Henry's been sick?"

"That, too. And riding herd on Earl."

"How's that going?" Bella clicked off the radio station that had begun blaring an oldies playlist.

"Some good, some bad. We had a little chat the other day. At least he isn't arguing with me as much. Leaves the sale table in place. Actually made some suggestions about what to place on it a couple of times."

"That's good news. Business is picking up?"

"It is. Another surprise. One that I hope makes Henry happy. I'm still going to have to talk to him about the profit margin—too slim—and his monthly costs—too high. But Earl's not the reason."

Bella raised an arm and pointed in the direction of Lake Geneva. "Turn here. We'll skirt the edge of the lake and then head toward the mountains."

He followed her directions and admired the lake against which Evergreen was nestled, the sailboats reminding him of vacation days spent with Henry, fishing, something he hadn't enjoyed in years. Minutes later, Bella instructed him to head east. She toured him through an upscale neighborhood of spacious homes on large lots that surprised him. He'd assumed only Seattle, much larger and to the northwest, would support this level of wealth. They drove along a tree-lined boulevard. Not far from those homes, they passed less well-off areas of town, though none of the neighborhoods qualified as run-down.

Then Bella instructed him to drive north through Evergreen's downtown. "You already know about the downtown near Henry's bookstore, and the courthouse. It was built in 1909—"

"You know that because …?"

"I looked it up. Zoe could give you chapter and verse on

the founding families of the town. In fact, one of her relatives, a great-grandfather, I think, was among the first to settle here in the 1800s. He was a logger."

He nodded, recalling that she'd mentioned moving to Evergreen sometime after her daughter had been born. He pulled the car to the curb.

"Okay. Time to change seats."

"Why?"

"I want to visit a dealership in Bellevue and I'd like you to drive in and park as close to the entrance as possible. Be a distraction, so I can look around. While I check out the cars on the lot, I want you to go in and ask for help. Like you're not quite sure how to get the roof up or the hood to release or something. Pretend to be helpless. See how they react."

"But the roof's easy. I saw how you did it the other day."

"Make up something. Tell them your boyfriend never showed you." He chuckled when the pink in her cheeks seemed to heighten.

"I'm to be a damsel in distress?" She chuckled. "Guess that means I'll have to put on my actress hat. Think I'll win an Oscar? Helpless is one thing I'm not." She gave him a wry grin then slid into the driver's seat and hit the accelerator before Gavin had fastened his seatbelt.

"Whoa! Take it easy, woman. I don't want to go home with dents in my fenders."

She laughed at him and continued to pick up speed when they reached the arterial that would take them to Bellevue. "Told you I could drive a fast car. You didn't believe me."

"If I apologize, will you slow down?" he asked.

"Maybe." Her smile warmed him.

Minutes later, they reached the dealership whose address he'd punched into the navigation system. Bella swung the car into a space near the front door.

"Not exactly a parking space. Maybe this'll do to show them I'm a ditzy lady," she remarked drily.

Gavin had to squeeze himself out of the car past the door he could open only halfway.

"So I see." He ambled in the direction of the parking area where used cars were parked, each showing off sale stickers. "Text me when you head for the showroom."

Bella nodded and walked toward the front door. Before she reached it, a salesman approached her, giving her a smarmy grin. The man's slacks were wrinkled and the shirt he wore, sans tie or suit coat, sported a stain of something greasy, as if he'd not been careful with whatever he'd had for lunch.

"How can I help you, ma'am? This your car? I would have figured you for one of our larger models. You know, big enough for groceries and the rug rats."

Playing along, Bella said, "Yes, well, I can't seem to re-member a few things and this car is new to me. Can you tell me how to get the hard top up?" She patted her hair after pushing a curl behind one ear. "I heard it's going to rain later today and I'm not sure I'll be home by then."

"Lots of shopping to do?" the man asked, as he slid his fingers along the edge of the driver's side door.

"Perhaps." Bella noticed dirt under the man's nails and his hair appeared greasy. *When was his last shower?* Not something she imagined Gavin would approve of, particularly if *his* sales-people arrived so poorly dressed.

"Well, I can help you with that."

"Good. Then I'll just watch while you do it." Bella crossed

her arms and stood back while the man seemed to fumble around under the steering wheel. She held the key fob in plain view, waiting for the man to request it. Instead, he walked around the car, his brow furrowed. Bella pulled out her phone and turned her back. "I just have to make a call," she said, "while you put up the roof."

She texted Gavin. *Doesn't seem to know how to get the roof up. Clothes dirty. Nails, too. Hair greasy. What else do you want to know?*

Out of the corner of her eye, she spotted Gavin trotting in her direction. He looked less than happy.

Bella approached the salesman. "I just remembered. Do you have an owner's manual? Maybe it'll tell me."

The man seemed relieved at her suggestion. "I'll get one," and he headed for the showroom.

Gavin grabbed Bella's elbow and slowed her down as she followed the man inside. "This place is a dump."

She nodded but smiled brightly at the salesman when he returned, an owner's manual in hand. He riffled the pages as he looked for information about the retractable roof and opened his mouth to speak.

Gavin interrupted him. "Darling, there's no reason to bother this man. Here. Let me show you. Remember? You just have to hit the key fob. Like this." Gavin turned toward the car and demonstrated, pulling Bella closer. The two of them watched as the retractable roof came up and out of the trunk and settled into place. "Hit it again and it hides away. So you won't forget." His eyes sparkled at her. "Again."

Bella resumed her smile for the benefit of the salesman. "Yes, sweetheart, thank you." She lifted her foot and placed her heel firmly on Gavin's recently shined left shoe and leaned her weight on him until he seemed to get the message about making her look less than intelligent. She released the pressure, and he pulled his foot out from under hers.

Gavin then turned to the salesman. "Sorry for taking up your time, sir." He held out his hand and the man shook it. "Mind if we look inside?"

"No problem. Come on in." He opened the door, edged past Gavin and tossed the owner's manual onto the cluttered desk of the woman Bella thought might be a receptionist.

"Been working here long?" Gavin asked.

The man puffed out his chest. "Started yesterday. Great place to work, don't you think? I just love these Beemers."

Gavin didn't smile at the comment. "Your supervisor around? I'd like to thank him for your help with my girlfriend here." He beamed in Bella's direction. With his hand firmly grasping her right elbow, he steered her in the direction of the back offices where the manager likely hung out.

"I'll—I'll get him," the salesman scurried in front of them.

"Be nice now," Bella cautioned under her breath. The almost predatory gleam in Gavin's eye was giving his intent away. He'd said he'd turned the Spokane dealership around in less than six months. Did he have that in mind for this establishment? Would he stay here then? The thought that he might not leave even though Henry was on the mend set Bella's heart to pumping and those pesky butterflies flitting.

Gavin plastered a smile on his face as he approached the manager, who looked to be about fifty. *He looks tired.* From the sad state of the cars on the lot, the man wasn't paying much attention to his inventory. Most sported dusty raindrops, evidence they hadn't been washed since the last storm had blown through. Not something Gavin allowed. "Nice place you have here," Gavin said.

"Are you interested in a new car?"

Bella stepped forward, her voice lilting upward slightly. "Oh no, sir. I already have a car. That red beauty out there. But your man here—" she gestured to the salesman who peeked over her shoulder at Gavin and his boss, "—he was *so* helpful when I had a question about the top. I haven't had the car that long and I forgot how to put it up and down, but now I remember. And I'm sure I won't forget." She beamed at the manager. "Excuse me, but would you happen to have a ladies room? I need to powder my nose."

Not her usual tone, Gavin thought, as Bella batted her lashes at the older man. *She's laying on the ditz factor pretty heavy.* But it seemed to be working. The eyes of the manager and his salesman were glued to Bella's delectable backside as she minced off in the direction the manager pointed.

"Nice lady friend you have," the manager said.

Gavin nodded, suddenly aware that he felt a frisson of jealousy at the way the man's eyes continued to scan Bella's body as she walked away. "You've managed this place long?"

"Long enough." The man's gaze narrowed slightly. "Are you looking for a job, maybe want to sell these babies?"

"Maybe."

"Great!" The man enthused. He shuffled a pile of papers on a nearby desk. "Arlene!" he practically shouted.

The woman Gavin had seen at the desk in the center of the showroom stood up and approached them.

"Where're the application forms?"

"I'll get one." She walked back to her desk and returned with a form. "Here you are." She handed it to Gavin, giving him an appreciative smile.

"Thank you, Arlene."

"You're very welcome," she simpered and stared boldly at him. He felt her gaze slide in the direction of his belt buckle and points south.

Gavin turned as Bella approached, swept her into his arms and planted a kiss full on her lips. "There you are, sweetheart. I think it's time we left." *That ought to set Arlene straight—and those men.* He smiled at Bella, who looked flushed and confused but chose to play along.

"Yes, thank you," she said, waving a hand in the general direction of the manager and the other salesman as they departed.

Gavin slid into place in the passenger seat and waited for Bella to start the car, *his* car.

"What exactly was *that* for?" Bella asked, her voice slightly breathy.

"Let's just say I was protecting my virtue." He chuckled when Bella's gaze shifted in his direction and she looked skeptical. "Arlene reminds me of a shark on the prowl for a meal," he explained drily.

Bella snorted but chose not to reply. For the next few minutes, she concentrated on driving through the heavier traffic. "Find out what you wanted to know?"

"That I did."

"Just in case you care, the women's room was filthy. I didn't dare use the towel to dry my hands. What are you going to do with what you now know about the place?"

"Not sure yet. Maybe make a couple of phone calls."

She nodded. "Do me a favor, will you?"

"What's that?"

"Give me a warning the next time you decide to play horny boyfriend."

Gavin laughed when he saw the corners of Bella's lips edging upward. "That would take all the fun out of it."

After dropping Bella off at her home, Gavin drove to Henry's house. He found the old man sitting in his lounge chair half asleep, the television providing background noise.

Henry roused when Gavin settled into a nearby seat. "How are you feeling, Uncle?"

"Better. You going to cook tonight? Anything'd be better than that hospital food."

"I'm not exactly a chef. What's your preference? I'll go pick something up."

"Anything hot and spicy. With real meat. But before you get something, tell me what you found out. About that dealership you've been meaning to see. That's where you went, isn't it?"

Gavin chuckled. "It's in need of a good cleaning, of staff and product. Reminds me of the one in Spokane before I took it on."

"You gonna buy it?"

"Don't know yet. I need to make some calls."

"It'd be good if you did. Take it on, I mean. You like a challenge. And if you stick around, you could get to know Bella better. And visit me some." Henry's eyes sparkled as if he knew something Gavin didn't.

"I already have a challenge, Henry. In Spokane. My own dealership."

Henry nodded. "Yes, well." He paused and waved a hand in the direction of the teacup just out of reach on a nearby table.

Gavin retrieved it, noted the tea had gone cold, and refilled the cup from the pot simmering on the stove.

"Did you take Bella with you?"

Gavin nodded, hoping the warmth of his neck was not noticeable. "She did a nice job distracting them while I looked around."

"She distracting you, too?" Henry asked.

"I enjoy being with her. Just like you do, Uncle." Gavin's pulse began to resemble a drumbeat rapidly increasing as he recalled how the manager and salesman had seemed to salivate over the librarian.

Henry nodded. "Too bad she's too young for me. But not for you. Or have you figured that out already?"

"Let's talk about your store. It needs work."

Henry groaned. "Isn't Earl following orders? He called today. Says you've been high-handed, ordering him around and all."

"I'm making sure we move your inventory. The doctor said you're supposed to take things easy. Which means you won't be spending all day there. Maybe just a couple of hours a day."

"Can't make any money if I'm closed more hours than I'm open."

"I'll keep it open the usual time, Henry, but we have to go over things. Your profits are negligible; your costs are too high. If we can't reverse that trend, you need to think seriously about selling the store, or closing it down."

"It's your aunt's store. How do you think she'd feel if we did that?" Henry looked indignant.

"Aunt Ina's gone, Henry," Gavin said, his voice gentle. "And she wouldn't want you to work yourself to death trying to keep it going if it's a lost cause." Gavin watched Henry's eyes fill, but he had to get him to face facts.

"Aren't Bella's kids comin' in to buy books?"

"They are, but that's not enough to keep the store's head above water."

"I want to talk to Bella about this. She knows books a lot better than you do."

"I'll talk to her," Gavin offered.

"No. *I'll* talk to her. Zoe, too."

"Want me to call and invite them over?"

"You do that," Henry grumbled then hauled himself out of the lounger and turned off the television.

"Did you know Bella has a daughter, Henry?"

His uncle turned and stared at Gavin. "When did that happen?"

"A long time ago. Her kid lives in Denver. Bella said something about going there to see her."

Henry nodded. "Maybe that's why Bella loves to work with the kids so much. You know, at the library. Because her own little girl is grown and gone. She could stand to get married, if you ask me. Have some more kids, a bunch of little ones. Just like you. Don't you want to be a father?"

Matchmaking again. It had been on Gavin's mind, too, though he was loath to admit how much. "Not for me to say, Henry." Before his uncle jiggled the reins of possible matrimony again, Gavin left the room. He spent the next several minutes ordering takeout before retreating to where he'd set up his laptop. It was time to talk to the man who ran the BMW franchises in Washington state.

Chapter 13

BELLA ARRIVED HOME AFTER AN ESPECIALLY TRYING DAY.

She opened the pantry door for dinner fixings when her phone rang.

"Is this Isabella Campbell?" The voice on the phone sounded uncertain, almost hesitant.

"Yes, this is Isabella." So few people in town called her by that name. This person had to be a stranger. Bella looked at the number, startled that the area code was the same as Destiny's. But the caller wasn't her daughter. Had something happened that required her to delay her upcoming flight to Denver? And if that was the case, why hadn't this person called Destiny's mother? "Who is this, please?"

"Vanessa Harris."

Tension wrapped around Bella's chest, squeezing her lungs, pushing her heart into her throat. *Vanessa?* O.M.G. "Is Destiny all right?" Bella croaked, her throat like a desert.

"She's fine." The woman's voice sounded not exactly angry, but not friendly either.

Bella saw herself as she had been so many years earlier, a pregnant teenager by turns sullen and then eager to please the couple who would take her daughter, wanting them to agree to maintain contact with her.

"Why did you call, Mrs. Harris?"

"I want to know why you contacted my daughter. Or did Destiny call you?"

"We've only spoken a few times. I wanted to make sure she was all right." Those words didn't come close to what she wanted, but Bella sensed Destiny's mother was near hysterics, her fast breathing coming through the phone, her words couched in fear.

"Of course she's all right. We've given her *everything* she ever wanted or needed. Did you ask her to visit you?" she demanded.

"Yes. You, too. But Destiny wants me to come to Denver instead. I just want to get to know her. That's all."

"She's *my* daughter," the querulous voice interrupted, now threaded with anxiety.

"Of course she is." *Mine, too.* But the woman didn't seem interested in sharing. "I gave birth to her. I was supposed to receive pictures and letters every year, twice a year, but when they stopped, I was so afraid she had died." Bella's frustration that she'd been left in the dark for so many years overwhelmed her intent to avoid challenging Destiny's mother.

"You were thousands of miles away, not even out of high school, and you couldn't possibly take care of a child," Vanessa countered. "We were a family. I—we didn't want you intruding on what we were trying to build with Destiny. Her security in our love."

"But how would a few letters and cards from me have made her less secure? I love her, too. Didn't she deserve to know that?"

"You gave her away!"

Those awful words that Bella hated singed her heart. "No, I didn't. I let you raise her because I wasn't in a position to do so at the time. I never gave her away. I've always loved her. Can't you accept that?" Tears burned Bella's lids as she flung her words back at Vanessa. *This isn't getting us anywhere.* Bella mentally fast-counted to ten then slowed and counted to twenty, forcing her voice to sound calmer, warmer. "Look, I don't want to fight with you, Mrs. Harris. I'm only interested in getting to know Destiny, and giving her a chance to get to know me."

Bella crossed her fingers, willing Vanessa to accept her words, if not her.

The woman on the other end of the phone seemed to be crying. Between sniffs, her voice sounded raw, raspy. "Her father keeps telling me she's old enough to decide for herself. I shouldn't have stopped Nolan from sending you pictures. I apologize. But I was so afraid you would take her away. You have to understand. Those horrible stories in the news about birth mothers doing that." Her last words ended in a forlorn sigh.

Bella's heart clutched. *She's afraid of me, of what Destiny might do.* "Destiny loves you. You raised her. I could never take her away. And I'm sure she'd never do anything to hurt you. I just want to meet her. If she doesn't want to see me after that, I won't ask her to."

"Oh." Was the woman accepting Bella's declaration? After another lengthy silence, Vanessa's voice now sounded stronger, more assertive. "Well, thank you for talking to me." After another pause, she added, "I had to find out what you wanted.

To protect her. She … she can be so impulsive. Always doing things without really thinking."

Bella gave a short laugh. "Maybe she gets that from me. Being impulsive, I mean. I had to talk to Destiny as soon as I could after I got that letter. The one your husband sent."

"Ex-husband," Vanessa replied huffily. "Yes, he admitted that." Vanessa cleared her throat before she asked, "Are you coming here? I'll bet Des asked you to."

"It's already scheduled. For this Friday. Didn't Destiny tell you?" Maybe Bella should invite Mrs. Harris to come along with Destiny, but she wasn't sure she wanted that. It wasn't likely she and Vanessa would ever become friends, but Bella wished they weren't so formal with each other.

"Yes, she did. For a minute there, I forgot." Then, as if Vanessa was reading Bella's mind, she added, "You can call me Vanessa."

Was the woman trying to be nice, maybe even setting aside her fears? "Okay."

After the call ended, Bella felt entwined in a web of conflicting emotions. Before receiving that letter, she'd never expected to meet Destiny. Now Bella had a second chance to cultivate the relationship she'd given up for dead.

But Destiny was entangled with her *other* mother, Vanessa, who seemed so fearful of Bella and her motives. Would she try to intervene? Maybe convince Destiny not to meet with Bella? Somehow, she sensed that Destiny wouldn't allow Vanessa to do that. But this wasn't about one woman winning and the other losing. This was about Destiny learning that she had *two* mothers, each of whom loved her. In spite of the different ways in which they'd become mothers.

Anticipatory tears slid down Bella's cheeks. She would see Destiny soon. And she would try not to step on Vanessa's ever-so-wary toes.

Bella reached for a tissue, then flicked on her laptop. She'd agreed to go to Denver to meet Destiny. Her ticket sat on her dresser, a reminder each time she saw it that she'd acted on Destiny's request. She texted Destiny to reconfirm her arrival, as she'd promised. *I'm arriving late on Friday evening. Could we meet some time on Saturday? At my hotel? Why don't you invite your mother? Perhaps she'd like to meet me, too.*

Her phone trilled again. *Gavin.* Her heart began to pitter-patter, recalling their shared kisses, the many times since his arrival to help Henry when he'd stolen time to be with her. And their little sojourn to the dealership, when he'd implied she was his girlfriend. That thought sent shivers through her. "What's up?" She smiled at the thought, wondering if Gavin caught the double entendre.

"Henry wants to talk to you and Zoe about the bookstore. Whether he should close it."

Bella sucked in her breath. "Whoa. Is he serious?"

"I'm not sure, but we need your honest opinions. Both of you. Henry insists."

"Of course, we'll talk to him. But, when?"

"You're still going to Denver?"

"In three days. And I'm swamped right now at the library. But Zoe could meet with you this week if it has to be soon. Want me to call her?"

"I'd rather both of you are there. When you're back is soon enough. It'll give me time to show him what needs to be done to turn things around. And to see if he's willing to make some big changes."

"Good luck with that. I have a feeling Henry isn't going to like your suggestions."

"Score one for Ms. Campbell, the clairvoyant." He paused. "Thanks again for going with me to the dealership. It helped that you … um … distracted the men while I looked around."

Glad that Gavin couldn't see how she flushed, Bella retorted, "Any time, as long as I can drive your car." She looked down at the book she'd been meaning to take back to the library, *Gone with the Wind*. "Not that I expect to have many chances."

"I can be bought." He laughed.

She imagined him morphing into someone like Rhett Butler, carrying her into her bedroom right before she tore off his shirt, the better to stroke his chest and other places.

Thrill bumps tickled the skin on her arms when he said, "Maybe I'll come up with another excuse to give you the wheel."

The flight to Denver finally landed, its last hour a challenge of bumpy air that jangled Bella's nerves. She reached the hotel shortly after dinner and ordered room service, but was unable to eat more than a couple bites. Too nervous to watch television, Bella called a cab after rejecting the idea of renting a car and risking getting lost in a city she'd never visited. *I have to see where she lives.* She pushed past the partygoers milling about in the lobby.

She sat stiffly behind the cabbie as he drove into an upscale residential neighborhood. All the homes looked well cared for. Children's toys and bikes were scattered in several yards, and signs supporting a local sports team were staked in three yards.

"Please drive slowly," she pleaded as they turned into a cul-de-sac at the end of the street. She checked the address on the paper she clutched in her lap. *There it is.* She stared at the white two-storey clapboard house, its front porch holding two wicker rockers. Flowers bobbed in the early evening breeze in two window boxes sitting below the front windows, one on either side of the double front doors.

A woman stepped onto the porch, her gray-streaked hair

gleaming in the porch light, as she agitatedly talked over her shoulder. Then Destiny emerged, her red hair falling in long waves past her shoulders, her hands gesturing angrily before she stomped off the porch. She pulled a black sweater around her shoulders and strode rapidly toward a decrepit sedan Bella hadn't noticed before. The girl's black skinny jeans seemed to elongate her slim legs. The cab stopped between the driveway and the neighbor's entry to a garage set well back from the street. Destiny seemed to stare briefly at the cab before focusing her attention on the driver of the beater car. Smiling at the driver, Destiny opened the passenger side door and climbed in. The car's tires squealed as the driver took off and rounded the corner almost on two wheels as it entered the thoroughfare.

Destiny. Bella's heart clutched. *Should I go after her?*

"If that's who you wanted to see, you just missed her, lady," the cabbie commented.

Bella looked back at the older woman, who remained on the porch, but whose gaze was now directed at the yellow vehicle still parked at the curb. Bella slid toward the center of the backseat. This was not the time to approach the woman standing on the porch. She had to be Mrs. Harris. Vanessa. And she looked to be in a black mood.

"We can go back to the hotel now," she said, her throat dry. Had Noah driven Destiny away? She now wished she'd ordered the cab driver to follow the beater. As they returned to the hotel, she peered out the window in hopes of seeing it again. Back in her room, her muted cell phone rattled on the dresser, an indication of an incoming message. She checked her phone. A text from Gavin.

Hope you landed safely. Let me know how your visit goes. G.

Butterflies invaded her stomach as she imagined seeing Gavin again. He was thinking of her. So kind, like when she'd first told him about Destiny. Bella rubbed her temples, eager to wish away the pounding headache that had progressed from a light snare to heavy bass drum throbbing, a sign of her nervousness about tomorrow's meeting. She glanced at her fingers, two of which were whitening again. *Damn that stress response!* She went to the sink, turned on the faucet and plunged both hands into the water as it warmed.

Minutes later, she checked the time. *I'll just send Destiny a text to let her know I made it.* Bella gulped down two aspirin and climbed into bed. Tomorrow she would see her daughter. In person. So much was riding on this meeting. A positive reaction from Destiny, and maybe even one from her mother, if Vanessa came, too.

The next morning, Bella jumped into the shower, forgoing her usual leisurely scrub, dried her hair, and climbed into an aqua skirt and white peasant blouse, an outfit she hoped was appropriately casual with black flats. She watched the numbers on the bedside clock slowly flip over, one after the other. Destiny had texted back that she would come to the hotel around nine. It was nearly ten. Maybe the girl had changed her mind.

I'll go downstairs and wait there. Bella grabbed her purse and walked briskly to the elevator. She wandered around the registration desk looking for someone who resembled Destiny, and mentioned to the desk clerk that she'd be in the restaurant should anyone ask for her.

The woman nodded and returned to checking in the businessmen and women lined up in the registration area, all in dark suits, who were awaiting room keys.

Bella walked into the restaurant. "Could you seat me near the windows, please?" She would watch for Destiny, maybe see her on the sidewalk as she approached the hotel.

After ordering her meal, Bella turned her gaze toward the

window. The people outside walked by as if they knew where they were going. *Business people and the occasional cowboy, assuming the boots and Stetsons aren't just for show,* she surmised. All ages, a microcosm of the city's population.

Bella's late breakfast was presented and she reached for the toast just before sharp words startled her.

"There she is." A young man stood next to her table. He reminded her of one of her library volunteers, dressed casually, his black hair held off his face in a man tail. Standing next to him was Destiny, grinning broadly. She was wearing a black tank top, black jeans, and black motorcycle boots. Even her earrings were black. But her hair, a bright coppery red, seemed to pull the sunlight around her body in a kind of halo. She clutched the boy's nearest hand.

"Hi, Bella." Her voice was soft, with a hint of a question. She slid into the chair facing Bella. "This is Noah. My boyfriend."

Bella set her toast back on her plate then raised her gaze sufficiently to address the tall young man and gestured for him to take the other chair. "Noah. It's nice to meet you. Why don't you have a seat, too?"

Bella reached for her teacup, her fingers trembling, before withdrawing her hand and placing it in her lap. Noah's gaze was more intent than Destiny's, reminding Bella of Gavin when he'd visited that car dealership. But she suspected this young man was nothing like Gavin, a professional who owned his own business, who had dropped everything to take care of his uncle. Still, she had to acknowledge him. Noah was here with Destiny, for moral support, she suspected.

Bella smiled at Destiny. "I'm so glad you came. Would either of you like something to eat?"

Noah's mouth slid into a smile that gentled his stern features.

"You look just like your picture," Destiny said, her cheeks flushed. "Of course, you would. That was so lame."

Bella grinned. "You do, too. I guess we're both a little nervous."

Noah plucked a piece of toast off the plate and began to chew. In between bites, he stared back at Bella as if memorizing her face. "You two could be sisters. You, older—" he pointed to Bella, "—and you, younger." He grinned at Destiny.

Bella liked the idea and from Destiny's expression, she did, too.

"Except she's my mother," she replied, playfully poking Noah in the ribs.

"But she's not that much older than you. Sorta like me and one of my big sisters."

Curious to confirm what she'd seen the night before, Bella asked, "Noah, do you happen to drive a dark blue car, rust on the back fenders, a yellow streak of paint or something like it on the driver's side door?"

"You saw my wheels?"

"If you were the one who drove Destiny away from her house last night."

He hunched his shoulders forward slightly. "That was me." He grimaced. "So. You're really her, her *real* mother."

His words, their incredulity that Bella was Destiny's mother, and his more relaxed posture tickled Bella's funny bone and she beamed. "Guilty as charged. Her birth mom. But her real mom is the one who raised her. Right, Destiny?" She was pleased that Destiny did not correct her. "Is that why you came with her, Noah? To see for yourself that I was real?"

The young man's head bobbed slightly and his mouth tilted upward again.

"I asked him to come," Destiny explained. "My mom …

she wasn't sure she wanted to."

"I'm sorry to hear that. I was hoping … Will you give her a message?"

"Depends on what it is." Destiny pulled the plate closer and picked up a slice of toast before Noah could take it.

"Tell her I was hoping—"

The approach of a woman with dark blonde hair and a prominent streak of gray at one temple interrupted Bella.

"You can tell me yourself," she stated, and took a seat next to Bella.

"Mom! You changed your mind." Destiny nervously brushed a curl behind her ear as she peered first at her mother and then at Bella.

The woman hung an oversized silver purse over the arm of her chair as she slanted a critical gaze in Bella's direction.

"I'm Destiny's mother," she announced without offering her hand. She wore a dress in a tasteful, toned-down shade of red. A pashmina shawl, in shades of gray and red draped across her shoulders.

Bella nodded and forced a smile, even as her pulse rose a notch higher than before. "I'm glad you came."

Destiny grinned at Bella. "I guessed you'd be wearing something casual," she remarked, as if hinting that her mother's dress was too formal.

Bella brushed a hand down one leg. "Yes, well …" She held out her hand to the older woman. "Mrs. Harris. Thank you so much for coming."

She nodded in response to Bella's words. The woman's palm was damp and her handshake limp when she reluctantly reached for Bella's hand.

"Would you like some tea?"

"How was your flight?" Destiny asked at the same time, seeming as unsure as Bella about what her mother would do.

Vanessa pressed her lips together and frowned at her daughter.

"A bit bumpy. But we made it," Bella replied, before silence wrapped around the four of them.

Destiny picked up the menu and stared at the offerings, acting as if meeting her birth mom for the first time, and in the presence of her adoptive mother, was an everyday occurrence.

"I'll have some herbal tea," Destiny requested, when the waitress approached the table. "Noah, what do you want, now that you've eaten the rest of Bella's toast?"

"Hey, she didn't seem to mind." He squinted in Vanessa's direction when she glared at him.

"And one of those fruit salads, too," Destiny added. "Mom?"

Bella watched as Vanessa gave a cursory glance at the menu and set it down. "Nothing for me, thanks." She then turned in Bella's direction.

"So." Her fingers darted from her lap to the table edge and back again. "So," she repeated, softly, and licked her lips. "We're here."

Bella nodded. "Yes. I'm glad you came, all of you." Her heart thudded against her ribs, her pulse racing. If only her throat didn't feel so dry, her face and neck so warm. "I wanted to meet you, Destiny, in person. We've talked on the phone, but I'll bet you still have lots of questions. Maybe your … mom does, too." She gestured toward Vanessa. "Go ahead. Ask. Whatever you want to know. My life's an open book."

Noah wiped his mouth with a napkin and rose from the table. "Hey, you three. I'm splitting. You can get a ride home with your mom, Des."

"Sure." Destiny half-stood and accepted Noah's quick kiss on her cheek. After he left the restaurant, she sat back down and replied to Bella, "I'm cool with what you've told me. You know, what we talked about before." But the way she was twisting her napkin suggested she might not be as relaxed as her tone implied. "You know, everything I already asked."

Bella smiled.

Vanessa cleared her throat. "Destiny tells me you're not married."

"No. I hope to be, someday." Bella thought of Gavin and she felt her cheeks heat.

"You live in an apartment?"

"My own home. I bought it about three years ago."

"You can afford that? I should think you'd want to save your money rather than risk the real estate market. Since it crashed not that long ago."

"Good grief, Mom. What does it matter where Bella lives?" Bella forced a quick smile at Destiny and then at Vanessa.

"Destiny looks like you," Vanessa finally stated.

Destiny snorted. "I told you that already, Mom. When I showed you her picture."

Bella chose to address Vanessa. "Do you have any questions for me, Mrs. Harris? It's been a long time since we last saw each other."

"I told you, call me Vanessa," she said, coldly.

But Bella felt uneasy using the woman's first name, implying a familiarity she doubted they'd ever share.

The waitress brought Destiny's fruit salad, herbal tea, and refilled Bella's teacup.

Bella squeezed a lemon wedge into her tea and waited, willing her pulse to stop jumping.

Vanessa's voice cut into Bella's gut as if with a knife. "I want to know what you *really* want. By coming here, I mean. You've already talked with Destiny. You said you wanted to know that she was okay, after not hearing for a long time. Well, you know that already, that she *is* okay. And she says she doesn't have any more questions."

Bella sucked in a quick breath. Zoe had warned her that Destiny's mother might not be welcoming. Her unpleasantness wasn't making this meeting any easier. Was she really here only to protect the daughter she'd raised all those years? Or was her presence a message that Bella wasn't welcome?

Time to be an adult, to show I'm not afraid of her. "I have no ulterior motives, Vanessa. All I wanted was to let Destiny know that I've always loved her and that, if she ever wants or needs anything from me—medical records, things like that— I'll provide them. That's all. And to talk, get to know each other a little better. Assuming she wants that."

She pulled out the pictures she'd brought with her. "I thought you might like to know more about me. When you last saw me, Mrs. Harris—um, Vanessa," she corrected herself—"I was still in high school. I put myself through college and this is where I work. I have a masters in library science now." She pointed to a picture of the front of the Evergreen Public Library. "That's Zoe, my best friend. She works there, too."

Bella paused and smiled first at Destiny and then at Vanessa, hoping the woman would relax when she saw that Bella had made something of herself. "One of my favorite activities at the library is reading to the little ones, under five, and a new group, for elementary school kids. One of those boys lost his mom to ovarian cancer a few years ago. His dad recently remarried. Eli calls her his second mom. Sort of like you, Destiny, sitting here with your two moms."

Vanessa reared back in her seat with a jerk that shook the table. "She has *one* mom. Me. I raised her. You gave her away. And you shouldn't have come here! It's not right that you want to insinuate yourself into our lives after so many years. Come on, Des. We're leaving." She grabbed her purse off the back of her chair as she stood up and reached for Destiny's hand.

"No, Mom. I'm not ready to go." Destiny clutched her chair and remained where she was, ignoring the hand that squeezed her upper arm.

Bella remained in her seat, horrified that her words, uttered so innocently, seemed so offensive. "I didn't mean to upset you, Mrs. Harris. Please stay."

But Vanessa shook her head and, casting her daughter one more disapproving glare, fled the restaurant. Bella and Destiny watched from the window as Vanessa half-walked, half-ran to her car.

"Sorry about that," Destiny said. "I guess she changed her mind about coming. That's why Noah came with me. I knew she didn't really want to meet you." She sighed. "She's so up-tight all the time, like I'm going to up and leave, maybe even move to Austin to be near my dad, or to Seattle near you."

"How are you going to get home, now that Noah *and* your mom have left?"

"I'll take the bus. No biggie."

"Or I could get you a cab. Destiny, I want to be clear. I would never ask you to choose between her and me. But if you ever need a place to stay—if you apply for a job in Seattle—or … whatever, let me know." Bella sipped her tea, glad that Destiny was still seated. "I'm betting your dad would take you in, too, if it ever came to that. He'd be your first choice, right?"

Destiny dropped her gaze, the corners of her mouth turned down. "Actually, my first choice would be Noah, but he and I had a big fight and he wouldn't even answer my texts for days. It must have been his curiosity that made him come with me today, to see you. We talked about that last night." She brushed a finger against the cheek Noah had kissed. "He gets in weird moods sometimes, says he needs space. Maybe 'cause his family doesn't like me that much. His mom calls me a spoiled rich kid. Which I am, I guess. But, I don't flaunt it. Maybe Noah told her I don't like the neighborhood where they live." She sighed. "But I never wear designer jeans, tons of bling, that sort of thing."

"If the clothes you're wearing now are your usual style, no, I wouldn't say you flaunt it. But maybe you do in other ways," Bella remarked.

"Like how?" Destiny's tone of slight belligerence reminded Bella of the teen girls she'd had to shush in the library the other day, when their laughter and animated conversation began to disturb the other patrons.

"Oh, maybe wanting Noah to do things *you* want instead of choosing what both of you might like to do."

Destiny set down her teacup and was silent for a long minute. She sighed. "Hmm. Like I want us to find a place away from campus." She glanced at Bella. "You sound like a big sister. You know, calling me on stuff, but not like a mom does."

Bella smiled. "Maybe."

"You said I might need medical information. Do you have a dread disease I should know about?"

Bella looked down at her hands. "When I'm stressed, I exhibit symptoms of Reynaud's Syndrome. That's about it for medical issues. I wrote down my blood type in case you need it. Here." Bella fished in her purse and handed Destiny a small piece of paper. "It's possible your folks already have that information, from the hospital, after you were born."

"They never said. Thanks." Destiny scanned the paper before shoving it into her jeans pocket. I'm sorry my mom was so nasty. Reacting that way when you talked about that little boy." Destiny stared at Bella for a moment. "Reynaud's happens to me sometimes, too." Then, without a second's hesitation, Destiny launched into a subject that set Bella's heart to racing again. "Did you really just want to meet me so you could tell me you loved me?"

Honesty here, total honesty. She nodded. "And to give you a chance to see that I'm an okay person." She stopped and reached for Destiny's hand. "I'll do anything for you. If you ever need anything and your folks can't help you—no matter the reason—call me. Maybe, just between us, since your mom wasn't happy about it, you might think of me as your second mom, or a big sister. Whatever you prefer. Someone besides your folks you can depend on."

"Chronologically, you'd be my first mom, and you're a lot closer to my age than she is," Destiny countered. "But we probably should just keep that between us."

"Vanessa raised you. She deserves to be your number one mom, don't you think?"

After an elongated pause, Destiny nodded. "I guess. I'm glad you came to see me, so we could really meet, not just talk on the phone."

"Me, too."

"Can I see those other pictures?"

"Sure." For the next several minutes, Bella showed Destiny the photos she had brought, including another one of Zoe and of the children's reading groups. "I'd like to ask you something, Destiny."

"What's that?"

"Now that I've come to Denver, would you be willing to come to Evergreen? Maybe after you graduate? I'll pay for your ticket so you don't have to ask your mom or dad for the money."

"To see where you live?"

Bella nodded, thinking of Zoe and the other women she felt close to. "I have a friend who owns a bookstore. You might like to talk with him, ask him what it's like. Maybe it will help you decide if you really want to work at a bookstore. I know he'd be thrilled to talk with you. Henry is such a sweet man."

"Are you in love with him?"

Bella laughed. "Not that kind of love. He's like a grandpa to me and Zoe." Gavin was another matter. Little Devil Bella teased her, turning her cheeks red.

"Let me think about it."

"If you don't have time this summer, maybe in the future. Whenever you decide, you'd be welcome." Bella finished her tea and stood up. "May I give you a hug?"

Her daughter's cheeks flushed. "Sure."

Bella hugged Destiny, clutching her loosely, but for a prolonged minute, imagining how it might have felt to do so every year since her daughter's birth.

"I was hoping you'd ask me about visiting," Destiny admitted. "But I'm glad you didn't while Mom was here."

"I didn't want her to feel uncomfortable. Will you tell her that? What she has done—raised you, loved you all these years—I can never repay her." Bella's eyes filled in spite of her plan not to allow her emotions to surface so obviously.

"I'll tell her." Bella and Destiny sauntered into the lobby. She gave Bella a relaxed wave as she departed.

Bella returned to her room, marveling that her daughter had finally come to meet her, that Vanessa had come, too, and that Destiny seemed to like Bella.

Gavin had wished her luck last night. He'd asked her to tell him how the visit went. Bella wanted to share how she felt, but hesitated. She waited another hour, savoring the moments she'd just spent with her daughter, then called him. He didn't answer. She texted him. *It went well*, wanting to say more, but not in a message.

The next morning, Bella rubbed her hand up her other arm to calm down the thrill bumps that rose when Gavin's name again appeared on her phone. "I wasn't sure you would call." She smiled into the phone.

"I told you I wanted to know."

"I know, but ..."

His voice sent another chill through her midsection. "You were testing me. With that message, three short words."

"No ... well, I guess I was," she admitted.

"What's she like?"

"Oh, Gavin, she's a delight. Her boyfriend is cute, too." Joy-filled excitement tinged her words.

"What about her mother? Did she come? You said you were worried about that."

Bella laughed. "She came late and left early. I guess she's just not ready to acknowledge me. I invited Destiny to come to Evergreen. I want her to meet Zoe and Henry and everybody," she bubbled.

"Not me?" he asked, sounding slightly disappointed.

"You, too." She felt her neck and face flush. "Yes, of course, assuming you're still there." But how would she introduce him? As her boyfriend, the word he'd used when she'd accompanied him to that Bellevue dealership?

"When's she coming?"

"We didn't settle on a time and it's up to her. If not immediately, perhaps next year." She caught her breath and the excitement that shimmered in the air as she recalled yesterday's meeting dimmed slightly.

"I'm glad your visit went well. Are you going to see her again?"

"I'm not sure." She sat down on the bed then stood up and repeated the up-down movements two more times, suddenly aware that she didn't want to end the call, but wasn't sure what else to say to Gavin. His call told her he was a friend, but those kisses he'd planted on her declared emphatically that he wanted to be more than a friend. Something she wanted, too.

Her cell pinged again, saving her from making a decision. "Oh! There's the phone. It could be her. I have to go."

"I'll talk to you when you get home." The warmth in his tone told her he knew how she felt about Destiny, about the call that could be her.

But the call was just the front desk, telling her they had something for her. When would she like it delivered?

"I'll come down," she replied.

When she arrived at the front desk, the woman handed her a beautiful bouquet of white and pink tulips. "Here's the card."

"Thank you." Who could have sent her flowers? Surely not Destiny. Her father, perhaps? Certainly not Vanessa. Bella couldn't imagine her apologizing for her hurtful words before she'd stomped off.

Bella cradled the vase and flowers in her arms, choosing to return to her room before opening the card. She set the flowers on the desk and stared at them for a moment. Her hands trembled slightly as she turned her attention to the card. She opened the envelope and her pulse skyrocketed when she read the words printed there.

"Good luck when you meet your daughter. I'm sure she'll be thrilled that you came to see her. All the best, Gavin."

Oh my gosh. Bella's lids pricked as tears threatened, tears of gratefulness that he cared enough to have ordered the flowers. *I'll call him back to thank him. He never even asked about them.* How did he know she loved tulips? If only they had arrived before her meeting with Destiny. Then she could have shared them with her.

Bella lay down on the bed, convinced that Gavin was nothing like Ethan, who never would have been so thoughtful, who'd never even asked her who that child was in the photo sitting next to Bella's graduation picture. But Gavin had noticed, and he'd encouraged Bella to get to know her daughter.

Bella's heart swelled. She imagined running her fingers through his thick, wavy hair, hugging and kissing him. Those images set her entire body humming. Was this what Zoe felt when Tör kissed her? Did Bella's kisses have the same effect on Gavin? He'd implied as much, more than once.

She picked up the phone and dialed his number, but he didn't pick up. *I'll bet he's at Henry's store.* "Gavin, it's me … um, Bella. Thank you *so* much for the beautiful flowers. The desk just alerted me of their arrival. I'm looking at them now. They're so beautiful. How did you know I love pale pink tulips? You were so thoughtful." She paused, aware that she'd almost said, "I love you." But did she? She'd only met him a few weeks ago. Instead, she said, "Bye."

Chapter 14

THE FRIDAY AFTER BELLA RETURNED FROM DENVER, SHE packed up a fresh apple cobbler still hot from the oven and drove to Books and More. Henry wasn't there, nor was Gavin.

"They're at Henry's," Earl muttered. "Probably going at the numbers. Again."

Bella set down the apple cobbler. "Would you like a piece, Earl?"

The old man raised his head enough to stare at the pan. "Smells good."

"Great. I'll cut you a piece and leave the rest in Henry's office."

"No, take it to him. Who knows when he'll be back, and he's got a soft spot for apple pie." Earl rummaged in a drawer near the cash register and pulled out a piece of paper. "His address, in case you've never been there." He handed the paper to her, but she shook her head.

Before she left, Bella took the time to wander around the upper floor of the bookstore. Months ago, she and Zoe had suggested that Henry move the children's books to the lower floor, so that mothers with young kids wouldn't worry about their babies falling down the stairs. But the children's section still occupied a dingy corner upstairs. *I'll mention it again.*

She left the store and headed for Henry's house. Willow Street wasn't far from downtown. She turned left after passing the Bean Blossom, a cheery coffee shop that had recently expanded to include tables set outside on a veranda surrounded by vine-covered fencing.

Henry's house sat near the center of the block, next to a pair of duplexes. The houses were small and well kept. She parked behind Gavin's roadster, opened the gate in the fence surrounding Henry's front yard, and walked to the front door. She shifted the still-warm pan into her right hand and knocked on the door.

Henry's voice rumbled. "Come on in, Mabel."

Bella grinned. *Mabel? One of Henry's neighbors?* "Not Mabel, Henry. It's me, Bella."

She heard a chair scrape and after a minute, the door opened. Gavin stood there in a University of Washington muscle shirt and jeans that hugged his frame. Bright red socks adorned his feet, prompting Bella to laugh.

"Is this a shoes-off domicile?"

"You got that right," Henry declared. "Gotta save my floors."

"They're beautiful," Bella replied. She handed the apple cobbler to Gavin, leaned down to remove her shoes, then followed Gavin into the kitchen where Henry sat at the table. "I brought you an apple cobbler." She angled a quick glance in Gavin's direction and lowered her voice. "Thanks again for the flowers." Her cheeks warmed when the corners of Gavin's mouth and his skillful lips angled upward.

"He sent you flowers, did he?" Henry looked askance at Gavin and then chuckled. "Now, wasn't that nice of him."

Gavin's tanned neck seemed to darken. "An encouragement," he said to her.

Bella motioned for him to resume his seat at the table. "Let me get you a dish."

"Bowls are straight ahead in the cupboard to the right of the fridge, spoons in the drawer just below," Henry instructed.

Bella found the bowls and spoons, and filled three bowls with the still-warm cobbler.

"I've got ice cream, too. Always love hot apples with ice cream, Bella. If you don't mind," Henry urged.

She spooned vanilla ice cream into the bowls and handed them to the men before taking her seat at the table. "I hope I'm not interrupting something important," she said. Papers were scattered on either side of the floor near Henry's seat. Stacks of file folders adorned most of the table, and an adding machine sat between the two men.

"Nothing that can't keep," Henry mumbled, with his mouth full.

Gavin glanced at Bella. One eyebrow arched as his smile broadened. "We needed a break anyway." His eyes seemed to burn a path through her clothes and into her heart. Bella's pulse rose.

"I'm glad." She picked up her spoon and began to eat the cobbler.

She'd have preferred a kiss, but she suspected Gavin wouldn't give her one in Henry's presence even though the flash in his eyes hinted at feelings she wanted to explore.

"Henry, I noticed that your children's section is still upstairs. Zoe and I will help you move it downstairs where it will be more visible."

Henry pointed to his mouth, conveniently chewing a bite of apple cobbler.

Gavin set down his spoon. "You saw that?"

She nodded. "When I stopped by the store, looking for you. Both of you. Left a piece of cobbler for Earl."

Gavin picked up a pen and jotted a note. "You think that change will move more merchandise?"

"Moms don't like worrying about their babies tumbling down stairs, and Henry's selection of kids' books deserves to be on the first floor, where it's safer and more easily seen. Even the young adult section—you know, for teens—would get more traffic at street level. It's so much better than the YA departments in other stores."

The old man frowned. "I don't have time for all that movin' and shiftin'. 'Sides, if I did that, where would the business books go?"

"Henry, Bella's right. The kid sections should be on the main floor. We can find another place for the business books," Gavin urged.

"I thought you just wanted to waste my time goin' through the numbers. Now you're wantin' me to rearrange things, too?" He pouted.

"You want to sell more books, don't you?" Gavin slid his chair back, his smile replaced by a slight frown. He crossed his arms over the hard chest Bella had been dreaming about, wondering what it looked like under the T-shirt that stretched across his shoulders, how it would feel pressed against her ...

Sensing the men were gearing up to butt heads, Bella raised her hand to get their attention. "Hey, I didn't mean to raise a sore point. If you aren't up to moving the books, Zoe and I will do it, maybe this weekend when we're not working. Tör might help, too, if he's not on duty."

"Good idea," Gavin seconded. "Count me in, too."

Henry stood up so suddenly, his chair knocked into the wall. "Not till I figure things out. After all, it's *my* store. Should be *my* decision. And Earl's."

"Of course," Bella backpedaled. She rose from her chair, placed her dishes in the sink, and stored the container with the remaining cobbler in the refrigerator. "I think I'd better leave so you two can finish what you were working on. Sorry I interrupted."

She gave Henry a peck on the cheek before heading for the door. She slipped on her shoes. "I'm glad you're feeling better. See you later."

"I'll see you out," Gavin said, and followed her to her car after donning his shoes. "Thanks for the dessert. I was hoping it would put him in a better mood."

"You're not happy about the numbers, are you?"

"Let's just say they could be better. That was a good suggestion you made."

"If he changes his mind, let me know. We need his store. I'd hate to see it go under."

He nodded. "Point taken." He opened her door for her. "If you're going to be home tonight, I'll stop by."

Those butterflies she'd felt earlier resumed their raucous fluttering, seeming to keep time with the pounding of her heart. "I'll be there."

"Okay. See you then." He touched his fingers to his lips and transferred a kiss to her nearest cheek, generating heat that Bella was sure had turned her face scarlet.

She watched as he strode back into the house.

That evening, Bella answered the door.

Gavin's stance seemed to shout testosterone as he leaned against the doorjamb.

She waved him inside. "You don't have to take your shoes off," she said, imagining other items she'd love for him to remove. *Mine, his, his, mine.* Maybe she should suggest a game of strip poker, not that she'd ever played it.

"Good to know."

She took two steps back before he closed the door then placed his hands on her arms and pulled her close. His kiss was as electric as the previous ones that had kept Bella up nights. "I've been wanting to do that since you got back from Denver," he murmured into the hair near her left ear.

"Yes, well …" she wasn't sure what else to say and didn't have to when he resumed kissing her. First her lips then the hollow of her neck, a spot just behind her left ear and then the right—who knew they had become erogenous zones?—before returning to her lips. Each kiss showed her better than words that he wanted her. His chest wasn't the only hard portion of his body and her pulse zoomed.

When his hand slid under the hem of her blouse, conveniently outside the jeans she'd pulled on when she arrived home, she seemed to stop breathing. *If he can cop a feel, so can I.* She ceased stroking his back through his shirt and pushed it out of the way to explore the skin that seemed to burn her fingers.

How they maneuvered to her couch, she couldn't have said. All she remembered was his skillful exploration of her body, ratcheting up her desire to do the same with his. But when his hand cupped one breast and her nipple hardened in reaction, Bella snapped out of her trance.

She pulled away. "Um, uh. Gavin?"

He seemed not to hear her whisper as he concentrated on stroking her into sexual oblivion.

"Gavin. Stop. Please. We need to slow down," she gasped, when his fingers found the snap on her jeans and eased between her clothing and her skin.

"You said something?" he murmured before kissing her again, forcefully.

Bella slid her hand from around his shoulders and pushed against his chest, now bare, so hard, so well-muscled. "Gavin. No."

His fingers stopped moving south. They eased out from under her jeans while his other hand maintained contact with her breast.

She pushed his hand away from her breast, replacing the heat of his hand on her skin with the evening coolness.

"What's wrong?" he asked. "You want it, too. I know you do."

Yes, I do. Parts of her body complained that her brain had called a halt to *things*. "I don't think we should start something we can't …" she licked her lips, "finish."

She almost groaned out loud at the pirate smile he laid on her.

"What makes you think we won't finish?" He dipped his head as if to resume kissing her.

She stood up. "We can't. You're going home to Spokane, and my home is here. In Evergreen." She paused. "Long-distance affairs … er, relationships, don't work for me."

The blue of his eyes seemed to darken to midnight at her words. He reached for his shirt and stood up. "We could make it work," he challenged.

"Let's talk about something else," she practically begged, desperate to stop thinking about how close they'd come to doing it right in her living room, on the couch, or on the floor. When had she lost all control? She knew when. When lust for this man had driven all other thoughts from her mind.

"Like what?" he asked, sounding a lot calmer than Bella felt.

"Henry. His store." She was grasping at straws, anything to distance herself from what she really wanted, what he obviously was capable of.

He nodded. "If you say so." When his gaze rose from studying the floor, the heat in his eyes almost bowled her over.

"I meant it when I said Zoe and I would help. Move the books, I mean."

"He's not thrilled with the idea. I'm giving him time to think it over."

She angled slowly toward the door, intent on easing Gavin out of her house, away from her arms. Hell, away from her bed!

But he didn't follow her. Instead, he wandered toward the bookcase. He pointed to the new picture in the frame containing Destiny's photos. "You said you were going to invite her for a visit. Is that still on?"

"She's kind of busy right now. College graduation. Going to see her dad and his new baby."

He nodded and finally moved toward the door.

"Thanks for coming over." She tried to sound calm, but her voice shimmered. His eyes narrowed as she opened the door.

Perhaps he sensed she was on the cusp of grabbing him and pulling him back into the house. "You said we had to stop," he repeated quietly. "I would never force a woman ..."

Before she changed her mind, he opened the door and walked outside.

Bella fell back on the couch, panting. *What is the matter with me?* This man brought out her desire. Lusty Devil Bella certainly recognized that. But her saner side knew she was right. Gavin wasn't a keeper. He couldn't be. His life would resume in Spokane. As soon as he got Henry's affairs in order, as soon as the bookstore began making money again and Henry was fully on the mend—Gavin would be gone.

Relieved that he seemed to have more self-control than she, Bella wondered what she was going to do the next time she saw him. *I have to talk to Zoe. She'll know what to do.* Bella chuckled to herself. *Probably tell me to renew my birth control prescription.*

Destiny clumped over to the baggage claim at the Austin airport, eager to see her father.

"There you are," he exclaimed as he swept Destiny into his arms.

"Dad, it's so good to see you. How's the new baby? I knew you were going to have a boy." She brushed his cheek with a quick kiss. "You look kinda tired. Not sleeping well?"

He beamed. "New babies have a way of keeping their parents up nights. Just like you did. Come on. Let's get you home." He grabbed her bag and headed for the car. "Erin loves the blanket you made."

As they drove to her father's spacious ranch house, Destiny mentally squirmed. Should she ask him or just tell him? So much had happened in the two weeks since Bella's visit.

"Something on your mind, Des? You're pretty quiet," her father observed. "You're not still on the outs with your mother, are you?" He placed a hand on her thigh and patted it.

She glanced his way as they sped down the highway. "I met Bella. Mom probably told you, right?"

He nodded, his eyes on the road. "Your mother did happen to mention it," he said, his mouth quirking up slightly on one side. "Along with you not doing as well in your marketing classes as she'd hoped. She was disappointed."

"Why is that not a surprise? She's always disappointed in me."

"You know that's not true. She's happy that you graduated. Aren't you?"

"Yes. But now I need a job. More than part-time."

Dad nodded. "Just like thousands of other graduates. Maybe I could find you something here, in the company."

"No, Dad. I want to find one myself. Nepotism's not for me. At least not right away."

He laughed out loud. "Good for you for wanting to do it on your own. Your mother loves you, Des, and wants the best for you. Just like I do." He glanced her way as the traffic thinned. "How did your meeting go with Bella?"

Des scrunched her face into a frown. "Well, *I* was happy, even if Mom wasn't. She's not thrilled about anything these days. I brought Bella's picture with me. To show you. Why didn't you tell me I look just like her? Or don't you remember?"

"It's been a long time, sugarplum. I remember she had red hair." He smiled. "Since you do, too, I guess you probably do look like her."

"Did you know she's a librarian? Even has her masters. Before she came to Denver, all Mom would say was she hadn't even graduated from high school." She huffed out a quick breath. "As if she never changed."

"I'm glad Bella's made something of herself." He smiled. "But I'm not surprised. Back then I sensed she had a backbone. Did she tell you she almost didn't go ahead with the adoption?"

"What do you mean?" Destiny's pulse shot skyward. "I thought Mom said she wanted you guys to have me."

"She did, but I got the impression if there had been any way she could have, she would have kept you. Something about what her father said, the way she tensed up whenever he spoke during our meetings." He paused and let out a small whoosh of air. "Then there was the way she looked when she handed you over. Terribly sad, but putting a brave face on it. Not a single tear. Unlike me. Did you know she breastfed you? It was in the nurse's notes, which were forwarded to your pediatrician. Did she mention that?"

Destiny nodded. "Only that she knew she couldn't take care of me, and that her folks insisted on, you know … what happened."

His voice sounded pensive when he asked, "How did you feel about that, when she told you?"

"It felt good knowing she didn't want to give me up, and that she wanted a family for me. I guess she didn't count on you guys getting divorced."

He patted her nearest hand. "No one wanted it, but it was for the best." They drove on for several minutes before turning off the highway and onto a residential road.

"Back to your mother. How is she feeling about you coming here?"

Destiny sighed. "Old news, Dad. Not happy, but accepting it. Mom didn't want me to come so soon after Bella showed up, but at least she didn't stop me." *I need to change the subject, get Dad to think about something other than Mom and me.* "Why'd you name the baby Nolan, Jr.? Couldn't be more creative than that?"

"Erin's idea. We'll probably call him by his middle name, Scott. He's your baby brother, Des."

"He is, isn't he?" She grinned. "Scott's a nice name. I like it better than having to call him *Junior.*"

"If he's at all like you, he won't be a junior anything. But you didn't answer my question. What's on your mind?" He pulled into the driveway and turned off the car.

Destiny grasped her father's hand as he started to open the car door. "Wait. Before we go in. I want to visit Bella. She wants me to see where she lives. And it'll give us a chance to really talk."

"I thought you did that when she came to Denver."

"She wasn't there long enough, and I only got to see her one time. I had to study the next day and then she left."

"How'd you do in your spring quarter classes?"

"Bs and As, mostly. One C. In Business Ethics. I hated that class," she added. "Mom wanted me to ace it."

He winked at her. "I hope it wasn't because you saw no point in staying honest in business."

"It was boring."

"I promised you a car after graduation. Have a particular model in mind?" he asked.

"No, and you don't have to get me one." Destiny sighed. "Dad, you didn't answer my question. About my going to see Bella."

"Because she asked or because you want to stick it to your mother?"

"Mom doesn't know. She'll freak. She was so rude; it was embarrassing. But Bella acted like it didn't bother her, and she invited me. Said she'd even pay my airfare. I was thinking if I just changed my ticket from here, it wouldn't cost that much. I want to see her before I get really busy, like with a real job. I'll bet her friends are nice, and I want to find out if she has a boyfriend. She never said." A flash of hurt echoed in her heart at the thought of Noah. What was he doing while she was gone? Who was he seeing now?

"What about *your* boyfriend? How is Noah?"

Destiny sucked in her breath, wishing her dad hadn't asked. "Okay, I guess. I haven't seen him in over a week."

"Why's that?"

"I think he dumped me." She pressed a nail into the palm of her hand in hopes the pain would stop her tears. "We had a big fight. When he finally called me, he said I was holding him back."

"Oh, baby. Maybe he'll change his mind." Her father patted her hand. "Does your mother know?"

Destiny shook her head. "I didn't tell her. Maybe she suspects. Since I haven't been going out with him, not staying over either."

Her father was silent for a moment. "Tell me more about Bella."

"What's to tell? She's my birth mother. Wants me to visit. Looks like me. She's nice, Dad. Said if I ever needed anything, she'd help me out."

He lowered his head in thought, and she waited impatiently for his answer. He was always so deliberate before he made a decision. Probably what made him such a good businessman.

"You should tell your mother about your change of plans. So she won't worry when you don't come home on time."

"No! She'll just say I shouldn't go. She's all bent out of shape about Bella. I'm almost twenty-two. And I want to go. I was hoping you'd agree that it's my decision." She leaned against the passenger door. "There's Erin." She grinned and waved at the beautiful woman with the flowing blonde hair. She was standing on the porch, holding a bundle that had to be Destiny's brother.

Destiny hopped out of the car, gave Erin a hug and looked down at the sleeping baby. His shock of thick dark hair made him look a bit like his father.

"Can I hold him?" she asked.

"Of course. Let's go in the house, out of the sun. Dinner is almost ready. I want you to tell me all about what you've been doing. Your dad says your birth mother has been in touch."

Through the rest of the evening, Destiny answered Erin's questions, held the baby, and told Erin and her dad about her job at the bookstore. She confided that she wanted to make it a fulltime job now that she had her degree. If the owner didn't agree, she was going to approach other bookstores.

The next day, after an extended discussion with her dad and Erin, she emailed Bella and confirmed she wanted to come for a visit. That evening, her cell phone rang.

"I'm sorry I didn't see your email earlier. I've been helping Henry at his store," Bella explained, sounding breathless. "But I'd love for you to come for a visit."

"Great! I'll call the airline, change my ticket and call you right back."

Two hours later, all was arranged. Destiny would stay with Bella for a week before flying home.

Destiny sank down on the couch next to Dad, happy with what she'd done. "I promise I'll call Mom from Bella's and tell her I've been delayed. She doesn't need to know where I am, Dad. Not until I get home. Then I'll tell her."

"I think you're making a mistake, hon, not telling her in advance." He frowned.

Destiny crossed her arms over her chest, determined to do things her way.

"You don't have to live with her, Dad. If she doesn't know, she won't worry. And if she calls here, just say I'm having too much fun with the baby. That I decided to spend an extra week here."

"As if that will help," he muttered, but he reluctantly agreed to go along with Destiny's plan. "One of these days, you're going to have to come clean with your mother. Tell her how you feel—about everything. Let her show you she loves you and that you love her. You do, you know. Even though you try so hard to hide it. You're a lot like her, Des."

"Oh, Dad. You know that's not true."

"You hide your true feelings, afraid she won't understand, that she won't accept them or you. Just like she does." He paused, glanced lovingly at his wife as she sat nearby, nursing the baby. "One reason we got divorced."

Destiny couldn't think of a thing to say to that.

Destiny waved at Bella as she approached baggage claim in the Seattle airport. Bella gave her a prolonged hug and hustled her outside into air far cooler than in Austin or Denver. "Are you sure it's summer here?" Destiny asked with a laugh. "I could almost use a sweater."

Bella chuckled. "June can be more like spring than summer some days. Never as hot as Denver or Austin. How was your baby brother? Cute, I'll bet."

"He looks a lot like Dad." She tossed her bag into Bella's trunk. "I promised to call my mom from your place. So she'd know when I'm coming home."

After they left the busyness of the airport area, Destiny gazed at the forested hills on a road with few cars.

"You live out in the country?"

Bella laughed. "Not exactly, but Evergreen isn't very big. I invited Zoe, and her fiancé, Tör, to come for dinner tonight. So you can meet them. I want them to meet you, too. But you'll have time beforehand to call your mom."

Minutes later, she pulled into the driveway of a small house, its style suggesting coziness.

As if Bella had read Destiny's mind, she said. "My house isn't quite as big as yours in Denver, as you can see."

"Oh, that's right. You said you drove by our place when you came to see me." *As if that matters.* "But your house looks nice."

"I like it." Bella opened the door and ushered Destiny inside. She scanned the living room with its colorful rug on the hardwood floor, the dining area off to one side. The table appeared to have been set for dinner already, with four place settings, each a different color.

"My mom has Fiesta ware, too."

"Great minds," Bella replied with a smile.

"What color's mine?"

"I chose red for you. Tör likes the blue, and Zoe's is the green. I'll use the yellow, unless you prefer it."

"Cool. The red's okay with me. It's what I use at home." She picked up her bag. "Where should I dump my stuff?"

"Let me show you. I hope you'll be comfortable." Bella led the way into a bedroom just off the hall. The multicolored coverlet on the bed reminded Destiny of a Jackson Pollock painting. Against one wall was a dresser. Next to the bed was a small table topped with a lamp and a clock radio. The room looked unused. Perhaps Bella didn't have many guests.

"Your bath is right across the hall. Feel free to freshen up. I'll just go back and check on things in the kitchen. Dinner should be ready soon."

Bella left and Destiny emptied her suitcase, placing her clothes in the dresser. She sat on the bed and imagined herself staying here in the future, maybe for an extended visit. The idea felt good to her. *But I have to get Mom to understand.*

A few minutes after Destiny returned to the living room, the doorbell rang, followed by footsteps and the sound of a man's voice and a woman's higher-pitched tone.

"Hi, guys. Come on in." Bella turned and smiled at Destiny. "I'd like you to meet Destiny. Here's Zoe, who works with me at the library, and Tör, Zoe's fiancé. He's an ER doc."

Destiny held out her hand to the tall man, his blond hair shining in the early evening sun. Tör reminded her of one of her professors, except that he was way hotter.

Zoe enthusiastically pulled Destiny into a hug. "Hi. I've been *dying* to meet you."

"It's nice to meet you, too."

The doorbell rang again. Bella looked up in surprise, then blushed at the man standing there, holding a multi-colored bouquet of flowers. "For Destiny. To welcome her," he said, his baritone voice luscious and ever so sexy.

Destiny stared back at him. *Are all the men around here major league hotties?*

Although he'd smiled at first, he now seemed to be assessing her, his expression serious. "Hi, I'm Gavin," and held out his hand. "Bella's told us so much about you."

Bella seemed to look askance at Gavin. She cleared her throat. "Why don't you all come to the table? I'll put on another plate. Gavin, would you help me with the cheesy potatoes?"

"I can help," Destiny offered.

"Good. Why don't you put this on the table?" Bella handed her a large salad bowl. As Destiny left the kitchen, she saw Gavin brush his lips against Bella's neck. "Sorry I crashed your party, but I couldn't help myself. Curiosity and all that."

"I thought you had to take Henry to the doctor, that it was going to take all afternoon and then some."

"The old coot cancelled the appointment. I was so mad I decided to come over here to cool off." He brushed past Destiny as he headed for the table with two more serving dishes.

Tör pulled out Destiny's chair for her.

"Should I call you 'doctor'?" she asked before glancing at Gavin again.

Tör shook his head. "Not necessary." He took his seat. "Did you have a nice flight?"

Destiny nodded. "Longer than I thought it would be. It's

a lot cooler here than in Austin."

Gavin grinned at Bella when she brought a platter on which a steaming slab of salmon rested. She placed it in front of Destiny next to a dish of green vegetables. "Bella says you'll be here for a week. Is she going to put you to work at the library?"

"I was thinking I'd take her to Henry's store. Destiny works at one in Denver," Bella replied.

"Is this your first trip to the Pacific Northwest?" Gavin gazed at her intently.

"We used to live in Portland, but we moved when I was little. I don't remember it at all."

Throughout dinner, Gavin asked Destiny one question after another. Tör was silent except when asking for another helping or making a comment to Zoe, and Bella spent most of her time glancing between Gavin and Destiny as she answered his questions.

After dinner, Gavin took a seat in the living room. Destiny helped Bella clear off the table, even though she insisted Destiny didn't have to. "You're a guest. Let us do that."

"My mom would expect me to help," she replied.

"Then thank you for the offer." Bella patted Destiny's arm.

"Tell me about this bookstore you want me to see."

After Zoe returned to the kitchen to help with the cleanup, she and Bella talked about Henry's store, informing Destiny how it was different from the franchises in town and how much they supported it.

"Henry was sick earlier this spring. If you'd like, maybe you could help him at the store. We've been trying to get him to take it easy, but he doesn't always listen," Bella said.

"Gavin is his nephew, here from Spokane. He wants Henry to think about selling the store or maybe even closing it," Zoe added.

"Oh, yeah? He's a real stud muffin. Are all the men here as good looking as those two?" She nodded toward Gavin and Tör, who seemed to be debating the Sounders' chances this year. Zoe laughed. "They are, aren't they?"

Color rose in Bella's neck and cheeks.

Bella really likes Gavin. Destiny glanced in his direction before asking, "Doesn't the owner want to keep running it?"

"It has to make a profit and some of what his wife used to do is just not something Henry's interested in," Bella explained, turning her attention to the pans still in the sink.

"I'd love to help out. Sounds like fun. I'm sure you don't want me just following you around the library."

"We'll have plenty of time for that, too," Bella assured her.

As she climbed into bed later that night, Destiny remembered she'd neglected to call her mom. "Damn!" Her dad was probably already fielding calls to find out why Destiny hadn't confirmed her flight time. Now she was in for it.

Chapter 15

THE NEXT DAY, DESTINY ACCOMPANIED BELLA TO THE library. At the first opportunity, she excused herself to go to the women's room. "Mom," Destiny whispered into the phone. "Please call me back. We need to talk. It's important."

The text she received from Noah when she returned to Bella's office sent her fleeing back to the privacy of the women's room. She burst into tears, shocking herself. She almost never cried. She'd been expecting something like this since their second big fight right before she left to visit Dad. Noah hadn't even waited until she came home.

Destiny returned to the office, her face tear-stained.

Bella asked, "What's the matter, hon? Bad news at home?"

"Noah dumped me, for real, this time," she moaned. She turned away from Bella, not wanting to fall apart in front of her. Bella reached for her, pulling her into a hug and rocking her as if Destiny was a small child. She seemed not to care that Destiny's tears were probably soaking into her blouse. After several minutes, she murmured, "The same thing's happened to me. More than once. I know it hurts now, but it'll get better. You'll see." She handed Destiny a tissue. "Maybe you'd like some private time while I talk to Mitchell."

Bella's boss had just knocked on Bella's open door and walked in, his gaze stormy.

Destiny nodded and returned to the women's room, allowing herself the luxury of another crying jag. Noah was her first love, not like those others guys she'd dated. She hated the thought that they were breaking up. Even after their first fight, he'd driven her to see Bella at the hotel. Destiny had assumed he wasn't mad at her anymore, after she'd apologized for insisting on doing things she wanted, for never giving him a chance to say what *he* wanted. But now he'd said they were through and not even to her face.

She suspected his folks' comments about her were behind it all, but when she'd accused him once of letting his mother run his life, he'd blown up big time, accusing her of using him to get back at *her* mother.

Destiny reclaimed a seat in the corner of Bella's office, glad the room was now empty. Bella was probably talking to her growly boss in his office. How Bella could stand the man, Destiny could not fathom. She would hate having a boss like him.

Bella opened the door and breezed in. "Feeling better?"

Destiny nodded. "You'd have made a great mom."

Bella's eyes widened. "I … um, well, thank you. Maybe I'll have a chance. In the future," she stammered, her cheeks turning bright pink.

"You should get married. Like your friend Zoe. To that hottie, Gavin."

Bella seemed to suck in her breath. "That's not very likely." She sighed and blushed again before changing the subject. "Zoe invited us to lunch at our favorite place, the Executive Dining Room. Want to come?"

Destiny glanced down at her black jeans and red T-shirt with the satanic face painted in black. "That place sounds fancy. Am I dressed okay or should we go home first so I can change?"

Bella chuckled. "We'll walk, and you're dressed just fine." She grabbed her purse from the lower drawer in her desk. "Come on. We don't have a lot of time, and it'll take us a few minutes to get there."

Destiny walked with Bella and Zoe across the park that bordered the library grounds. Several people were clustered around a food truck parked across the street. Smells of something delicious wafted in their direction.

"Why don't we eat there instead?" Destiny pointed to the truck.

Zoe laughed. "That's where we're headed. See?" She pointed to the words written in fanciful script on the side of the truck.

"Oh!" Destiny grinned. "That is so cool."

Zoe motioned toward an empty table. "Why don't you grab that table? We'll get the food. I hope you're into steak sandwiches with pepper and onions. Today's offering."

"Sounds good to me." Destiny trotted over to the table and sat down. Zoe followed with three icy drinks and napkins. Destiny scooted over to make room for Bella when she approached the table, balancing three sandwiches in her hands.

"Quick, Zoe. Grab one. They're really hot," Bella said. She took a seat next to Destiny. "Welcome to the Executive Dining Room. Tyrone outdid himself today. He gave us extra onions and peppers in honor of you joining us, Des." Bella chortled. "I hope you don't mind. If you don't want all of yours, Zoe and I will take them, right Zo?"

"You bet!"

"How long have you known Tör?" Destiny asked Zoe.

"A little over a year."

Destiny bit into her steak sandwich, moaned in appreciation and concentrated on the delicious flavors exploding in her mouth. "This sandwich is fabulous." She wiped her mouth then added, "And now you're getting married. For the first time, right?"

"The only time," Zoe replied, her eyes sparkling.

"Don't you think Bella should get married, too? I mean, you guys are the same age. Way past when most people are married."

"Lots of women wait until they have established careers before walking down the aisle." Zoe winked at her friend. "Bella and I are just picky, that's all. We wanted to make sure we found the *right* guy. I just happened to find mine first. Doesn't mean Bella won't meet *her* Mr. Right." She gave Bella a conspiratorial grin.

"Oh, yeah?" Destiny stared intently at her birth mother.

"She's seeing someone, but I'll bet she won't admit how much she likes him," Zoe said.

Before Bella could respond, Destiny asked, "It's gotta be Gavin, that guy who couldn't take his eyes off her at dinner." Destiny wiped her hands and took another sip of her soda.

Zoe snorted. "In my book, he definitely qualifies." She elbowed Bella, whose eyes were following a squirrel as it scampered up a nearby tree trunk.

"Then I think Bella definitely should marry him," Destiny blurted to Zoe's hoot of laughter.

Bella finally spoke up, her voice somewhat hoarse. "Let's not jump to conclusions, you two. Gavin's not staying here.

He's going back to Spokane as soon as Henry no longer has to see the doctor. You know that, Zoe." She gave her friend a piercing look.

Destiny laughed. "If it were me, I'd want a guy who's really hot. A real stud, someone who makes my friends jealous that he likes *me* and not them," she declared, thinking of some of the comments her BFFs had made about Noah.

Bella turned serious when she replied, "Looks aren't everything, Destiny. Having an education and a good job is important, too."

"What about Gavin? Is he 'educated'?" She asked, air-quoting. "Does he have a good job?"

"Owns his own BMW dealership," Zoe offered. "Wait till you see the wheels he drives. A red-hot car. Maybe he'll give you a ride."

"Sounds good."

Bella smoothly changed the subject. "Tomorrow I'll take you to the bookstore to meet Henry."

Destiny looked down when her phone pinged a familiar tone. She hauled it out of her pocket and swung her legs over the seat. "It's my mom. I need privacy for this call."

"Of course," Bella replied, her smile receding slightly.

Destiny trotted away from the table. "Mom? Can you make this quick? We were just sitting down to lunch."

"You said to call. What's the problem? And when are you coming home? Your dad said you've extended your visit for another week. Surely the baby isn't that interesting, or has your dad finally convinced you to apply for that job with his company?"

Dad kept his promise not to tell her. "No, Mom. Actually, I'm at Bella's."

"What?!"

"Dad helped me change my ticket so I could spend more

time with her. And she's taking me to a bookstore tomorrow. Seeing it, talking to the owner, might help me decide if it's what I want to do as a career. You *do* want me to get a job, don't you?"

"Yes, of course, but why do you have to see a bookstore where Bella lives?"

"It's an independent, like the one at home. Bella says the owner might even let me help him while I'm here. I could make some money. He's been sick. I really want to do this, Mom. Please don't be mad."

Silence followed. Was her mother holding her breath? Maybe she'd dropped the phone.

"Mom?"

"I'm here," her voice no longer as shrill. "Why didn't you tell me you wanted to see Bella again?"

"I didn't think you'd agree, and I wanted to see where she lives. It doesn't mean I won't come home. I just want to get to know her better. In her own space. She has neat friends, and she talks to me like I'm an adult. Just like Dad." She hesitated then added, "Noah broke up with me. I need some time away so I don't run into him or any of his friends." She gulped and tears again threatened to slide down her face. "I just wanted you to know that I'm okay. I'm sorry I didn't tell you first. I should have."

Her mother was silent again before adding, her voice gentle. "You're forgiven, honey. And I hope you have a good time with Bella. Tell her hello for me."

"I will. Thanks, Mom." Destiny hung up. She wiped her face, hoping her tears hadn't left tracks on her cheeks and returned to the table.

"Is everything okay with your mom?" Bella asked.

Destiny nodded, relieved that her mom hadn't exploded and demanded that she come home, still stunned at her last words. "She says hello."

The next day, Bella introduced Destiny to Henry. "She wants to know about running a bookstore. Perhaps you could show her around the store, let her know how long you've been in business. That sort of thing."

Henry beamed at Destiny. "Oh my, yes. You are a sight for these old eyes. A beautiful girl and you want to help out old Henry. What do you think, Earl? Should I send you home now that I have a new helper?"

Earl snorted dismissively, shoved his Mariners cap onto his head and grabbed a magazine before stomping to the back of the store.

"I don't want him to be mad at me," Destiny said.

"Don't mind him. He's just jealous. Come along with me, darlin'. Old Henry will teach you all there is to know about runnin' a bookstore." He looked up briefly. "You need anything, Bella? Those books workin' out okay?"

"I'm fine. When would you like me to come back?"

"Give us till lunch time, at least." He reached for Destiny's hand. "We'll start here on the main floor."

"Is Gavin here, too?" Destiny asked.

Her question generated a frown and harrumph from Henry. "I 'spect he'll be around soon enough. Said he had an errand to run this morning. 'Sides, he doesn't know a thing about runnin' my store."

Bella returned to the library, pleased that Henry seemed to be his old self, flirting with Destiny, and eager to show her his beloved store. Minutes after she arrived in her office, she wished she had stayed with Destiny. Her boss stormed in, raving about a child that had been injured while attending a story hour.

"Mitchell, I had no idea. When exactly did this happen? The mother never told me."

The library manager gave her another thunderous scowl as he rubbed one hand agitatedly against the arm of his chair. "She threatened to *sue*, Bella. I want you to talk to her, get the details, beg forgiveness, offer to pay for her kid's injuries. Do whatever you have to do. The Council is going to *demand* that I explain what happened and I wasn't even *there!*"

Bella gripped her hands in her lap, wishing she could be anywhere but here. "Give me the mother's name, Mitchell. You said her daughter was in the new Story Time?"

He nodded. "McIntosh. The child's name is Nickie. I don't recall the mother's name. *Mrs.* McIntosh."

Little Nickie McIntosh? They've been patrons forever. "Fine. I'll talk with her mother."

"Now you know *why* I'm always hesitant about having so many groups come to the library. This *new* group … those children are simply too disruptive, noisy, rambunctious. I won't take the chance of—"

"But, Mitchell, when I was with them, the children were very respectful, quiet. They listened to the story and then we made the brooms so we could have a Quidditch match. Outside, well away from the building. Tell me again what Mrs. McIntosh said to you. So I can speak to her, knowledge-ably." She couldn't remember even a minor skirmish between the children. But she'd left early, right after the end of the Chapter Read Along, to pick up Destiny at the airport. *Maybe I should have asked Zoe to stay late.* As best she could recall, the children had dispersed normally.

Mitchell gave a put-upon sigh. "She *said* that bigger girl,

Roberta, whatever her name is, smacked her child in the face and knocked her down. Then one of the boys took after Roberta and chased her away. *Her* mother yelled at me, too. You know how I hate fighting, antagonism. That other mother as much as *accused* me of allowing *delinquents* to frequent the library. That new group of yours has to go."

"I'll call Roberta's mother, too," she said, hoping her willingness to talk to the mothers would mollify Mitchell, the milquetoast.

"You do that, since this happened during *your* new program." He rose from the chair, and departed, shutting her door behind him.

After *the program, Mitchell.* Thank God the children had already left the building, but the thought did little to assuage Bella's sense of impending doom.

Before Bella could pick up the phone, her cell pinged and Destiny's image appeared. "Yes, Destiny?"

Her voice bubbled with enthusiastic excitement. "Hi, I'm outside so Henry can't hear me, but I just *love* him *and* the bookstore. Is it okay if I work here instead of coming back to the library after lunch? Henry said my idea of putting the kids' books and even the YA section on the main floor was a *great* idea. What do you think of that?"

Bella grinned. *When it was our idea it wasn't acceptable, but now it's coming from Destiny, it's worth doing?* Wasn't that just like Henry, the old flirt? "Go for it, sweetie. When do you want me to pick you up?"

"Gavin came in and he's helping me move things. Bella," Destiny's voice lowered to a whisper. "That man is to die for in the hotness department. Too bad he's too old for me." She paused and giggled. "I'm *so glad* you went out with him. Isn't that what Zoe said? Fan me quick! Oh. Gotta go. Gavin's knocking on the window for me to come in so we can get started. He'll drop me off when we're done. The library or your house?"

"Why don't you give me a call before you leave and I'll let you know."

"Okay. Bye."

Bella sat back in her chair, glad Destiny was happy to help Henry. Gavin, hotness, a date or something? Bella's body tingled at the thought. Good thing Destiny didn't know what she and Gavin had already engaged in during their last encounter and where it had almost led. The man was too enticing.

Time to get back to business. She looked up the McIntosh file, picked up her office phone and punched in the local phone number.

"Hello?" a girl's voice answered.

"Is this Nickie?"

"Yes. Who's this?"

"Nickie, it's Ms. Campbell, from the library. May I please speak with your mother?"

"Moommm! It's for you."

Muffled voices could be heard before the mother answered. "Ms. Campbell?"

"Yes. I understand there was a problem after the last story hour. Could you fill me in on what happened?"

The silence that followed—was the woman gathering her thoughts or gearing up to refer Bella to a lawyer?—worried her enough that Bella brought a finger to her lips to nibble on a nail. She halted and looked at her fingers. Two were turning white, as if in anticipation of Mrs. McIntosh's words.

"Nickie was attacked by another child. Roberta Belfore. For no reason. I spoke with Mr. Hargrove."

"Yes. He said Nickie was hurt. How badly? Does she need stitches?" Bella crossed her fingers in hopes the child's injuries were minor.

"She has a split cheek. But the doctor said he'd closed it so the scar wouldn't show very much. But I'm not going to allow Nickie to attend if that other child is there."

"Totally understandable. I'll speak with Roberta's parents. Is there something you would like them to do, to show how sorry they are? Perhaps cover Nickie's visit to the doctor?"

The woman snorted. "I doubt it'll do any good. I've watched that child on the soccer field. That girl, Roberta, is just plain mean when she doesn't get her way."

"Do you know why she got into it with Nickie? Please let me speak with her." Bella rubbed her whitened fingers against her skirt while she waited for the girl's mother to call her back to the phone.

"Ms. Bella, I didn't do anything," Nickie's voice sounded. "Roberta tried to take my book away. It wasn't one of the library's. It was my very own copy, but she didn't believe me." The child sniffed.

"Okay, Nickie. I'm just trying to sort out what happened. I'm sure you didn't do anything wrong. Let me speak with your mother again." Bella jotted down a note to make sure that the library copies were prominently identified, perhaps with a sticker on the outside cover, not just on the inside. "Mrs. McIntosh, if you could please send me a copy of the doctor bills? We will get to the bottom of this. The library doesn't allow fighting in the building or on the grounds. I'm so sorry I wasn't there to witness what happened to Nickie, but I can assure you, it won't happen again."

"Thank you for calling, Ms. Campbell. I'll have my husband email you a copy of the bill. Maybe then he'll calm down." She gave a soft laugh. "I have to say he wasn't very nice when he spoke with Mr. Hargrove. I'm sure you know how fathers can be when their little girls are hurt."

"I can imagine." Would Gavin be as protective of his children? Somehow, she found it easy to think that he would.

She took a quick break to brew a cup of tea in the small kitchen at the back of the library. She wrapped her hands around the mug, willing her fingers to warm up before she called the Belfore home. Roberta's mother was not likely to be as pleasant as Nickie's mom.

The last time Roberta caused trouble in the library, Bella had been confronted by the woman who refused to believe that her "precious R.J." could possibly have been the culprit who had pulled several books out of the shelves and stomped on them. Bella had refused the little girl entrance into the Preschool Story Land until she apologized. Two weeks of no story hour convinced the child to behave, at least temporarily. But her mother wasn't one to help. She had glared at Bella when her daughter begged to return, in a whiny higher pitched version of her mother's voice. Bella hoped Roberta had learned better manners in the intervening years.

I have to be pleasant. Maybe Mrs. Belfore would take the hint and reciprocate. Bella glanced at the calendar one of the teachers had given her. It included notations for those days when the children had vacation days while the teachers worked. Roberta was likely to be home today, just like Nickie.

"Mrs. Belfore? This is Isabella Campbell. From the library."

"Oh, yeah? Mitchell Whatever, that manager who called me to complain about R.J., couldn't be bothered to call back after I threatened to sic my lawyer on him."

Bella's stomach clutched. *Oh, dear.* She decided to plow on ahead. "I don't know about that, but I'm calling to tell you that we can't have fighting on the library grounds. You do know what Roberta did to Nickie McIntosh, don't you?"

A heavy silence followed before she bellowed, "R.J.?"

Maybe she doesn't know. Bella pulled the phone away from her ear. She listened while mother and daughter had a testy conversation that sounded like demands to know the *whole* story.

"The other kid hit her back, she was just protecting herself. Especially after that *boy* knocked R.J. to the ground."

"What boy was that, Mrs. Belfore?" This was getting more complicated by the minute. The woman repeated the question then said, "Eli. Don't know his last name."

"I'll speak to his parents about this," Bella replied. She'd never known Eli to be aggressive and doubted he'd done so without provocation. "I'm sure we can get all this taken care of without having to resort to a lawyer, Mrs. Belfore."

"Is that why you called, to beg me not to take action against you and that weak-kneed little boss of yours?"

Bella bumped her back against her chair, anger building. It was one thing for *her* to think of Mitchell as a milquetoast, but not the patrons, especially this particular one. She looked up at the quiet knock that sounded. Destiny's chatter sounded, followed by a much lower, masculine reply that set Bella's stomach butterflies flipping around again. Gavin poked his head into her office, his raised eyebrow asking a question. Bella covered the phone with one hand and shook her head. She mouthed, "In a minute."

"Mrs. Belfore. I'm sure we can come to an equitable settlement regarding all this. Nickie's doctor bills are something—"

The woman's voice was shrill. "We're not paying no doctor bills, so just get that out of your head! And you'll be hearing from my lawyer, for sure." The call ended with what Bella imagined to be a slam of the phone onto something solid.

Gavin knocked again. "Is it safe to come in?" he asked, his mouth quirking upward. "Sounds like you were dealing with something unpleasant."

She sighed. "You could say that."

Destiny walked past Gavin and claimed the chair near the

window. "You should *see* all the work we did in the bookstore. It's starting to look really good. We still have a bunch of stuff to move, but we'll do more tomorrow. Right, Gavin?"

He nodded, his eyes on Bella.

"Perhaps I could help, too," she replied.

"You're not working tomorrow?" Gavin asked.

Bella shook her head. "A good thing, too. I need some time away before I have to talk to Mitchell again." She glanced at Destiny, who was humming to herself. "If the two of you could just give me a minute, I have one more call to make."

"Okay," Destiny said, her voice bright. "I'm going to call my mom and let her know what we did."

Bella nodded. "Zoe's working in the basement today. I'm sure she won't mind if you use her office next door."

Destiny nodded and left.

"What about me? Where do you want me to go?" Gavin asked. "Or would you prefer that I rub your back while you make the call?" Something about the way his eyes twinkled sent shivers skittering up Bella's spine. "Not if I'm to concentrate," she murmured in an almost whisper. "What I'd prefer has nothing to do with this call. I need privacy. Library business."

"Of course." He stepped away from the door and shut it behind him.

Several minutes later, Bella leaned back in her chair and rubbed her forehead. At least that call had ended more pleasantly than the one with Mrs. Belfore. Eli had insisted that he'd just been protecting Nickie, his friend. She was on his soccer team and a lot smaller than R.J., who was a big old meanie, Eli kept assuring her. And he only pushed her. His stepmother had confirmed what Eli said, repeating that she'd come on the scene about the time Nickie was on the ground, crying and holding one hand over her cheek, blood seeping from between her fingers. Eli had shoved the bigger girl away and then helped Nickie to her feet. Eli's stepmother had called Nickie's mom and waited with the child until her mother arrived to take her to the doctor.

Bella called Mitchell. He didn't answer his phone. Bella pushed herself out of the chair and left her office, eager to go home. Her daughter was seated at a nearby table, chatting with one of the other library workers, a young woman about the same age as Destiny. At least Destiny was happy, and Bella had been hoping they would be able to spend a pleasant week with each other. Now, it seemed, Destiny was looking forward to spending more time at Henry's store than with her.

Her daughter waved a note in Bella's direction. "From Gavin. He had to leave."

Bella nodded, slipped the note into the pocket of her skirt. "Let's go home. It's been a long day. Over dinner, you can tell me all about what you did at Henry's store."

Perhaps it was a good thing Destiny was so taken with helping Henry, given what Bella now had to face. She fingered Gavin's note, eager to read it, hoping it would improve her mood. *After I get home.*

Chapter 16

DESTINY TOOK A SEAT AT THE SMALL DESK IN BELLA'S guest room while she called home. "Mom? I'm so glad I caught you. I have so much to tell you."

"Slow down, Des. Take a deep breath. I haven't heard you so excited in a long time. Did you meet a new boy? Is that what this is all about?"

Destiny gave a short laugh. "No. I couldn't care less about dating. I've spent almost all week at the bookstore. Books and More. I told them I'd work for free in exchange for learning how to run the store, but the owner, Henry, said he wouldn't let me work unless he paid me."

"I thought you wanted to spend time with Bella."

"I do. I am. In the morning and when we're done. But she's so busy at the library, and I don't want to get in her way. Some of the parents are giving her trouble. Their kids fighting, I think she said." She waved one arm in the air, dismissively. "Henry's store is so cool, Mom. We're rearranging things, and his sales have gone way up. Gavin told me, even thanked me."

"Gavin? He owns the store?"

"The owner's nephew. I think he has the hots for Bella." Destiny laughed. "She blushes just like me when I tease her. You know, bright red."

"Hmm. So what are you doing at the bookstore?"

"Everything. Earl lets me work the cash register and Gavin has this new system for tallying all sales, so we know what sells and what doesn't. On the computer. Earl won't use it, so I've taken that over. Now we know what inventory to reorder and everything. And guess what, Mom?" Her enthusiasm was beginning to carry her away again and her words sped up. "I made posters for the downstairs windows, to entice people to come into the store. Marketing stuff! And we're getting more customers every day." She paused. "I want to stay here longer. So I can keep working at the bookstore. Using my marketing degree like you said I should."

Her mother's silence suggested she wasn't happy about Destiny wanting to delay her departure. Bella had urged her to talk to her mother about it. Henry wanted her to stay. He hadn't exactly said so, but she knew he'd be happy if she did. Every morning when she entered the store, the old man beamed and called her his special girl worker, said that she reminded him of his late wife, Ina.

"Mom, please say yes. I'll save the money Henry's going to pay me."

"If you weren't working at the store, would you come home, Des? After seeing Bella, like you wanted."

"Yes, but I'm really needed here. And I'm learning so much. Enough to maybe even run my own store someday. You said I needed to concentrate on getting a job now that I have my degree, and I have one. Right here. Henry's really old. He was sick before I came. Bella called his nephew and *made* him come to help out. Henry can't do half what he needs to do to keep the store going. I heard him telling Gavin that I was helping him out of the hole, making more money, and that means he won't have to sell the store or close it down. What Gavin wants to do."

Her mother sighed into the phone. "It's not your responsibility to keep that store open, Des. I don't like that the owner seems to need you so much. Have you talked with your father about this?"

Destiny ran her fingers along the edge of the desk where she was sitting, unwilling to consider her mother's questions or acknowledge the concern she heard in her mother's voice. "Bella says I'm welcome to stay as long as I want, maybe even through the summer. But she said I should talk to you." Destiny stood up and began to pace, afraid her mom was going to insist that she come home. "I've been so busy … and having so much fun."

"What about your dad?" her mother repeated. "You should call him."

"Already did. He said it's my decision, that he was proud of me for wanting to stand on my own feet. I think he said he was going to call Bella, too." She laughed nervously. *To make sure Henry isn't some serial killer or worse, he'd said.* "And maybe Henry, too."

"Hmm."

"Please, Mom. I really want to do this. It'll help build my resumé. Something else you said I should do." *What else can I say to convince her?*

Destiny looked down at her nails, which she'd stopped chewing. Bella had taken her to get a manicure and pedicure. Now her nails were polished a light pink shade. Bella had urged her to start wearing clothes in a variety of brighter shades. She'd even taken her shopping and helped her pick them out. Like a mother would. What her mom had despaired of doing after Destiny had insisted on wearing only black. And not just jeans and tank tops, but dresses and skirts and blouses that made Destiny feel more professional when she talked to the customers who came to the bookstore, who now were as likely to ask her as Earl about which shelves carried certain book titles and when they might receive books that had been on order before Henry became ill.

Her mother's prolonged sigh dissolved Destiny's fantasy of working in Henry's store, maybe even owning it. "Oh, all right. If your dad is watching out for you. I'm sure he would object if he didn't think it was safe. And if Bella thinks it's okay … But I want you to call me at least once a week and tell me how things are going. Will you do that?"

"Yes! Thanks, Mom. Yes, I'll call. I've been texting Dad about what I'm doing, too. I'll text you, too."

"You know I don't like texting, dear. Phone calls will do."

"Okay. Bella says hi. Gotta go. We're going on a picnic with her best friend, Zoe, and her fiancé. You should see the men around here, Mom. They are *so* hot." She giggled. "But, I don't need a boyfriend. I want to concentrate on my *career*."

She ended the call and rejoined Bella in the kitchen. "What can I do to help?"

"Everything's all packed. Why don't you take it to the car? I promised Zoe I'd text her when we left." Bella picked up her phone. "Those shorts look good on you, Des."

"Thanks." She smiled back at her birth mother who had so recently begun using Destiny's nickname. But only after asking if she was okay with it. Destiny reached for the large picnic basket.

Gavin pulled up to the lakeshore parking area and looked toward the water. Bella had texted him an invitation. Minutes later, Zoe had insisted that he come—bring Henry, too, she'd said—that Bella had made more food than they could possibly eat, and besides, Tör was coming, so Gavin wouldn't be the only guy there.

Bella had seemed distracted for the better part of the week, probably because of that woman who'd made such a stink at the library and then sent her lawyer to threaten not only the library, but the manager *and* Bella, according to Destiny. Bella assured him that she could handle things, but Gavin felt like decking both Mitchell—whose comments had inferred the problem was of Bella's making—and the woman who'd made the threats. Henry said she was a pain in the ass, her daughter not any better. Earl had claimed he'd refused to wait on the woman when she'd come into the store to buy books for her "brat." Not exactly the way to win customers, but Gavin couldn't fault the man for wanting to distance himself from Mrs. Belfore.

He brushed his forelock out of his eyes as the lake breeze picked up. *There they are.* Zoe and Bella were waving at him, having spotted his car, standing out among the more subdued hues of the nearby vehicles. He waved back and grabbed the box of fried chicken he'd ordered, along with two containers of potato salad and coleslaw. He and Tör would polish off what he'd brought if the women didn't want the grease or carbs.

The doctor was bent down, leaning over a fire he was trying to start in a sand pit as Gavin sauntered up the beach.

Bella was facing the lake as she placed items on a blanket on the sand.

"Hey," he said softly. "Have you got a minute?"

She glanced over her shoulder and smiled, setting his heart to pounding and his blood flooding south.

"Sure. I'm glad you were able to get away. How's Henry? I guess you couldn't get him to leave the store?"

Gavin shook his head. "He finally agreed to try out the new computer system I set up. Destiny made a bet with him that he'll be able to use it when she comes in on Monday. That if she could learn it, he could, too. My money's on Destiny."

Bella barked a quick laugh. "I'm glad he's doing better. We'd really hate for you to have to close the store. Des told me you're still thinking about it."

"That decision is on hold for the time being. We may have to revisit it after Destiny leaves. Henry says she's planning to stay all summer. Is that true?"

Bella chuckled. "She finally called her mom. Her dad called me and gave me the third degree about Henry. I assured him Henry loves his daughter, treats her like his favorite grand-daughter, and that her ideas about fixing the store to be more user-friendly were much appreciated. He asked me to let him know if things don't work out. He thought it a fine idea for Des to be away from her mom for a while. On her own is the way he put it."

"Good. Then maybe you'll say yes to my idea." His nervousness that she might not agree began to tell. He raked a hand through his hair for the second time since leaving the car, hoping Bella hadn't noticed.

"I can't say yes if I don't know what it is," she replied softly. "And I'm sorry we haven't had much time lately … you know, for us," she added, her cheeks pinking up.

"You've had it rough the last few days at the library," he

began, hoping she'd want to get away from the unpleasant-ness. "And I knew you'd want to spend time with Destiny." Bella had refused all but his lunch invitations since the girl's arrival and only agreed to them after Destiny began working at Henry's store.

She nodded.

"I'm leaving town next week. Back to Spokane. Have to keep my hand in my own business, you know."

"Oh." Her voice lost its warmth. "Well, then I guess that means you're here to say good-bye."

In spite of their increasingly passionate conclusions to sev-eral dates, she'd insisted they couldn't get serious, because he'd been so clear that he wasn't planning to stay in Evergreen. That topic had ended his getting to second, or was it third, base after their last dinner date before Destiny had shown up. Hadn't he said they could still enjoy each other's company while he *was* here? And what if he decided not to leave, he'd hinted. Her eyes had widened under brows raised in surprise at his declaration. He hadn't planned to make a public pro-nouncement, but he didn't regret telling her if it meant she'd still see him, in spite of Destiny's continuing presence. Was Bella now pulling away from him? It wasn't what he wanted, not how he hoped she'd react. Far from it.

"Not to say good-bye. I'm here to enjoy our picnic and … I want you to come with me. To Spokane. Just think. In my wheels that you like so much. Might even let you drive part of the way. Over the mountains with the top down. The sun on your face, the breeze in your hair. Say yes, Bella. There's a winery near Chelan where we could have a late lunch or maybe an early dinner."

Her eyes were a brilliant green when she gazed at him again. "Where would I stay?" She seemed to have jumped right over the enjoyable ride in his fast car to being with him in Spokane.

"You know where I'd like you to be," he murmured, keeping his voice low. He cleared his throat then whispered. "Wherever you want. My place. I have a guest room. Or," he gulped, "if you insist, I'll get you a motel room."

"But—"

"Destiny won't miss you. Besides, she's old enough to take care of herself and Henry will watch out for her. Or you could ask Zoe to check in. If her parents trust her with Henry, why don't you let stay on her own? And it'll only be for a few days. One to go, a couple for me to make sure all is well at the dealership and one more to come back. Four days. A long weekend, Bella. Just for us." He reached out and grasped her hands, rubbing his thumbs against her skin. "I've missed us not being together."

He hadn't planned to beg, but if that's what it took, he was willing. *Groveling.* What Tör had urged him to do when he'd asked the ER doc what he thought of his plan. Tör had given him a slow smile, told him to go for it.

"When are you leaving?" she asked, folding and unfolding one of the napkins she was holding.

"Tuesday. There's less traffic over Stevens Pass midweek."

"Isn't Snoqualmie faster?"

"Maybe, but there's the winery." He allowed the corners of his mouth to slide upward. "And that highway is a prettier drive."

"Can you give me a day or two to think about it? And talk with Destiny and Zoe?"

"Sure."

He left her and angled in Tör's direction. "Want me to help with those hot dogs?"

The blond doctor grinned. "Here you go. I can tell you brought chicken. You must have read my mind."

"Potato salad, too."

"Perfect. We'll let the women chew on what I just burnt to a crisp after they fill up on the greens and other veggies," Tör retorted.

Bella yawned and stretched both hands over her head, her fingers splayed to catch the wind as Gavin drove east.

"You're awake. Good. We're almost at the winery. You missed some great scenery about an hour back."

She smiled. "I needed the nap more. I figured I'd just miss the big trees and those places that look down into deep canyons. Not my idea of restful scenery." She studied his profile as he drove, one hand on the wheel, the other resting just inside the open window on his side of the roadster. He'd picked her up wearing a sharply creased pair of Dockers and a jacket that no longer covered his shoulders. The top button of his short-sleeved shirt was undone, showing off his tanned neck. Bella couldn't seem to get enough of Gavin. His strong chin and even stronger personality. The way he seemed to genuinely care for his aged uncle, at the same time insisting that they take a pragmatic approach to the store and whether to keep it open.

Destiny's remarks about hunky men were a constant reminder of Gavin. But Bella had no desire to engage in a long-distance romance unlikely to portend a future of togetherness, even though she knew she was falling in love with him. *What am I going to do?* She shook her head to dislodge her questions, her fear of getting her heart broken, and concentrated on the feel of the wind as it lifted her hair off her neck. "Tell me about this winery you want to visit."

He slowed the car and turned right. "Great timing. Here it is. Remind you of anything Old World?" he asked as he pointed.

She gazed up the hill at a building that seemed to glow in the sun. Its red-tiled roof and second-floor balcony with a chocolate-brown railing contrasted with the beige exterior that seemed to nestle into the side of the hill.

Gavin parked the car and helped her out. She turned and stared at the lake on the other side of the highway, its blue-green waters sparkling. "No wonder you wanted to stop here. What a gorgeous view."

"You ain't seen nothin' yet," he drawled. "Wait till you see the inside. Since you're not driving, what's your pleasure? White or red? I'll buy a couple of bottles we can open after we get to my place."

"I'll hold off deciding until I check the menu."

Gavin grasped her hand and they walked up the brick-faced steps to the entrance of the winery. The interior space continued the tasteful Tuscan theme.

Bella stared at the rows of bottles to the left of the entrance. They were nestled in diamond-shaped squares behind a long counter, along with displays of accoutrements wine aficionados might like. The back wall sported numerous pictures of the grape-laden vines, the casks in which the wine was stored, and before- and after-pictures of the building.

"Welcome!" A woman greeted them.

"We're here for a late lunch." He looked around. "Unless you're not serving today."

The woman nodded. "Only in the small dining room, where we're rearranging the tables. The large one is being prepared for a private event later this afternoon and evening. If you'd like to explore the grounds, I'll get you in a few minutes."

"Thank you." Gavin grasped Bella's hand. "Let's check out the patio."

They walked across the flagstone patio to one of three small bridges leading to a grassy island surrounded on two sides by waterfalls cascading down from a cliff face dressed in vines and small evergreens. The waterfalls fed a circular streambed in which large, colorful koi lazily swam about. When Bella held a hand over the water, several of the fish swam closer, a sign they expected to be fed. Butterflies flitted between the flowers that decorated the vines covering the fence enclosing the large pond feeding the upper watercourse. She closed her eyes, easily imagining a wedding occurring on the island, serenaded by the sounds of the water and the birds that sang in the larger trees.

She glanced in Gavin's direction. His gaze was soft as he smiled back. "Like it?"

She nodded. "So beautiful."

"Our hostess just signaled we can go in and eat." He escorted her into a small dining room whose entrance was at the back of the winery, its windows looking east onto brownish-green hills.

"I'm surprised we don't see vines there."

The woman stood next to their table with two large menu books. "That soil is being prepared. Next year, you'll see new vines there," she explained. "Bringing our total acreage in vines to more than forty acres. We own nearly two hundred. All the way up the hill behind us and across the road to the lake."

Bella nodded. "What a gorgeous site for a winery." She accepted the menu from the woman and listened to the specials available for lunch. After she and Gavin ordered, she sipped a glass of sempre amore, a white blend that she declared delicious.

Gavin nodded. "I'll get us a bottle."

After a relaxed lunch, Gavin insisted on showing her the grounds. They spent the next two hours wandering around the winery and gazing at Lake Chelan in the near distance. Bella waved to a boat laden with passengers as it chugged by, nosing across the deep-water lake.

"You've never been here before?" Gavin asked.

"No. But I've read about it: how long it is, how deep. Maybe I'll have to plan a trip here. What about you?"

"When I was twelve, my Scout troop had an overnight near the north end, at a place called Stehekin. Hikers often head out from there."

"I'm glad you said we'd stop here. I never realized how beautiful it is."

"Come on, let's go pick up the wine I bought. I want us to make Spokane by dinnertime and we have another three hours to go."

As Gavin and Bella entered the winery, she saw that the large dining room had been set up for a reception. Bella sucked in her breath when she saw a bride emerge from a room near the small dining room. Another young woman and a child who looked to be about three emerged from the same room. The child skipped past the bride holding a basket overflowing with what looked like rose petals. The woman accompanying the bride followed the child and reached down to lift the train and the lace overlay of the bride's dress off the floor of the winery as they headed toward a large grassy area. The seats set up there were arranged to face a Tuscan-style gazebo.

As Bella watched, the groom, his attendant and the officiating minister took their places in the gazebo. Music sounded and the bride's attendant, in a pale peach cocktail-length dress, began walking down the aisle. The little girl followed her and then stopped. She looked back at the bride, the basket tipped, and several rose petals fluttered onto the ground. The unaccompanied bride reached out a hand, which the tiny flower girl grasped, and together, they walked toward the gazebo to delighted murmurs from the onlookers.

"Beautiful, don't you think?" Gavin whispered in Bella's ear.

She wasn't sure he was referring to the bride or to the wedding scene. Her heart pressed into her throat and her eyes threatened to tear up at the thought that perhaps the child was the bride's daughter. *That might have been me if I'd kept Destiny.* "So sweet."

The bride reached for her groom, who led her up one step into the gazebo to exchange vows. The flower girl was coaxed into the lap of an older woman sitting on the aisle. It was easy for Bella to imagine Destiny taking such a walk, looking resplendent in a dress just like the bride's. *Some time in the future*, Bella thought, *on her father's arm.* Not like this bride, who'd traversed the aisle alone until the little girl joined her. *I wonder what her story is.*

"You ready?" Gavin finally asked. A bag holding two bottles of wine dangled from the fingers of his left hand. "We need to get out of here before that reception starts and the fireworks begin."

Bella nodded. When she'd dated Ethan, she'd thought she might get married. But that dream had died when she realized they could never be happy together. She sighed.

"Wishing that was you?" Gavin asked as they walked to his car, past a stretch limousine decorated in pale peach and white streamers.

"A dream of my youth," she rasped then cleared her throat. "Weddings always make me weepy," she explained as she fumbled in her purse for a tissue to blot her eyes.

"You're not exactly a senior citizen," he said as he started the car. "Happy tears, I hope."

Gavin glanced at Bella. He hadn't expected to see a wedding, but had the bride's hair been a deep burnished red, it could have been Bella under that gazebo, staring into her groom's eyes. The man under the gazebo hadn't taken his eyes off the woman since she'd begun that little walk up the aisle. *Probably thinking she'd never been so beautiful.* He recalled similar feelings when he was a groom. His image of Eileen morphed into one starring Bella, who was so different from Eileen. Bella was too kind, too caring, so unselfish. She'd welcomed her long-lost daughter into her life so easily.

Gavin had observed her with the little kids in the library, when she'd comforted a small boy, his first day at the Preschool Story Land without his mother. Bella had wrapped an arm around the child's shoulders and kept him near her through the entire session. When she called a halt, the child was no longer unhappy and ran to his mother to show her the book they'd been reading. Bella had even taken on that awful Mrs. Belfore, insisting that the city attorney sit in on one of the Chapter Read Along sessions so that he could see how she ran it. Those gatherings couldn't possibly have contributed to the fighting that had occurred. Bella was strong; she had made a life for herself. Without her parents' support. Gavin couldn't imagine Bella needing to lean on a man, though he felt increasingly protective of her, *wanting* her to lean on him, wanting her to want him. As she seemed to whenever they'd exchanged kisses and caresses.

Gavin knew he'd lost his heart to her. Something he'd vowed would never happen. But Bella was right. He had no plans to leave Spokane, even if he took over that dealership in Bellevue. He shouldn't have begun to imagine they could be a couple permanently, but he was no longer able to think of life without her. Why he'd invited her to come with him to Spokane. What he was feeling for her wasn't just lust, though she brought that out in him. He knew she was as attracted to him as he was to her, but how—

An air horn from an eighteen-wheeler interrupted his thoughts and he eased back into the right lane to let the big truck pass. Bella had closed her eyes and appeared to be napping again. Something she probably needed, what with those sleepless nights she'd mentioned after she'd spent so many hours talking with Mitchell, meeting with the city attorney, and with Nickie's and Eli's parents. According to busybody Destiny, the Belfore bitch's attorney had refused to allow her to meet with anyone from the library so that they might come to a satisfactory conclusion to the unpleasantness generated by her daughter.

I'll let her sleep. Gavin enjoyed glancing Bella's way as he drove. She'd worn a dark green sundress that complemented her skin tones. Her hair, previously in a ponytail, now flowed down her shoulders, almost covering her breasts. Before they'd left the winery, he'd closed the car windows and hit the button to set the roof in place. Those rain clouds to the east looked ominous. No way did he want his woman getting wet. *My woman.* He sensed she'd be upset if she knew he was thinking so possessively. Hadn't she told him, more than once, that theirs could only be a temporary relationship? Gavin sucked in his breath. His brain agreed. Logic demanded that he accept her words. Too bad his heart and the rest of him disagreed.

Chapter 17

"WHY DON'T YOU OPEN THE DOOR WHILE I GET OUR suitcases?" Gavin handed his keys to Bella.

She stood aside as he entered, carrying her suitcase and his, her heart thudding in her chest. Gavin had given her options, even been a gentleman about it, but going to a hotel seemed a colossal waste of money. She picked up her suitcase and wandered into the hall. The door on the left, to Gavin's bedroom, was ajar. *Wrong room.*

His voice sounded from behind her. "Guest room's on your right."

Bella felt her cheeks heat as she opened the door to a room that looked more like an office than a guest room. The desk in the corner was cluttered with papers. A gooseneck lamp was canted at an angle, as if to throw light on the nearest wall.

"Here are sheets and blankets for you." He stood in the

doorway. "I need to call Zeke. I'll help you with the bed in a couple of minutes."

"Take your time." She closed the door, shoved her suitcase to the side and began to tuck the sheets around the bed. Their words in the car, *his* words, his actions, too, told Bella he was a good man, a caring man. Not just for Henry, but for her. Zoe had urged Bella to focus on the present *and* the future, what Gavin represented. A man Bella had come to trust, who hadn't judged her when she'd told him about Destiny. As simple as that, he'd wormed his way into Bella's heart. He thrilled her with a look, or a quiet touch, like that night when they'd walked in the park after their business dinner. A dinner where they'd talked more about Henry than about the bookstore. That first kiss into her palm should have warned her he was also a lady-killer. Her bones had nearly melted into a puddle of longing for what that kiss hinted.

Bella finished dressing the guest bed with a dark blue duvet and pillows in similarly hued cases, belatedly aware that Gavin's conversation in the other room had stopped.

He opened the door and pointed to the bed. "You finished already?"

"I saw no point in waiting for you. Did you find out what you wanted to know?"

Gavin nodded. "I need to stop in the office tomorrow. Early. Want to come with me, or would you prefer to stay here? I could drop you off downtown if you want to shop. You know." He pointed to her feet. "In case you want to look around, buy new shoes ... whatever." His neck seemed to redden.

Why is he nervous? Bella cocked her head at him and smirked. "What's on your mind? Never mind. I think I know." Was he as aware of her choice of the guest room as she was?

His lopsided smile confirmed what she'd guessed. "I guess

we men are easy to read. And I *am* a man. Red-blooded and all." He backed toward the door. "Come on. I'll give you the tour."

The living room, with a large-screen television screen on the wall, contained furniture likely to appeal to a bachelor. Bella admired the new appliances in the kitchen and laughed when he admitted he had barely broken in the stove. She was jealous of the spacious master bath. "Now that's a room I'd love to have in my house."

When he opened his bedroom door, she saw that his bed sported a covering in three shades of brown and beige. The plush carpet repeated those colors along with a bright blue that barely tamed the darker tones. The dresser was massive and oak, as was the headboard of the king-size bed. Even the side table was oak, sturdier-looking than her furniture at home.

Bella stepped out of the room, ignoring Little Devil Bella's appreciative comments and suggestions about how best to test out Gavin's bed. "Are we going out to dinner, or should we rustle up something here?"

"I don't have anything fresh, after being gone so long. I'll order in, if that's okay with you."

Gavin and Bella ate a light dinner and topped it off with the red wine he had purchased at the winery.

"Let's take a walk before the sun goes down." He reached for her hand and led her outside.

"It's pretty here. I didn't know what to expect," she said as they began to walk.

"Another place you've never visited?"

"Right."

Keeping his tone casual, he asked, "Ever given any thought to leaving Evergreen? Maybe moving here where it rains less, has more sun?"

"And is hotter in the summer and snowier in the winter." Bella shifted her eyes off the horizon, now glowing with hues of purple, red, and gold as the sun moved behind the mountain peaks to the west. "I like the western part of the state. Evergreen's where my friends are, my job, my house."

"You're pretty definite about that."

"Why wouldn't I be? Aren't you settled here? You said you don't plan to move. After all, your dealership's here. That's why you needed to come back."

Frustrated that she hadn't picked up on his hint, Gavin kicked at a stone lying on the path. "I'd never let a job keep me from ... you know, learning about another place, having an adventure, maybe even settling down. What about you, Bella, if you met someone, fell in love, and he didn't live in Evergreen?" He dared to ask, his gaze on the tops of their shoes as they left the sidewalk and entered a little pocket park.

Bella slipped her hand from his. "I doubt that will happen." But her voice was tinged with wistfulness he wanted to sweep away in a kiss, whose passion he hoped she would return.

"Why not? You're the kind of woman any smart man would want. Or don't you plan to have a family? I saw how you looked at that little girl in the wedding party. Don't you want children of your own?"

"I already have a child."

"But you never raised her. You know what I mean." Images of two children, a boy and a girl, each with Bella's red hair swam in his mind, and a third one, too, a little girl with Bella's eyes and Gavin's hair color, maybe taking after him in wanting to be an entrepreneur.

"Can we talk about something else?" Bella pointed to the darkening sky. "Don't you think we should go back soon? It's getting late and you said you want to be at the office before it opens tomorrow."

He stifled a sigh, grasped her hand again and turned toward his condo. "You're right."

Gavin listened as Bella turned on the shower in the guest bath. He forced himself to review Zeke's last message about the dealership and failed miserably when all he could think about was himself in that shower with Bella, soaping her down, she soaping him down, each sliding their hands in and around sensitive places. He was relieved when the water stopped and silence again surrounded him.

From the hall several minutes later, Bella called out. "I'm going to bed, Gavin. See you in the morning."

He remained in the living room. "You don't have to get up when I do. Feel free to sleep in. I'll call you for lunch."

"Okay." The guest room door closed.

Gavin listened as Bella moved around his office qua guest room. Bella had surprised him when she didn't object to his bringing her suitcase into his place. But she didn't offer to sleep with him, either. Her being in his guest room was better than nothing, he figured, but how was he going to nod off, knowing she was on the other side of the wall?

The squeaky floorboard on the far side of his desk near the window sounded again. Maybe Bella was looking out the window. Gavin heard a muffled voice and concluded she had called Destiny. Not the first time she'd done that since they'd left Evergreen. She was a caring mother, even though she'd had little experience in that role.

He shifted uncomfortably in his chair for the third time, his arousal more painful than when he'd first sat down. Unable to decide what to do, when to say that he loved her—never his intent, but he'd fallen hard and wanted her to know—he rose from his chair and adjusted his trousers. Again. He walked past the kitchen, thinking fleetingly that maybe he'd invite her to join him. He imagined her draped in a satin robe, beautifully nude under it, and knew his invitation would be going back on his vow not to introduce her to his larger, much-too-cold-and-empty bed.

Bella invaded his thoughts day and night. Was this true love, the forever kind that was strong enough to stand up to the variety of crises that could occur? He knew what he felt for Bella was different from how he'd felt about Eileen. The times he'd spent with Bella told him she wasn't the love-'em-and-leave-'em kind. She was a woman his uncle called a "keeper." More than once. Probably why Henry had made that comment in the hospital. *Damn Henry's words.* The old man's prediction had thrown Gavin off his game, unsettled him.

But did he really want a long-term relationship with Bella? His experience with Eileen had killed his interest in any relationship with even a whiff of permanence. Well, that wasn't exactly true. He'd wanted his marriage with Eileen to last, but circumstances made it easy to end that unholy alliance before it destroyed him.

When he was with Bella, he felt … different. With Bella, he sometimes saw himself floating on air, like champagne bubbles sliding up a tall flute, enjoying a bright, fun, and exciting present *and* future. Something he wanted more of.

Was this what love was *supposed* to feel like? If so, he'd lost his battle not to give his heart away. But should he tell her how he felt? She'd reminded him more than once that she would never fall in love again. That it was too dangerous, like what had happened when she'd fallen for Taylor, that brainless teenage scumbag she'd told him about, or Ethan what's-his-name that Tör had mentioned in passing. Ethan must have done a real number on Bella. But did she also mean that she couldn't love *him*?

Gavin slowed his steps as he approached her door and knocked quietly. "Bella? Is everything okay? Is the bed too hard, too soft? Do you need anything, want anything?" *Like me?*

The soft murmuring he'd heard stopped and footsteps told him she must have approached the door. He placed his hand on the knob, intent on preventing her from opening it and seeing how much he desired her.

But she didn't open the door. "I was just talking with Destiny. She and Earl created two window displays today, in between taking care of more customers than last week." She laughed softly. "I think Destiny has Earl wrapped around her little finger. She said he barely opened his book all day, what with all the changes she insisted on making in the store, moving shelves and changing out where books are displayed, how they are displayed."

"Where was Henry? Didn't he help?"

"Des said he was tired, so she sent him home early. Convinced him that she and Earl could handle things."

Gavin heard the squeak of the bedsprings. *She must be sitting on the bed, or maybe climbing in, losing the robe.* Was it shimmery? Perhaps moving like flickering flames if red or like water falling if blue as it shifted around her body? He didn't have to look down to know how his thoughts were affecting him.

Her voice turned firm. "Good night, Gavin. I'll see you in the morning."

"Okay." He backed away from her door, entered his bedroom, tossed his clothes into the hamper, and headed for the shower, a long cold one, as if that would help. He climbed into bed minutes later, intent on going over his plans for the next day in spite of the thoughts that continued to intrude. Of Bella.

In the light from the side table next to his bed, he reached for the notes that told him the Bellevue dealership was ripe for new ownership. The current franchise holder had encouraged Gavin to make an offer, that the manager wasn't doing the job. Turning the page, he jotted down issues he planned to address tomorrow, first with Hortense and then with Zeke. Hortie would let him know if what Zeke had already sent him was an accurate picture of how the business was doing in his absence. He hadn't planned to be gone so long, a short week that had stretched to eight.

A half hour later, he was reaching over to turn out the light when a soft knock sounded.

"Are you asleep?" Bella asked, her voice almost a whisper.

"Not yet. Come on in," he invited, shoving his papers onto the side table.

Bella opened the door, wearing a pale blue satin robe that she clutched tightly across her breasts. Her feet were bare and the robe opened enough to give Gavin a glimpse of her legs from just above her knees to her toes. "I just wanted to say that I've been thinking about what we talked about today. In the car. At the winery. Over dinner." Her robe shifted as she stepped into the room, displaying more leg.

"Oh?" His chest was bare and his brow arched as he scanned her form. He looked as if he was trying to recall their conversation.

Bella wondered briefly if he slept in the nude as she noted the breadth of his bare chest, the width of his shoulders that straightened and pressed against the headboard. She loosened her death-grip on her robe and it slid off her shoulders and shushed quietly to the floor.

Gavin took in an audible breath as he stared at her in her black teddy and matching bikini panties.

She felt her neck and face flush, hoping he wouldn't think her too forward, but she'd been unable to stop thinking about this trip as an opportunity to "take life by the balls and enjoy it for once," as Zoe had so succinctly declared when Bella asked her what she thought of Gavin's invitation to go with him to Spokane. Now here she was, not in a motel room, alone and lonely. Not even in his barely-there guest room that was really an office. In *his* room. A testosterone-filled room that seemed to fit Gavin perfectly.

"Your guest room is very nice," she began, feeling the need to explain, aware that her voice was raspy, her throat dry. "I know you and I—we've been walking around this attraction we seem to have, that I have, that I can't seem to deny—"

"Me, either," he interrupted.

"So ... I just decided, we need, we *deserve* to test whether it's real, even if you're not going to be with Henry much longer ..." Her voice seemed to trail off. "And, um, I was lonely," she murmured. "In that bed all by myself." She took a tentative step toward him. "So ... I ... are you lonely, too?"

Gavin cleared his throat. "As a matter of fact." He slid a bare foot out from under the covers.

Bella had never thought of men's toes as sexy, but she couldn't stop eyeing Gavin's as they seemed to reach for the floor, followed by his foot, then his ankle, and his right leg. A long leg whose muscles confirmed his strength. She pondered for a moment whether he was a runner. He'd mentioned how he missed using the gym when he was in Evergreen, how he'd visited the Y several mornings before going to the bookstore.

"Maybe I could solve your loneliness problem. Mine, too." He patted the side of the bed next to where he sat. "Or would you like this side?"

"Yes, please."

He smiled at her, tossed back the covers and stood up, naked, an adult male ready for action and proud of it.

Even better than I imagined, and her heart seemed to seize. She stepped closer.

Gavin took her in his arms and welcomed her with a kiss that sent her pulse soaring, the heat of her cheeks encompassing her entire body as he pressed himself against her curves. For the next several minutes, they kissed and caressed each other. When he eased her onto the bed, she no longer wore the teddy or the panties.

"I couldn't stop thinking of you," she murmured when she reached for him. "I hope you don't mind."

"Not at all," he said as he stroked her, prompting little gasps she couldn't seem to stop and that erased from her mind all thoughts other than of this beautiful man, this man who seemed as taken with her as she was with him. *I could love him,* she thought and gave herself over to doing just that.

Dawn broke shortly after they made love again, or was it the third time? Gavin had given up counting the number of times Bella had come apart in his arms. He'd slept little, but he didn't care. Their lovemaking had been soul-satisfyingly pleasurable. He should have been exhausted. Instead, he felt energized. He looked over at Bella. She was curled against him, asleep, a light smile on her face, as if still relishing their last orgasm. Gavin pulled the blanket up over her shoulder and gathered her close. She murmured and slid one leg closer to his. He closed his eyes and slipped into sleep, happy to doze another hour before preparing to go to the office.

Gavin woke with a start, the sun blinding him with its intensity as it poured through the window, whose blinds were now open. The smell of coffee curled through the air, tempting him to get up to greet the day. He yawned and dropped his feet to the floor. "What time is it?" he mumbled and grabbed his watch.

"You're awake. Good. Ready for breakfast?" Bella wore her silk robe, over which she'd wrapped an apron tied tightly around her waist. She looked good enough to eat. She handed him a steaming mug. "You'd better hurry. It's almost eight. Didn't you want to be at the office before anyone else?"

"Why didn't you wake me?" He bounded out of bed, grabbed the mug, and took a quick sip.

"You looked so cute sleeping like that, your hair all rumpled and … and everything." She blushed.

"No time for breakfast. I'll just grab a quick shower." He dashed into the bathroom, finished his ablutions in record time, not bothering with a shave. He'd take care of that while driving to the office, using the spare electric razor he kept in the glove box. Wouldn't be the first time he'd multitasked on the I-90 between his condo in Spokane Valley and the dealership in downtown Spokane.

Bella handed him a muffin topped with egg and a slice of bacon. "Take this with you. Business always goes better when you've had some protein."

He smacked a kiss on her lips as he headed out the door, stopped, and raced back for those notes he'd studied the night before. "You're a genius. Beautiful, too," he crooned. "I'll call you later."

"Take your time. I think I'll go for a walk after I clean up."

He waved as he dashed outside to his car. *She's too good to be true.* After he checked on the business, he'd get her to see that they *could* be a couple. Before they drove back to Evergreen and he took on that other dealership.

Gavin stared at the computer screen on his desk then back at Zeke and Hortense seated in front of him. "These summaries tell me everything went smoothly," he finally stated. "Better than those weekly emails."

Hortense smiled, a bit smugly, Gavin thought.

"What about Farley and Irving? Have they been minding their manners?"

Zeke spoke up. "Well, uh, when they got into it again, I fired them. Hortense told me I could."

"With pay for what they earned before you canned them?"

Hortense nodded. "Of course. Along with a statement that they shouldn't expect a recommendation from you. Not that I think Farley would ask. I hear he's working at a used car place in Lewiston."

Gavin nodded. *A real comedown from this place.* Too bad for Farley. "What about Irving?"

Zeke cleared his throat. "He asked me if he could talk to you. Says he's real sorry. Wants his job back. He's called me every day since I gave him the axe."

Gavin leaned back in his chair, and raised his arms to cradle his hands against the back of his neck. "What do you think, Hortie? Has Irv learned his lesson?"

"You'll know better if you talk to him. His wife just found out she's pregnant again."

"How many kids does that make?" Gavin asked, mentally

counting past one hand's worth.

"Six or seven. Ask him yourself." She chortled. "Seems he knows better how to make babies than to stay out of fistfights in the showroom. I think Farley dissed his wife."

Gavin fought the urge to utter good riddance to them both. He leaned over his desk. "Okay. Hortie, call Irving and tell him I want to see him here at five sharp. No excuses, even if he has to leave dinner with the rug rats. Tell him it's up to him to convince me to take him back." He was about to say something else when the intercom buzzed.

"Want me to get that?" Hortense offered.

Gavin shook his head. "What is it, Darla?"

"I have a woman here who says she's meeting you for lunch. Shall I send her on back?"

Gavin glanced at his watch, surprised the morning had sped by so rapidly. "Tell her I'll be right out." Bella and images of their night together flashed through his mind, generating heat that raced upward, coloring his neck and face, then downward with a groin-filling sensation that threatened to embarrass him if he didn't regain some control.

He pushed his chair back from the desk, but hesitated to stand and give himself away. "Zeke, before you leave this afternoon, we need to talk. Hortie, have all the sales numbers in front of me when I come back from lunch. The ones broken down by salesperson, not just these overall ones. Which look good, by the way. Zeke, you did a great job. Appreciate the effort."

He reached over his desk and shook Zeke's hand, noting the man's palm was damp, like he'd been expecting to have been found wanting. He must not have known that Hortense would have alerted Gavin in her twice-a-week texts if things had gone from bad to worse. What she called the mice playing.

Hortense stood up and headed for her office. "Those reports will be on your desk when you get back. Oh, look at that pretty thing!" she exclaimed, and pointed a manicured finger in Bella's direction.

She was wearing a casual pair of dark blue Capri pants that hugged her hips and legs. Her blue and white striped V-necked blouse tastefully hinted at her upper curves. A matching scarf held her red curls off her face. She waved at him and smiled, then wandered toward one of the new cars in the showroom, a black number Gavin had ordered moved off the lot earlier that morning. Now that it was polished and shiny, it was drawing buyers like bees to honey as they entered the expansive area designed to put stars in the customers' eyes—and an itch to spend money for the privilege of rescuing the merchandise from others who coveted the fancy wheels.

Gavin left his office, strode over to Bella and gripped her elbow as he gave her a quick peck on the cheek. "How'd you get here?" he asked quietly.

"Took the bus."

"Let's go." The sooner she left the showroom, the less likely Hortense was to demand an introduction.

Later that afternoon, Gavin was satisfied that his current business would support the additional outlay of funds needed to take on the Bellevue dealership. He gave Zeke a promotion in recognition of his continued management of the Spokane business. If Gavin's plan for the Bellevue business panned out, within six months he'd offer partial ownership of the Spokane dealership to Zeke as incentive for keeping things going smoothly. He faxed an offer to take over the Bellevue franchise and leaned back in his chair.

After lunch, Bella had borrowed his car to drive around Spokane. She planned to pick him up at six if he didn't call her sooner. How long he intended to listen to Irving plead his case depended on his former salesman. Gavin looked up when the man knocked on his office door.

Gavin waved him in. "Have a seat. Hortie tells me your wife's in the family way again. How many does that make?"

"Seven, assuming we only have one. The last time, we got twins." The man gave Gavin a rueful smile and sat down, wearing what looked like a new suit. His shirt was blinding white, his tie a subdued brown stripe that looked good with his dark brown jacket and trousers. Unlike the salespeople in the Bellevue dealership, Gavin's people knew how to dress.

"Tell me why I should take you back." Gavin listened while Irving took responsibility for his actions and assured him it wouldn't happen again.

"You have my word, Gavin. You'll see. I need this job, want to do good here. And my wife's counting on me. The kids, too."

Gavin nodded. "Okay. See you tomorrow, Irv. Eight sharp. By the way, that suit looks good."

Gavin watched as the man left. He seemed to walk taller as he left the showroom, proceeding directly to the front door. He waved to one of the saleswomen before climbing into his car, a broad smile on his face.

Grabbing his suit jacket, Gavin spied Bella parking his car in the side lot. He left his office congratulating himself on successfully avoiding Hortense and those questions she was sure to ask about Bella the minute she got the chance.

Chapter 18

DESTINY SCAMPERED UP THE STEPS AND INTO HENRY'S office. The old man smiled as he looked up from the sales sheets of the past week. "Looking good, Henry? Better than you thought? I told you we're doing better."

He nodded. "You're a miracle worker, pretty girl. Let's see ol' Gavin try to shut us down now."

"He can't do that. *You're* the owner. Don't you think he'll be happy when he sees those numbers?" She leaned against the doorjamb and rubbed her shoulder against the wood, hoping Gavin would be in a good mood when he returned from Spokane. Especially since he'd taken Bella with him. They deserved each other. And, if Henry was right, Gavin liked Bella as much as Bella seemed to like him. *It takes all kinds,* Destiny mentally shrugged. He for certain wasn't her favorite person.

"Your back still hurting you from all that moving and shifting you and Earl did?"

"Don't worry about me. After a hot shower tonight, my back will be fine. You should take a break and come see all the people in the store. It's practically standing room only downstairs."

The murmur of customers could be heard over the soft music Destiny had insisted they play over the outdated sound system she'd found hidden in the storage room behind a bunch of boxes. Miracle of miracles, Earl had been able to get it working.

"In a little while. I want to finish checking that order for new books you slapped on my desk yesterday."

Destiny grinned and planted a quick kiss on Henry's shiny forehead before she walked out of the room. "Okay. But you *have* to see what we've done, especially those big posters Earl put up and the window displays and *everything*," she enthused.

"Yeah, yeah ..." he mumbled.

She looked back in time to see him rubbing the side of his head. "Do you have a headache, Henry? I'll bring you some aspirin."

Before Henry could reply, Earl called Destiny's name, asking for help at the register. She flew back down the stairs and spent the next few minutes helping customers with their book purchases and answering questions about when the local author of the latest bestseller would be doing a book signing. Her books were now prominently displayed on one of the front tables.

"We're going to start a website next week, and it will have a spot for people to sign up to receive our newsletter. If you want, I could take your name and email so you'll receive it."

"Good idea." A woman and two men signed up.

After they left, Destiny teased one of the regulars, urging him to buy a book this time. He was a businessman who came in every day to pick up three newspapers. "This book is full of that information you're always looking for to keep you ahead of the competition."

"You're a born saleswoman, Destiny." He smiled at her. "You could teach my daughter a thing or two if she would only get her nose out of her iPad."

"Well, bring her in. We could use more help around here."

"She's only fifteen. Doesn't know the meaning of work."

"I'm sure Earl and I can find something for her to do, and we could pay her in discounted books unless she wants cash." She giggled, thinking of herself when she'd first begun working in the bookstore in Denver. "Excuse me, Mr. Chalmers. I have to help this nice lady here."

Forty minutes later, the crowd at the register thinned. Earl was walking around, per Destiny's orders, asking people if they needed help finding what they were looking for. *Wait till I tell Bella what we've done.* She suspected her birth mother would be proud of her. She'd call her mom tonight to thank her for insisting that Destiny major in marketing. She'd barely tolerated the classes, but what she'd thought was a waste of time had come in handy when she'd spied the posters in the storage room. *They really work!* Books were moving out of the store at a record pace and she'd heard compliments from two nearby store owners who'd noticed how she and Earl had spiffed up the place, washing the windows and brightening the walls with colorful fliers. Why Henry had never put them up, she couldn't fathom, but he didn't object when she did so.

Destiny walked slowly up the stairs to insist that Henry sit at the register and talk to people. He liked doing it, he'd finally admitted, because Ina had told him it was important. He'd turned that duty over to Earl when their customers had dwindled. But not anymore. More people were coming in to see what they had and how they'd changed the store. Word was getting out that it was under new management, as a large banner proclaimed.

Henry had laughed heartily when Destiny had shown it to him. "Maybe not totally new, but better'n before." Even Earl had smiled.

"Henry?" Destiny called. "Time to show your face. Your public is waiting."

He didn't reply.

From the landing, she looked out over the railing at people roaming the aisles on the first floor, the hum of conversation almost drowning out the music. "Henry?"

She walked into his office, surprised the old man was slumped over his desk. He looked as if he was sleeping. She gently nudged his shoulder, but he didn't move.

"Henry?" Something about the way he was staring with half-open eyes, as if seeing nothing, jolted her. She shook his arm forcefully. "Henry!"

She backed away from the man's still form, her heart racing as if she'd just finished a marathon.

"Earl!" she screamed. "Earl, get up here!" She bumped into the chair she'd perched on so many times while convincing Henry to let her make changes in the store and slid onto the seat. Earl lumbered into the office, his breath sounding harsh in the silence that now seemed to envelop the second floor. Several customers followed him and looked with concern over his stooped shoulders at her, then at Henry.

Destiny pointed wordlessly as tears flooded her eyes and slid down her cheeks.

Earl leaned over Henry. He placed a hand against his friend's neck and checked his pulse before muttering, "He's gone."

"I'll call 9-1-1," someone said from the doorway.

Sudden conversation erupted when word that Henry had

died filtered down the stairs. One of the regulars, a woman who worked at the delicatessen three doors down, approached Destiny and pulled her into her ample arms. "You stay right here, honey. There are people downstairs still wanting to buy books. I know how to work the register. I'll take care of that while you and Earl tend to dear Henry. Poor old man, to die at his desk like that."

Destiny nodded, unsure what to do. The woman's arms reminded her of Bella when she'd hugged her after Noah dumped her, and her mother whenever Destiny had needed a hug. Even times when she didn't.

It seemed forever, but it couldn't have been long before a siren sounded and two EMTs pounded up the stairs, one of them hefting equipment boxes, the other carrying what looked like a folded-up stretcher. They checked Henry, and confirmed what they'd been told. At a word from Earl, one of them approached Destiny.

"You're shaking," he said as he checked her pulse. "Let's get you into a blanket."

Earl mumbled, "Looks like she's going into shock. She's so pale."

Was that why she felt dizzy, nauseous, too weak to get up?

"Here. Let's get you down on the floor," the EMT suggested, easing Destiny off the chair and onto the floor then lifting her legs and resting them on the chair. "So the blood will go back where it belongs," he explained.

"Stay with her, Earl," the first responder said. "We'll take her in, too."

Earl sat down next to Destiny and reached for her hand. "You're going to be okay, honey. Just don't pass out on me. Medic stuff freaks me out."

Minutes later Destiny watched as the EMTs opened a collapsible stretcher to its full length, and lifted Henry's limp body onto it. They covered him with a blanket, strapped him down and carried him out of the office, their boots thumping on the stairs as they left the scene.

When they returned, the EMTs each took her by an arm and lifted her onto the chair. "You feeling better now?"

"I have to go with him," she said, wiping her eyes. "Earl, help me. We *have* to go with him, but not in the Medic One truck." She struggled to her feet, wobbled for a moment and reached for Henry's old friend. Earl placed an arm around her waist. He'd said Henry would never implement the ideas she had thrown at the two of them over the past few weeks. But when asked, Earl had helped her, had convinced Henry to give her ideas a try.

"I got 'er. You guys can leave now. We'll meet you at the hospital."

"You sure? We can transport her in the rig," one of them offered.

"No. Earl'll take me," Destiny replied. "I have Bella's car."

Earl seemed doubtful, but didn't object when Destiny clung to his other hand. "Okay, kid. Let's go."

On their way out, Earl nodded at Opal, who was still manning the register. "You'll lock up?" He handed her the key.

"Don't worry about a thing. You can come get it at the deli. I work late tonight. And I'll put a note on the door."

For the first time since Destiny had begun working at the store, Earl walked her to her car and insisted she let him drive. He who wouldn't ride a bus, who rode his bike to work. *Does he even know how to drive?* Destiny sensed this was not the time to ask, and she was too shaky to do it.

He took her key, hesitated for an instant then climbed into the driver's seat. He closed his eyes for a moment, took two big breaths and turned the key. He jerked when the car's engine turned over.

"Are you okay?" Destiny asked.

He stared at the street as he eased out of the alley and onto the thoroughfare. "Let me think. Right turn then left and straight," he said, his voice a croaking whisper, as if reading an invisible map, breathing audibly.

"Have you been there before? The hospital?"

He nodded. "On my bike. When Henry was sick."

Destiny closed her eyes and leaned against the seat. She had to call Gavin. She rummaged in her pocket for her phone and scanned the contacts stored there but couldn't find Gavin's name. *Maybe Bella will tell him.* She stifled another sob, not wanting to distract Earl who was driving so slowly, hunched over the steering wheel he was holding in a death grip. When another driver honked and swung around him, Earl jerked and swore under his breath.

"It's okay, Earl. You're doing fine. It's that big white building. Straight ahead."

He drove into the ER loading zone and shut off the car, not seeming to notice that he wasn't in a regular parking spot. He trotted around the car and reached for Destiny's hand.

She took it and together, they walked into the building. Earl seemed to be shaking as much as Destiny. They approached the desk, gave their names, and asked for information about Henry.

They were told to have a seat.

Destiny watched as a nurse left the desk and went into another room. Was that where they'd taken Henry?

Bella stifled a yawn as she drove to Gavin's work. He'd promised to show her Spokane Falls before dinner. After two nights of lovemaking with Gavin, she felt like she needed a nap and it was barely three in the afternoon. She pulled into the lot at the dealership and parked in the back, out of sight from the cars on the lot and the customers eyeing them. She debated asking Gavin if they could stay in Spokane through the coming weekend instead of leaving for home as originally planned, to enjoy the privacy they had here. *I'll ask him at dinner.* She smiled, imagining his response.

She'd checked in with Destiny every day and all seemed fine at home. She reached for her phone to do so again, but before Bella could punch in the number, Destiny's face appeared as the phone pinged.

"Destiny," Bella welcomed her. "I was just getting—"

A sob cut her off, followed by a wail that ended in another sob. "Oh, Bella. It was awful. You have to come home. Right away."

Bella's heart stuttered to a stop. "What's the matter? Were you in an accident?"

"It's Henry. He died." Another paroxysm of sobs followed. *Oh my God. Henry?*

She climbed out of the car and began to walk slowly toward the back door through which she could reach Gavin's office. "What happened? Where are you?"

"At the hospital. Earl's here, too. He drove. He said to call Gavin, but I don't have his number. Will you tell him? He needs to know."

"Yes, of course, I'll tell him." She spotted him through the window and waved in his direction. "How did Henry die, honey? I need details."

A spate of sniffs preceded Destiny's next words, but at least she sounded like she was in better control and the background sounds of what Bella thought to be a busy emergency room reception area had faded.

"Did you go outside, Des?"

"I'm sitting in your car. It's not parked right. I need to move it." She blew her nose again. "Earl and I were so busy today. Henry was in his office. I said he had to come and see what we'd done, how much the customers like it—you'll never believe how much business we're doing now. Even Earl was convinced we should move the business stuff upstairs. Anyway, Henry said he'd come, but when he didn't, I went to get him." Another sob followed, then a sniff and more nose blowing. "I thought he was asleep. Right on the desk. He complained he was tired yesterday, so I didn't think anything of it. Except he didn't look right. So I touched him, but he didn't get up. And that's when ... oh, Bella. I've never seen a dead person before."

Bella's eyes filled as she imagined Destiny finding dear Henry, dead at his desk.

"Someone called 9-1-1," Destiny sobbed. "We probably shouldn't have made so many changes. Except for yesterday afternoon, Henry was helping us move the last of the shelves and the tables. He must have overdone it. Because I asked him." Destiny's words faded into a soft moan. "I must have ... I shouldn't have asked him ..."

Gavin opened the back door and waited for her to enter.

"Was it a heart attack?" Bella asked, wanting an explanation, more than that Henry was ... just ... dead. As if that wasn't bad enough.

"The EMTs never said. And the doctor hasn't told us."

"Okay. We'll leave right away. I'll talk to Gavin and get back to you."

Bella wished she could put her arms around Destiny, soothe her, tell her she'd done everything she could, that Henry's death wasn't something she'd brought on. Even if Henry had helped move shelves and carry books up and down the stairs. Until he'd contracted pneumonia, the man had been so vigorous. Not acting eighty, whatever "acting eighty" meant.

Bella plucked a bloom off the bush near the building. "Des, honey? Will you be okay until we get there?"

"Yes," but her voice sounded wobbly.

"Why don't you call your folks?"

"I'll leave Dad a text."

"I'm so sorry this happened and you were the one to find him." What else could she say?

"Earl said you'd know what to do."

"Is Earl there? Let me speak to him."

"He's in the ER, waiting for the doctor."

"Then you go in and stay with him. We'll be there as soon as we can." Bella hung up, stunned at the news. She met Gavin at the door and followed him into the building. Gavin shut the door of his office and pulled her into a quick clinch before kissing her.

She returned his kiss then pulled away. "It's not that I don't want to kiss you, but there's a problem."

"I knew something was wrong the way you were frowning. What is it?" His voice rumbled seductively as he brushed a finger across her forehead, as if to smooth away the worry lines. "Tell me." His tone turned serious.

No sense trying to cushion the blow, but she hated having to tell him. "Des just called, practically in hysterics. Henry died. We need to go home. Tonight."

Gavin was silent for a long minute. "We'll fly."

He punched the intercom on his desk and said to Hortense, "I need a flight for two to Seattle. Tonight. As soon as possible."

Hortense's tinny voice replied. "I'm on it."

"Can she can get a flight, just like that?"

"Hortie's son is a pilot for Alaska. She hates to fly. Gives me all the vouchers she doesn't want to use. Maybe she can call in a favor. For what she calls 'mother rates.'"

Bella smiled. "Convenient."

Hortense knocked once and opened the door. "I got one seat for tonight. Two won't be available until late tomorrow."

"You take it," Bella said. "I'll drive your car back. Destiny and Earl need you."

"But—" Gavin protested.

"I'll confirm." Hortense left the office.

Gavin nodded. "Okay. I'll have Hortense drop me off at the airport." He paused for a moment. "What a way to end our time together," he murmured.

"I was hoping we could stay longer," Bella said, almost in a whisper. "But what's important now is Henry, and Earl and Des. I'll go home and pack so I can get on the road."

"Do me a favor, Bella."

"What's that?"

"No testing how fast my wheels can go. I don't want to lose you, too."

"You're not going to lose me. Just because I know how to make that little red engine go."

"I'm serious." He pulled her close and lowered his head as if to kiss her. "I love you, Bella."

The door opened and Hortense entered. Gavin released Bella and she moved out of the comfort of his arms, his words echoing through her, sending such a shock wave of feeling she wasn't sure how to respond. Oh, she wanted to say she loved him, too, but she hadn't expected him to say it. At least not in his office. Even though she ached to dream that they could be a couple. Permanently, now that they'd become one for the last two days. But she'd forced herself to think of their time together as a respite from her regular life, a respite that included the best sex she'd ever had, something that would end after he made a decision about Henry's store.

Hortense peered at Gavin. "Sorry to interrupt," though she didn't look sorry. "You're on the flight that leaves in forty minutes. Better get moving."

Gavin nodded and reached for his suit coat.

Bella gave him a quick smile and left the office, but not before she heard Hortense chuckle.

"You are so hooked. Like a big fat king salmon, hooked and ready to be tossed on the grill."

Bella stopped outside the closed door of Gavin's office.

His yummy baritone held the hint of an insult. "What are you talking about?"

"This is the second time I've seen that woman driving your car. You never let any woman drive your wheels. Must be true love. I've been praying it would happen now that nasty Eileen isn't around to set you to growling. About time, if you ask me."

As Bella drove back to his condo, Gavin's words echoed, their import sending her pulse zooming as her cheeks flushed what she imagined to be full-on red. *He loves me?* But didn't she feel the same about him? Hadn't she shown him during their time together? But she'd never followed up her actions with words.

Bella shook her head to clear her brain. *No time for that now.* She needed to get her things, Gavin's things, too, and head home. Bella entered Gavin's bedroom to throw clothes into a suitcase. She did the same with her clothes and carried both suitcases to Gavin's car, tossed them into the backseat, locked the door of his condo, and left Spokane, determined to go at least the speed limit, in order to get home as soon as possible.

Gavin strode into the hospital waiting room after enduring a too-fast, bumpy ride from Sea-Tac Airport. Destiny and Earl occupied two seats near a window. The girl was leaning against Earl's shoulder, asleep. The old man also appeared to be dozing, his scruffy Mariner's cap perched on one knee.

"Earl?" Gavin asked and shook him gently.

The old man turned a bleary gaze upward. "You're back."

"Have you talked to the doctor?"

He nodded.

"What did he say? And why didn't you go home?"

Earl grimaced. "Didn't trust myself with the car." He pointed to the desk where a nurse was holding forth with two doctors. "You can ask him yourself. I think Henry's doc is still here." One turned in Gavin's direction as he approached.

"I'm Henry Quackenbush's nephew. Can you tell me what happened?"

"We can't be sure, but we suspect a heart attack or a stroke. His friend said no one was with him when he died. If you want to know definitively, that requires an autopsy. Will you authorize it?"

"Let me think about it." He glanced over his shoulder at Destiny, still sleeping, and at Earl, who looked like he needed to be tucked in, too. "Could you tell if he suffered?"

The doctor shook his head. "It was probably pretty quick."

Gavin nodded. "I take it Henry's in the morgue?"

"Not yet. The young woman over there said you were coming, that we had to wait. So you could say good-bye."

The nurse edged around the corner of the desk. "Come with me."

Gavin followed the nurse through the nearly empty reception area, aware of the squeaks her shoes made on the floor tiles. She held back a curtain and Gavin entered the small space, mostly taken up by the bed holding Henry's body. Gavin moved closer and pulled the sheet off the man's face. He looked peaceful, like he'd simply gone away, quietly and without a fuss. Unlike Gavin's mother, who had fought so valiantly against the cancer, a disease that had ravaged her body and left her too weak, finally, to hang on any longer.

Gavin leaned over and kissed the man's forehead. "Henry, old man. You had a good life. I'm sorry I wasn't here when … you … decided to be with Aunt Ina and Mom." He sat down heavily on a nearby chair he hadn't noticed when he entered the curtained-off space. His heart seemed to close in on itself for a long minute as he bowed his head. What to do now? His mind was blank. Then tears spilled onto his hands as he recalled the times he'd spent with his uncle growing up. He'd taught Gavin how to tie flies, how to send a line flying out into a river at just the right spot to lure a trout to strike.

Henry had loved the store, too, and vowed to keep it going after Ina's death, but his age must have caught up with him. Only after Destiny volunteered to help him had Henry begun to show some enthusiasm for the store the way he had with Ina so many years earlier.

The store was a problem Gavin would have to deal with now. He suspected it was still operating in the red. Earl couldn't possibly manage it, nor could Destiny, at least not on her own. Henry had said he'd put her on the payroll, which was a good thing. After he closed things down, Gavin would make sure she received what she was due, maybe even a bonus along with a major-league letter of thanks. She deserved it for all she'd done.

He wiped his eyes before standing and patting Henry's

shrouded shoulder. "You were a good man, taking care of your war buddy, showing Destiny the ropes. Giving books to Bella." The woman Henry had said Gavin would marry. The idea had buried itself deep in his brain and he'd been unable to dislodge it, not that he'd tried all that hard after their first business dinner. They'd known each other for such a short time. Barely two months. He couldn't imagine life without her, but did she feel the same?

Henry was right. Gavin *had* been gob smacked that day in the hospital when he'd bumped into Bella and she'd landed on the floor, her face as flaming as her locks, her luscious curves beckoning him to touch them, to stroke them, and those legs of hers that went on forever.

Gavin glanced at his watch, wishing Bella had come with him. She was probably still three hours out, driving his car, hopefully without risking a speeding ticket.

He'd take Earl home, and drive Destiny back to Bella's place. They'd wait up for her. Together. Gavin ached to hold Bella, to feel the steady thud of her heart against his chest, the softness of her skin as she brushed his cheek with her lips, her heated passion and release when they … He shook his head. How could he be thinking about *that* at a time like this? But he knew why. He wondered if she thought of their time together as often, as joyfully, as he did.

Chapter 19

GAVIN RETURNED TO THE WAITING ROOM AND ROUSED Destiny, who took one look at him and began crying in between repeated gasps of "I'm sorry."

He pulled her into his arms and hugged her tight. "Listen, it's okay. You made Henry's last days happy." He motioned to Earl. "I said good-bye to Henry. Let's get you two home."

"Where's Bella?" Destiny asked.

"On her way. She's driving my car. We'll drop Earl off and wait up for her."

Destiny led the way to Bella's car, no longer parked in the loading zone. Gavin took the keys from her. Earl climbed into the back seat and huddled there. Destiny slid in next to Earl and put her arms around him. Gavin drove to the bookstore, loaded Earl's bike into the trunk, and drove him to his little apartment.

Earl's voice was gravelly. "I'll go in extra early tomorrow and let people know."

"No need to open at the regular time," Gavin replied. "People will understand."

Earl frowned. "Henry likes us to open at eight." In the lamplight, the old man looked bereft.

"Destiny and I may be in a little later."

"So you can check the account books again?" Earl angrily pushed his bicycle into the side yard, giving Gavin a scowl before clumping up the two steps to his apartment door.

Gavin chose not to argue.

At Bella's house, Destiny slumped into a seat in the living room and stared intently at Gavin.

"Something on your mind, Destiny?" he asked tiredly, as he sat down on the couch. "Henry, maybe? The bookstore?"

"I didn't like you much, when I met you." The jutting of her chin reminded him of Bella when she'd argued with him about their relationship, how they couldn't have one. Even though they did. At least as far as he was concerned.

And you like me now? But the way Destiny seemed to be staring holes through his chest didn't seem all that friendly.

"You interrogated me," she accused.

"I asked you questions," he countered, recalling that introductory dinner at Bella's with Zoe and Tör.

"You thought my being here would hurt Bella. I'm right, aren't I?" The stiffness of her shoulders dared him to contradict her.

"I just wanted to be sure your coming here was a good thing. For her. For you." Keeping his voice calm, wanting her to keep talking, he chose not to meet her gaze for a moment. "I'm glad you came. Bella wanted to spend time with you. It meant a lot to her that you were willing."

"To make up for the years she didn't know me?"

"That, too. But I'm not sure she'd think of it as making up for anything. You're a young woman now. She knows she'll never have the kind of relationship you have with your mom."

Destiny looked skeptical as she jumped up from her chair and stomped into the kitchen. "It's so hard waiting. I can't just sit here. I'll make hot chocolate. Want some?"

"Suit yourself." He watched her prepare the drink. "If there's enough for two, I'll have some."

"I'll make enough for *three*. You said Bella'd be here soon."

Gavin looked at his watch. "Assuming she didn't run into traffic." *Or get pulled over for speeding.*

Destiny brought him a mug of hot chocolate. "I hate that you're going to sell Henry's store. He loves it. Loved it," she corrected, her chin wobbling slightly.

"There's no point keeping a business going when it's swimming in red ink, Destiny. Surely, you know that, from all those business courses you took."

"But it's not! Not now. You've hardly paid attention these last few weeks." Her eyes seemed to shine in the light as she challenged him again. "All you think about is Bella."

Gavin took a gingerly sip of the hot chocolate, aware of his heated reaction to Destiny's words. *All I think about? More like feel her in my arms. Love her in my bed.* "Who I think about is no business of yours."

"But if you'd paid attention, you would have *seen* how many more customers we have. Especially the last couple weeks. But you went off to Spokane to check on your *precious* car place. Bella didn't need to go with you," she added dismissively. "I *know* why you asked her."

He was about to make a comment that she shouldn't disparage his thriving business, unlike Henry's barely-hanging-on bookstore, when Destiny slammed down her empty mug.

That it didn't shatter on the counter seemed to surprise both of them.

"Henry told me about you and Bella, what he told you. He was hoping you'd stay here to help him with the store. Maybe even take over that *other* car place, the one you visited so many times." She air quoted her words with a slight snarl. "But now, with Henry gone," she sucked in a quick breath, "you're just going to close the store. And I'll bet you're happy he can't stop you.

"What's going to happen to Earl? I'll bet you don't even care about him. Do you know his background? Why he won't go near cars or buses? How he almost died in a big truck when he was in Vietnam where he met Henry? How Henry saved him? When we went to the hospital, he drove Bella's car because I was so upset. Even as scared as he was, probably having flashbacks the whole time. Earl won't have anything to take his mind off the bad stuff if there's no store to work in."

What she said explained a lot.

"Look, Destiny. What happens to the store is a *business* decision. Not a reflection on Henry or you. Or Earl." He leaned forward, peered more closely at her, and softened his voice. "You may not believe me, but I appreciate everything you did at the store. Henry did, too. Earl's an adult. He'll find something else to do."

She stood up, her hands gesticulating, her voice rising. "No, he won't. He's *devastated* that Henry died. That store was his safe place, especially in the quiet corners. That's why he likes it so much. Since it's gotten busy, he doesn't sit at the cash register as much. Now he goes upstairs and reads in one of the corners up there. I set up a little desk and chair just for him. He talks to the regulars who read the newspapers up there. It's his way of connecting on his own terms. He'll *die* without the store."

Gavin met her glare with a small nod. "Maybe he will, but that's not my responsibility nor yours." He willed himself not to show how her words were affecting him, giving him the guilts for focusing on the business, for giving her the impression he was cold-hearted, something he wouldn't allow in any of his salespeople. Injecting warmth into his tone, he asked, "What about you? Are you going home if I close the store now that Henry's gone?"

"I want to *run* the store. It's making money now, maybe not as much as your *precious* car dealership—"

He couldn't help that his voice rose, offended at how she characterized—*precious, for God's sake?*—what he'd worked so hard to accomplish. "*My* business makes a profit."

"That's all you care about, isn't it? That and Bella? Well, if you care so much about her, why don't you marry her, like Henry said? She deserves to be happy, to have a husband and a family, what she never got because of me." Her voice hitched and tears shone on Destiny's cheeks as she picked up her empty mug.

"How Bella's lived her life isn't something you created. You can't take respon—"

Gavin recognized the distinctive sound of his roadster's engine. Bella's arrival was confirmed when headlights flashed in the windows before she stopped the car and climbed out.

Destiny raced to the front door, flung it open, and ran down the steps into Bella's arms.

Gavin watched the two women hugging each other, their hair blending into a single fall of red curls, their voices similar, too, he realized. Were both of them now weeping? For Henry? For the store?

He walked outside, detoured around them, both of them talking, not seeming to notice that their words were entangled, like their hair, in a single blend of womanly emotions.

He opened the backseat, pulled out Bella's suitcase, and carried it into the house.

"Thank you." Bella said as he preceded her up the steps.

"In your bedroom?"

"Please."

He walked past what had to be the guest room, where a pile of Destiny's mostly black clothing lay on the floor, on the bed, even draped over the desk chair. He belatedly realized she wasn't wearing all black anymore. When had that changed?

By contrast, Bella's room was a haven of soft greens, neat like she was, the coverlet sporting a striped green and white pattern that contrasted with the decorative pillows, some white, others a dark forest green, nested together next to the headboard. Her furniture was of modern design, with clean lines, its polished wood gleaming in the light he flicked on.

Gavin set Bella's suitcase on the end of the bed and turned to leave the room, trying to ignore the image of Bella in that bed, beckoning to him. Destiny's words, her accusations about his plans for the bookstore had finally succeeded in resizing his pants into the comfortable zone. He clicked off the light and shut the door.

Destiny was right on both counts. He needed to come to a decision about the store *and* Bella. At least about the store. Bella was her own woman. She would decide if what he felt was something she felt, too, if what he wanted to say to her she wanted to hear.

A thought came to him that sent his heart rate skyrocketing. If Destiny knew what Henry had declared so smugly weeks earlier, had she shared that with Bella? Would she, now that she figured Gavin was going to shut down the store? And how would Bella take that news? She seemed to be assessing him as he walked toward her.

"Act! Don't just stand there looking like a love-sick mule," his administrative assistant had urged. "Tell her how you feel. How you *really* feel. Stop assuming she knows." Hortense's words haunted him. As she drove Gavin to the airport, she'd repeated what she'd said in the office, that she knew he was in love, for real this time. She wanted him to be happy, knew that the dealership couldn't be his entire life, that Bella was a breath of fresh air, the kind he needed to live a full life, one that included a loving wife and children. Then Hortie had kissed his cheek and waved him onto the plane, with the shouted order, "Don't you dare come back without putting a ring on her finger and a wedding date on the calendar."

Gavin settled his gaze on Bella, still standing near the door. Destiny had taken a seat and was again watching him. He took several steps and stopped, then several more until he was standing close enough to feel the warmth of Bella's body. She had to be tired. Who wouldn't be after six long hours in the car? She looked beautiful when her gaze met his and then seemed to slide downward toward his lips. He lifted her chin with one finger, took her in his arms and kissed her with all the pent-up passion he'd been unable to quell while standing in her room, imagining them together, like the previous two nights, like he wanted for all future nights. Days, too.

She melted against him when she kissed him back, not seeming to notice that Destiny was in the room.

After they came up for air, Destiny snickered. "You two should get a room. Or maybe I should just leave." She walked to her room and shut the door behind her.

Destiny pulled out her phone. It was really late in Denver, but it couldn't be helped. She dialed, silently urging her mother not to be mad.

"Mom?"

"Des? Good Lord! It's after midnight. What's wrong?"

Keeping her voice down so Bella wouldn't hear, Destiny sucked in a deep breath. "Henry died"—her mother gasped—"but that's not why I called. Well, sort of. I need your help. So Gavin won't sell the store. I know he wants to, but it's doing a lot better than before. All those marketing things you and I've been talking about—they're working, but I need more of them, so we can keep the store open."

Her mother sounded more awake. "I gather this means you don't plan to come home anytime soon."

"I'm needed here. And Earl needs me. All I have to do is convince Gavin to let me run the store. He wants to go back to Spokane."

"If he doesn't want to run it and you do, what's the problem?"

"Well ..." How could she say this without opening a huge can of worms? Destiny hugged the pillow to her chest, willing herself to just say it. *Mom, it isn't my fault. Not really.* "He hates me."

"Your boss hates you?"

"He only became my boss because Henry's ... gone." Destiny wiped away the tears that began to slide down her cheeks. "I sort of, well, I accused him."

Silence greeted her admission.

"I was upset. After Henry died. And Gavin doesn't really know what we've done, Earl and I. How many customers we have now. Opal, at the deli, says we're doing almost as much business as when Aunt Ina was alive."

"Sweetheart, it's never good to be at odds with the boss."

"I know, Mom." She punched the pillow before grudgingly adding, "I'll apologize tomorrow. While we're driving to the store. I know he's going to check sales receipts. Maybe that will convince him, when he sees how much more money we're bringing in."

"Have you talked to your dad about all this?"

"No."

"Maybe he'll have some ideas."

"But, what do *you* think? You're the marketing genius."

Her mom chuckled softly. "Years ago, I would have agreed with you. Whatever you've been doing is what you need to keep doing, Des. What you said is working."

"That's all?"

"That and an apology."

"Right. Okay. Thanks."

"You're welcome."

"I love you, Mom." Guilt that she hadn't said it in months, maybe years, forced another gush of tears onto Destiny's cheeks.

"I love you, too, honey."

The next day, Gavin arrived at the bookstore shortly after nine with Destiny in tow. Several regulars were purchasing morning newspapers and other customers were scanning the best-seller tables. Earl waved at him as Gavin walked up the stairs. He'd promised himself he would look over the most recent bank deposits before concentrating on Henry's funeral, tentatively planned for the end of the week. He'd wanted to have it sooner, but Bella said they needed time to make sure all of Henry's friends and customers were informed so that they could pay their respects.

He yawned, realizing that his sleep last night had been too short. All because he'd stayed up with Bella to talk and then gone back to Henry's and picked up the phone to talk with her again, well into the early morning hours. He'd have preferred to be tired from lovemaking until dawn, but that wasn't to be with Destiny in the guest room. Not unless Bella chose to join him at Henry's place, and those digs weren't exactly ideal for romance.

Two hours after reviewing the information left for him by Earl and testily pointed out to him by Destiny, Gavin was pleasantly surprised at how well the store was doing. He hadn't needed a guide to recognize how much Destiny had changed the store. Earl, too, seemed happy to work with the customers, several of whom gave him hugs and chatted with him about Henry, wishing him well. Still others asked Destiny if she was going to be staying on.

Gavin was standing on the landing when the phone rang. Earl picked it up while he manned the register. "It's for you!" he shouted over the hubbub of customer conversations.

Gavin returned to Henry's office. "Hello?"

"Is this Gavin Cambridge?" a man asked, the sounds of a baby crying in the background.

"Yes. Are you calling about Henry?" *Another person wanting to offer condolences?* The store had been full of that sort of thing all day.

"Actually, I'm calling about the bookstore. And my daughter. Destiny Harris."

"Oh. Would you like to speak with her? She's downstairs. I can get her."

"Perhaps later." The man cleared his throat. "What I need to know are your plans for the store. She's terrified you're going to shut it down."

Gavin rose and shut the office door. "She made that clear last night. A final decision hasn't been made, but from what I've just reviewed, the need to sell may be premature." The increase by more than twenty percent over the previous week, and the recent sales of the past few days were up, too. Destiny was right. He'd focused only on costs.

"I'm sorry. I should have introduced myself. I'm Nolan Harris."

"Destiny's father," Gavin replied.

"Yes, and I was wondering if you felt the store might benefit from a silent partner, assuming you feel it needs an infusion of funds to bring it fully back to what it should be." The baby sounds seemed to have devolved from cries to delighted coos.

The man continued. "Destiny wants to keep working in the store. I'm happy she's found a meaningful job and a career. I want Destiny to be able to chase her dream and she seems quite happy there."

"She called you," Gavin declared.

"She kept me up half the night," Mr. Harris added. "As if I don't miss enough sleep."

"Hmm. A silent partner?" The idea had merit. It would enable him to hire a manager, someone with experience running a bookstore, someone who could ride herd on Earl and on Destiny. Young as she was, as ambitious as she was, she didn't have what Gavin knew was needed to keep the bookstore afloat in the long term. Not yet, anyway. "Mr. Harris?"

"Call me Nolan."

"May I call you back about your offer?"

"Certainly. Let me be clear about one thing."

"What's that?"

"Destiny didn't ask that I call you. In fact, I'd prefer that she doesn't know. It was my idea. I figured if there was a financial cushion, you'd gain enough time to get the store back in the black. Destiny seems dedicated to the store, and wants to work up to owning it or a similar place someday. This is the best possible training for her. But she's afraid you'll sell it to someone who won't keep her on, who might actually fire the other fellow who works there—Earl I think his name is. She seems very protective of him."

"I see." Gavin needed to think all this through. "Thanks for calling. Give me your number. I'll call you in the next forty-eight hours with my decision. If that's okay."

"Certainly."

Gavin left the store and drove to the Bellevue dealership. He wandered around the grounds, taking pictures on his smart phone. The manager had fewer salesmen on staff than when Gavin had first visited. He checked the social media sites for mentions of the dealership, saw how poorly they were rated, and made a call that left him smiling. His next stop was at the local bank where Henry had made his deposits. What he learned there convinced him that additional funds were necessary if he was to keep the store open. When he returned to the bookstore, he asked Destiny to come to the office.

She walked into Henry's office and perched on the chair to one side of the desk, nervously nibbling on her lower lip. "It feels kind of funny to be in here again."

Gavin nodded. "If you'd be more comfortable at the coffee shop across the street, or at the deli, we can talk there."

She shook her head. "That's okay. Are you going to fire me?"

Gavin snorted. "Why do you think that?"

"You haven't exactly agreed with me about how well we're doing. And I sort of went off on you last night. Because I was upset. Since you want to dump this place, I figured that's what you were going to say."

"What I want to know is if Henry was paying you."

Destiny's brows rose. "Oh. Well. Sort of."

"Either you're being paid or you're not."

"He covered my lunches. Most days he paid me something," she finally admitted. "But I've learned a lot since working here. That was pay enough. Really."

"No, it isn't. You should be on the payroll, like a regular employee."

"Does that mean you're not going to close the store?"

"I haven't decided yet. Before you leave this afternoon, I want you to give me a list of the hours you've worked since you started here and how much you've been paid. Then I'm going to write you a check to cover what you should have received."

"And *then* you're going to fire me?"

Gavin leaned back in the chair. It squeaked in protest, mirroring the words he refrained from saying. "Then I'm going to talk with Earl. You can go back to work." He smiled at her, hoping Destiny was reassured. "Ask him to come up, please."

"You're so mean," she muttered under her breath as she left the office, scowling.

Earl entered moments later. "I guess this is it, right?"

Gavin laughed out loud. "I'm not sure what you're referring to and I don't want to know. I need a straight answer. Do you like working here, or were you doing it because Henry needed you? And you needed him?"

"That's three questions." The old man peered out from under his Mariner's cap, shuffling his feet as he stood in front of Gavin.

"Well?" Gavin motioned toward the chair. "Take a load off, Earl."

The man eased into the chair. "Okay. Yes times three."

"Since you like working here, do you want to continue?"

"Sure, but I ... Destiny said you thought we were going

belly up. Even though that's not how I see it."

"The store isn't going belly up, Earl. But I need to hire a manager."

"Won't Destiny do? She's young, but she's full of ideas. It's because of her that we're seeing so many customers."

"She's too young. Not experienced enough. Yet."

Gavin watched Earl's mouth turn down at the corners, as if insulted that his friend was thought incapable of running the store. "Not what I think."

"It's what *I* think, and now that Henry's gone, I own this place. So, it's my call." Then, to soften that particular blow, he added, "Maybe you know someone who could manage the store. Someone with more experience than Destiny."

"Opal might. At the deli. She knows all kinds of people."

Gavin nodded. "Okay. I'll talk to her. You can go back to work."

Two days later, Gavin called Nolan Harris and thanked him for his offer, but it wouldn't be necessary. Then he finished detailing a business plan, one that he was certain the bank would approve when he sought a small business loan for the bookstore. The next day, he received the answer that had him humming in the shower before going to Bella's to pick her up for dinner.

She was waiting for him on the porch, wearing a pale cream sundress that called attention to her tanned arms. Her hair was piled on top of her head like a frothy red crown.

Thank you, God, he thought, as he pressed his lips to her swan-like neck. She wore a fragrance that reminded him of dogwood blossoms in the spring. When Destiny came out on the porch to tell Bella good-bye, the girl gave him a sly look, like she knew what he was up to. He just smiled at her.

After a dinner that his nerves prevented him from fully

enjoying, he drove to the park on a hill high above Evergreen with a view of Lake Geneva. He offered a seat to Bella near the gazebo overlooking the rose garden.

Hortense's exhortation echoed in his head as he sat down next to Bella and turned to her. "I never thought I'd ... Bella, do you like me? Think I'm an okay guy? Enough to spend the rest of your life with me? 'Cause I can't see myself living another day without you."

Her eyes widened. "What are you saying?"

He hesitated for a moment then dropped to one knee. "The last time I did this, I made a big mistake," he continued. "But you're not a mistake. You're who I've been waiting for. Henry told me I ... never mind." He gulped, gave up trying to explain and uttered the words he'd never expected to say a second time. "Will you marry me?"

It was Bella's turn to stammer. "Oh! Is this why you were nervous at dinner? I was so afraid you were going to say you were going back to Spokane, that you were going to say good-bye."

He shook his head. "No chance of that." He swallowed once, twice. "Well?" he croaked.

She beamed. "Of course I will ... marry you." She pulled him up to sit next to her. "How could you think I wouldn't?"

Thinking of their recent lengthy nighttime conversations, he replied, "Just dumb, I guess." He pulled out the box that had been pressing against his left chest all evening and opened it. "I hope this fits. Destiny guessed it might."

"She knew about this?"

"She probably guessed. I asked her to check your jewelry box for a ring. To get the size right."

Bella laughed. "She kept humming 'Ring Around the Rosie,' last night. I kept asking her why that song, and she refused to say."

"You have a smart-ass for a daughter." Gavin kissed Bella and slid the diamond solitaire onto her finger. It fit perfectly.

She kissed him back. "So, you're really going to stay in Evergreen like you said the other night, or do I need to tender my resignation at the library?"

"I'm staying. That old dealership in Bellevue, the one I've been wandering around for weeks, needs me a lot more than the one in Spokane. I just picked up the franchise. After Henry's funeral, I'm going over there to clean house, hire new salespeople, fire the ones that don't measure up. That sort of thing."

"You're going to be busy."

"Yes, and I'm hiring a manager for Henry's store. Someone who agrees to teach Destiny how to run a bookstore so it makes a profit. And is willing to keep Earl on as the in-house example of a reader." He chuckled.

"Henry would be so happy." She kept glancing down at the ring and back at him, the rim of emerald in her eyes widening in the light.

"One more thing. We need to help Destiny find a new place to live. She needs an apartment of her own, don't you think?"

Bella laughed. "Funny you should mention that. She said her dad told her the same thing the other day."

Gavin stood up and pulled Bella into his arms for a kiss and impromptu hug, followed by a slow dance among the rose bushes. "I hope she agrees. So we can celebrate in our own special way." He kissed her neck where her pulse jumped before concentrating on her lips.

"Looking forward to it," she murmured a few minutes later.

Epilogue

DESTINY WAVED AT BELLA AND GAVIN WHEN HIS SHOUT caught her attention in baggage claim. She was back in Evergreen after visiting her mom. Once in Gavin's car, she resumed her conversation with Bella, begun on the phone before she left Denver.

"My mom finally agrees that having my first job away from home isn't a bad thing."

"I'm glad." Bella patted her hand.

"We're back to what we used to be. Close. Like moms and daughters are supposed to be, according to my dad."

Bella chuckled. "Good."

As he drove Destiny to her new apartment, Gavin asked, "You never did say how you like the manager at the store. Is she as good as Henry about accepting your suggestions?"

Destiny folded her hands in her lap. "She asks more questions, makes me explain *why* we should do it, but she likes my ideas. Most of them, anyway. She loves the store. And I think she loves Earl, too. He blushes whenever she talks to him."

Gavin laughed. "Think there'll be another wedding?" He beamed at Bella, leaned over, and kissed her when he stopped at a light.

"I doubt it, but you never know."

Gavin carried Destiny's suitcases into her apartment. "Nice dress you have on. You look good in blue."

Destiny felt her cheeks heat. Since meeting Hardy, the UPS driver, who delivered so many of their new book orders, she'd decided to wear more girly things. Her mom had been thrilled to help her shop for new clothes. "Thanks. Mom says this one brings out the color of my eyes."

"Speaking of weddings, I hear your folks are coming."

Destiny nodded. "They both want to be here to wish Bella well. Besides, it gives them a chance to see me and my new digs."

Bella gave Destiny a hug. "I'm looking forward to seeing them again. You look really happy about your folks coming to visit."

"I am. And that you're getting married. I'll bet Henry's looking down and saying, 'I told you so' in Gavin's ear."

Gavin smiled. "I'm sure he is."

A week later, Destiny peered out from the door in the room where Zoe was making final adjustments to Bella's headpiece. Destiny giggled behind her hand when her last-minute invitee to the wedding, Hardy, smiled and waved at her from the back pew where he was sitting.

Destiny glanced over her shoulder at Zoe and Bella. "It looks like everyone's here. And your mom's waiting, Bella."

Zoe, herself a recent bride and Bella's matron of honor,

wore a pale blue dress whose cut mirrored Bella's ivory gown. Destiny, as her bridesmaid, wore a slightly darker version that set off her red hair dramatically. Her pulse picked up when she spotted her parents, seated on the right side of the church. Vanessa Harris was seated on the aisle, behind Destiny's father and his wife. They'd left the baby downstairs in the nursery with an attendant who was watching several other small children, many of them younger brothers and sisters of the children Bella read to in her story hour sessions. The administrative assistant for the Spokane dealership, whom Gavin had introduced as Hortense—she'd corrected him and said she was his second-in-command—was dabbing at her eyes where she sat across the aisle from Destiny's mom.

Destiny opened the door and approached the entrance to the sanctuary, where Bella's mother waited, pacing nervously.

"She's ready? I *so* wish she had let me help her get dressed," she whispered to Destiny.

"She really didn't need any help," Destiny offered. "Here we are." She waited until the music changed then nodded at Zoe and Bella. Then she began slowly walking toward the front of the church where Gavin and his best man, Zeke, from Spokane, and Earl, who'd proudly ushered, waited.

Destiny imagined herself as a bride and couldn't quite see it. She had refused to go out with Hardy until he asked her a third time. But they weren't serious, just friends, though the way he sometimes looked at her made her blush and wonder if maybe, some time in the future, they'd get serious. For now, she looked forward to working at Books and More and picking the new manager's brain. *Maybe I'll go to grad school and get an MBA, like Gavin.* Today she just wanted to enjoy being part of her birth mother's wedding to Gavin, Bella's really hot groom.

Destiny turned and watched a beaming Zoe make her way

to the front, followed by Bella, on her mother's arm.

I wonder if I'll look like that when I get married. Bella was radiant, her eyes shining as she gazed at Gavin, who stepped forward to take her arm.

Throughout the ceremony, Destiny's mind wandered, coming back to the present when Gavin kissed Bella to the applause of the congregation. They then turned and walked down the aisle together, to laughter and shouted congratulations from the crowd. It wasn't a huge gathering, but all seemed to know and love the members of the bridal party.

After Gavin and Bella left for the airport, Destiny returned to her apartment with her parents and Scott. The little guy gave her a drooly grin whenever she said his name.

Destiny thought back to Bella's first call, ten months earlier. It seemed like she'd known Bella, her birth mom, forever. Somehow, getting to know her had helped Destiny to make up with her other mom, finally acknowledging how much Vanessa loved her, worried over her, and wanted Destiny's life to be free of difficulties. Not like Bella's had been so many years earlier.

After showing her parents the bookstore the day before the wedding and telling them about all the changes she and Earl had made with Henry, her dad had smiled and said he was proud of her. Her mom had said she'd done a good job with the posters and the arrangement of books that encouraged buyers to take them home. She had even pronounced brilliant several of Destiny's marketing ideas. Destiny wasn't so sure about that, but she was pleased that her parents seemed to think she had a future as a bookstore owner.

She picked up the *Harry Potter* book she'd brought home from the bookstore and showed it to her parents. "It's for Scott. When he's ready to read it. For now, I picked out some other cool cloth books. Ones he can't make holes in while he's teething."

Her dad laughed. Scott cooed and reached for the book she was holding. Destiny took it as a sign her little brother would be a reader, too, just like her.

Questions for Book Clubs and Reading Groups

1. Bella was a teen when she had her baby. Have you known teens who relinquished their baby for adoption? Was their reaction to doing so the same as Bella's? How was it different?

2. How would you describe Bella's relationship with her daughter's adoptive parents? How is it different/the same as her relationship with her own parents? In what ways might her parents have helped her to come to terms with her grief at losing her child?

3. Bella stops hearing from her daughter's adoptive parents after five years. If you were Bella, what would you have done under the same circumstances?

4. How does Bella's recent breakup with Ethan affect her expectations for finding love again? In what ways does her best friend Zoe's engagement to Tör influence how Bella feels about herself?

5. When Bella receives the letter from Mr. Harris, she wants to contact Destiny immediately. Had you been advising her, what would you have recommended and why?

6. Bella likes Henry Quackenbush, the owner of the bookstore. How does her friendship with him fill a void, now that she no longer has much contact with her mother and never made peace with her father before his passing?

7. How would you describe Henry's relationship with his nephew, Gavin Cambridge? If you were to meet Gavin on the street, what would you think of him? If you visited his automobile showroom, how would he appear to you?

8. When Gavin meets Bella, his uncle declares that Gavin is going to marry Bella. Why do you suppose Henry makes that comment? Should he have done so? Why or why not?

9. Bella first writes Destiny a letter and then she calls her, but only after contacting Mr. Harris first. Would you agree that this was the right way to approach her birth child? If not, how would you have done so, and why?

10. What is it about Vanessa that makes her so distrustful of Bella? When is this first apparent? And what did you think of her actions in hiding those letters from Destiny for so many years?

11. How would you describe Nolan and Vanessa's marriage? Before they adopt Destiny? After the death of their second adopted child, a son? After their divorce?

12. Why do you suppose Destiny starts dating Noah and then becomes his lover? How strongly does she love him?

13. When Gavin first learns about Destiny, he seems very accepting of Bella's action in giving up her daughter. Why, then, does he question Destiny so much when she comes to stay with Bella?

14. When Bella goes with Gavin to Spokane, she approaches him when she enters his bedroom. Was that wise? In what ways does it show how she feels about him?

15. When Bella learns of Henry's death, how does she support Destiny? Gavin?

16. What do you suppose Gavin talks with Bella about later that night and after they return to Evergreen?

17. How does Bella's relationship with Destiny aid in Destiny's relationship with Vanessa?

18. What do you think of Earl? Why do you suppose he keeps to himself, refuses to take a bus or drive a car? How else

might his behavior reflect his wartime experience when he met Henry?

19. Is Gavin correct in concluding that he needs to hire a manager for the bookstore after Henry's death? Or should he have simply closed it down? Had he done so, how might that have affected his relationship with Bella? Destiny? Earl?

About the Author

KATE VALE LIVES IN THE BEAUTIFUL FOURTH CORNER OF northwestern Washington state. She enjoys the slower pace of a small city located between Vancouver, BC, and Seattle, WA. Her stories reflect the many different careers she has experienced and the crises that confront real men and women. Helping her characters get to a happily-ever-after is a continuing goal.

Reviews, a link to her blog and first announcements of new titles appear on her webpage: http://katevale.com. Feel free to visit it.

You can contact Kate at ...
katevale@sent.com,
tweet her at http://twitter.com/katevalewriter; or, on
Google+ at katevalewriter@gmail.com